∽ A fine friend in Hell. ∽

"You cheatin' son of a b—"

Mike's insult was cut off by the roar of a shotgun at close range. The blast took a chunk out of his torso and spun him around.

Every face turned to stare at Caleb, who stood over the messy remains of Loco Mike Abel.

"Jesus Christ," came one voice from near the bar. "He shot him."

"I saw it, too. Damn near cut him in half."

"I think I'm gonna be sick."

The bottom of Caleb's stomach dropped out, and soon the floor seemed to tilt beneath his feet. Almost immediately, he felt a steadying hand on his shoulder.

"It's all right," Doc Holliday said in a low, soothing voice. "It's all over. You did good."

THE
Accomplice

Marcus Galloway

BERKLEY BOOKS, NEW YORK

THE BERKLEY PUBLISHING GROUP
Published by the Penguin Group
Penguin Group (USA) Inc.
375 Hudson Street, New York, New York 10014, USA
Penguin Group (Canada), 90 Eglinton Avenue East, Suite 700, Toronto, Ontario M4P 2Y3, Canada
(a division of Pearson Penguin Canada Inc.)
Penguin Books Ltd., 80 Strand, London WC2R 0RL, England
Penguin Group Ireland, 25 St. Stephen's Green, Dublin 2, Ireland (a division of Penguin Books Ltd.)
Penguin Group (Australia), 250 Camberwell Road, Camberwell, Victoria 3124, Australia
(a division of Pearson Australia Group Pty. Ltd.)
Penguin Books India Pvt. Ltd., 11 Community Centre, Panchsheel Park, New Delhi—110 017, India
Penguin Group (NZ), 67 Apollo Drive, Mairangi Bay, Auckland 1311, New Zealand
(a division of Pearson New Zealand Ltd.)
Penguin Books (South Africa) (Pty.) Ltd., 24 Sturdee Avenue, Rosebank, Johannesburg 2196,
South Africa

Penguin Books Ltd., Registered Offices: 80 Strand, London WC2R 0RL, England

This is a work of fiction. Names, characters, places, and incidents either are the product of the author's imagination or are used fictitiously, and any resemblance to actual persons, living or dead, business establishments, events, or locales is entirely coincidental.

THE ACCOMPLICE

A Berkley Book / published by arrangement with the author

PRINTING HISTORY
Berkley edition / February 2007

Copyright © 2007 by Marcus Pelegrimas.
Cover illustration by Bill Angresano.
Cover design by Steven Ferlauto.
Interior text design by Laura K. Corless.

ISBN: 978-0-425-21420-6

BERKLEY®
Berkley Books are published by The Berkley Publishing Group,
a division of Penguin Group (USA) Inc.,
375 Hudson Street, New York, New York 10014.
BERKLEY is a registered trademark of Penguin Group (USA) Inc.
The "B" design is a trademark belonging to Penguin Group (USA) Inc.

PRINTED IN THE UNITED STATES OF AMERICA

10 9 8 7 6 5 4 3 2 1

*In loving memory of
my grandmother Martha.
She taught me to play cutthroat poker and said,
"Shut up and deal, kid,"
when I wanted to go to sleep
after winning a few hands.
Thanks, Ma-Mu.*

Going to bed early never got anyone anywhere.

Author's Note

In writing this book, I have tried my best to stay true to the spirit of John Henry "Doc" Holliday. Wherever possible, I have kept the actual names, places, and dates intact. Even some details that might go unnoticed are historical fact. However, this is a work of fiction, and some things needed to be altered a bit for the sake of the story. My real intention is to entertain but also give an accurate portrayal of one of the Old West's most well-known figures. Doc was a character in every sense of the word, and hopefully this book will let that shine through. If it's true history you're after, I would suggest books like *Doc Holliday: A Family Portrait*, by Karen Holliday Tanner, or *The Frontier World of Doc Holliday*, by Pat Jahns. With that said, turn the page and enjoy!

Dallas, Texas
～ 1873 ～

The Busted Flush Saloon wasn't the biggest place in Dallas to go for a drink. It wasn't even the best. It was, however, the closest when approaching the town from the southeast, and that was good enough to bring plenty of folks through its doors. The saloon was cobbled together from splintered, weathered wood and leaned slightly to one side. In that way, it resembled the drunks who stumbled out of it after a long, rowdy night.

It was the end of summer, and waves of heat from the ground made the Busted Flush appear to waver in the breeze. Grit covered the ground after having been blown or tracked into each and every building. Everyone in Dallas knew only too well the feeling of their teeth crunching upon the dust that had coated the backs of their mouths. It was hot. Everyone knew it. Even so, that didn't stop some folks from needing to drive the point home even more.

"I'll be damned, it is hot!" the tall fellow bellowed as he

strutted into the Busted Flush. He was a big man with long, wavy hair encrusted with dust, tangled with briars, and tossed about by the wind. He gazed around at the half dozen or so others inside the place, waiting for some kind of answer to his statement.

Finally, a portly figure standing behind the bar obliged him, twisting a cloth through one mug after another as he said, "You got that right. What can I get for you, Mike?"

The big fellow's proper name was Mike Abel, but he went by the name Loco Mike. He hadn't exactly earned the nickname or gotten it from someone else. The name, along with the three guns holstered on his person, were overly obvious attempts to gain respect or at least some degree of fear. Judging by the tired glances he got from the others around him, he might have needed to try a little harder.

"I'll take a beer. Jesus, it's so hot I think I feel my gullet baking in me," Mike said as he strutted up to the bar. Slapping the shoulder of an old-timer standing there, he asked, "How 'bout you, Orville?"

"Sure, Mike," Orville said without even glancing in the bigger man's direction. "But I felt a whole lot worse when I was out digging. You ain't never felt heat like the kind that gets reflected off the top of a tin pan."

The barkeep took a mug out for him and filled it with beer from a rusted tap. "Any luck playing cards last night?"

Mike had both hands flat upon the warped wooden surface and looked at the barkeep as though the man had just insulted his mother. "What the flamin' hell is that supposed to mean?"

Freezing for a moment, the barkeep topped off Mike's drink and set the mug down in front of him. "Nothing, Mike. Just making conversation is all."

"Well conversate about something other than my goddamn losing streak!"

"Sure, Mike."

The old-timer was chuckling and shaking his head.

"What're you laughin' at?" Mike grunted.

Without flinching, the old-timer stared straight ahead and ignored the growling menace beneath Mike's question.

"He's probably laughing at those sorry hands you tried to bluff with last night," came a voice from the Busted Flush's front door.

Mike, as well as one or two others in the saloon, turned around to get a look at who'd just spoken. What they saw was a solidly built figure wearing the black suit and string tie that might as well have been the uniform of a professional gambler. He carried a polished cane, which seemed to be more of an accessory than a necessity. A wide-brimmed hat cast a dark shadow over the well-dressed man's face. Beneath that veil of shadow, the man was smiling.

Taking hold of his mug roughly enough to spill at least a quarter of its contents upon the bar, Mike shifted on his heel until he was facing the new arrival. He glanced around at the other drinkers, not even seeming to notice that they were already leaning forward with their elbows in the grooves that they'd worn into the bar.

"You all hear that?" Mike asked to nobody in particular. "Seems like the dandy over there's got a sense a' humor. Well, come on over here and tell me another one, Dandy. I'd love to have a laugh."

The well-dressed man walked lightly across the room and sat down at one of the tables. He kept his back to the wall and his cane within arm's reach. "I apologize, Mike. That was rude of me. Enjoy your drink. In fact," he added, flipping a coin through the air, "have the next one on me."

Mike caught the coin and then stared down at it as though it had bitten him. With a sneer, he threw it back to the well-dressed man's table and said, "Buy a fuckin' drink for yerself. If you want to hand out money, you should give me back the hundred dollars you cheated off of me last night!"

When the gambler snatched his coin from the air, he did it with a gesture that fell just short of a flourish. He held it for a moment, rolled it over the back of his fingers, and then pocketed it. "Any time you want another game, I'm your man."

That was too much for Mike to bear. Hearing those words come at him was like having a punch land squarely on his nose. He glared about with disgust and still seemed to miss the fact that most everyone else in the bar had already lost interest. "You talk to me like that in front of my friends?"

The gambler shrugged.

"You gonna put up with this bullshit?" Mike asked the barkeep. "After all, he did cheat me in your place!"

"You got proof?" the barkeep asked.

Mike gritted his teeth and said, "Fetch the asshole in that office. I want to have a word with him. Or maybe the law ought to know what goes on in here."

"No need for that," the gambler said. "You have a problem with me, you can take it up with me."

When Mike wheeled around to get another look at the well-dressed man, he found the gambler was already on his feet and walking toward him. Mike's lips curled into a humorless grin, baring a yellowed set of crooked teeth. "I do got a problem with you. And I think I can settle it right here. Right now."

Mike's arms dropped to his side, making a jerky wave toward his guns as if the weapons weren't already on display well enough. "You wanna know why I'm called Loco?" Mike asked, patting the pistol on his right hip. "You're about to find out."

The gambler stood his ground. With a flip of a wrist, his coat was opened just enough to reveal the Colt housed in a finely tooled leather holster at his side. "You lost at cards, friend. See that you don't lose a whole lot more."

Mike wasn't the only one to feel the impact of those

words. All the others at the bar had taken notice and were backing away from the pair, getting ready to either run for the door or jump for cover. The barkeep had stepped a few paces back and was reaching for something with a twitching, desperate hand.

Words swirled around inside Mike's head like whiskey at the bottom of a shaking glass. Before any of those words could be spoken, they were swallowed up by the nervous breaths leaping back and forth at the top of his throat. The corner of one eye twitched, flaring the nostril on that same side.

The gambler read Mike's expressions as though he was reading a book. Sensing approaching danger, he let his smile fade as the muscles in his gun arm tensed beneath his skin. "Tell you what, Mike," the gambler said evenly. "We can play again tonight. Bring your own cards for all I care. I'll front you the money I won last night as half your stake. That way, if the fates are on your side, you can double what you risk tonight."

"Double it?" Mike snarled. "You mean I'd win back what you cheated from me as well as what you put up tonight?"

Nodding, the gambler said, "Either way you want to think about it, that's the only way you're getting your money back. That is, unless you want to try your luck right here and now."

When he'd said those last few words, the gambler's voice dropped to a dangerous pitch. It wasn't a dramatic change, but it was like the shift in a wolf's eye. When another man spotted a change like that, he tended to think twice before taking his next step.

Mike's jaw clenched, and the muscles in his arm relaxed a bit. Finally, he nodded. "All right then. But if'n I see the first sign that you're cheating, I'll blow you straight to hell."

"Fair enough. I'll see you back here tonight, and we'll

have our game. In the meantime, I think I'll seek my re-
freshment elsewhere." The gambler tipped his hat and
started to leave.

Only then did the barkeep finally get a response to the
insistent rapping of his knuckles against the narrow door
behind the bar.

When that door swung open, it revealed a small back
office as well as a man that nearly filled out the entire
frame. He was of slightly better than average build and carried himself with a quiet confidence. Dark brown eyes
darted back and forth, quickly taking in the situation
within the saloon.

"Hold on here," the man said as he stepped through the
door. Addressing the gambler more than Mikc, he asked,
"Is there a problem?"

The gambler shook his head and continued out the door.
"Not at all. I'll be back later."

Seeing that it was too late to say anything to the well-
dressed man, the bigger fellow behind the bar shifted his
attention to the barkeep. "What's so urgent?"

The barkeep nodded toward Mike with a pained expression.

"Ain't no problem here, Caleb," Mike grunted. "Just get
your ass back into that office like a good little bookkeeper."

Annoyed, the taller of the two men behind the bar
stepped forward, pushing the door shut behind him. "If
you're chasing off my customers again, Mike, I'll have you
run out of here for good."

"Yeah, yeah. That's what you always say." The more
Mike talked, the more steam he put into his words. And
when he saw that nobody around him was heeled, he found
even more courage. "If you think I'm taking orders from
some goddamn Injun, then you've got another think coming."

Those words dropped through the air like dead flies.
Everyone else in the saloon who'd just been starting to

relax now once again backed away. As Caleb stepped up closer to the bar, his boots knocked against the floorboards like hammers. When he got close enough, he placed his hands upon the bar and leaned forward.

What little sunlight that could make it through the smoked glass of the windows fell upon his face in a grimy wave. His skin was darker than most, carrying the underlying tint of desert clay. Coal-black hair sprouted from his scalp in irregular clumps, not one of which was longer than a brush's bristles. The intensity in his eyes was powerful enough to light a campfire.

"What did you say to me?" Caleb asked.

Mike leaned forward. At this point, he was either too cocksure to care about the glint in Caleb's eyes or too stupid to notice it. Slapping a coin onto the bar, he said, "You heard me, Injun. Now shut yer hole and give me some firewater."

As Caleb reached out to accept the coin, he felt a calming hand on his shoulder. The barkeep eased him away from the bar and sidled in front of him.

"With all the heat we've been getting," the barkeep said, "it's no wonder tempers are flaring. Here's your whiskey, Mike, and how about a round for the rest of you?" Glancing back at Caleb, he asked. "That all right?"

"Sure," Caleb said. "I think I could use a drink."

Caleb stepped away from the bar so Mike could get to his bottle and spout off to someone else. After filling up a mug of beer for himself, Caleb didn't even get a chance to raise it to his lips before he heard Mike's voice booming out yet again.

"This ain't whiskey!" Mike shouted after spraying the liquor out at both men behind the bar. "It tastes more like piss to me! What's the deal, Caleb? Did your squaw momma squat down on top of this here bottle and piss in it, or do you just need a lesson in how to run a goddamn saloon?"

Stopping just short of the narrow door leading to his office, Caleb pulled in a measured breath and let it out. He wasn't at all surprised to hear the taunt coming from an asshole like Mike Abel. Unfortunately, the bottle thrown at him by that same asshole was a bit more of a surprise.

The bottle knocked against Caleb's left shoulder blade and rolled down his back before hitting the floor. Although the impact wasn't enough to do any damage, it was the spark that had landed too close to a powder keg.

The bottle hadn't even come to a stop on the floor before it was snatched up again by Caleb's hand. Shoving past the barkeep, Caleb glared straight into Mike's eyes and slammed the bottle back onto the bar in front of him. The impact was hard enough to send a series of cracks through the glass.

"You'd best calm down, Mike," Caleb snarled. "Or so help me . . ."

Mike's smile was deceptively calm as he reached out to grab the bottle one more time by its neck. "Or you'll what?" Mike taunted. "I've had enough grief for one day, so I sure as hell won't take no more from some Injun bartender." Without another word and before Caleb could say anything else, Mike brought the bottle up and around in a quick arc that was aimed directly at Caleb's head.

Caleb's first thought was to reach for the shotgun beneath the bar. He could also have picked up a thick length of timber that sported plenty of dents from cracking against the skulls of men like Mike Abel. Instead, Caleb stepped back after too much deliberation and almost tripped over the barkeep behind him.

The bottle slammed into Caleb's jaw with enough force to snap his head to one side and rattle his brain. Caleb could feel the bottle folding around his jaw as the cracks deepened and eventually shattered it completely. When the bottle exploded, Caleb's world became alight with intense, throbbing pain.

"How'd you like that, Injun?" Mike taunted with a grunting laugh.

Before he knew what was happening, Caleb felt the floor teeter beneath him. His arms reached out for support, but his backside found the closed office door instead. As he bounced off the door, Caleb pulled in a breath while trying to right himself before he gave Mike the satisfaction of seeing him fall over.

That breath felt like his jaw was being sawed off, but at least it kept him upright.

"Get the hell out of here, Mike," the barkeep said while bringing up the thick piece of lumber that was dented and bloodied at one end. "Or I'll knock you into tomorrow."

Mike held up his hands and backed away from the bar. "I'll be back tonight for my game. And I expect to have my whiskey replaced with some proper liquor." Before anyone could say or do anything else, Mike turned his back on the bar and walked out of the saloon.

"Jesus Christ," the barkeep said as he rushed over to lend a hand to Caleb. "Are you all right?" While he was genuinely concerned with Caleb's well-being, he was also raising his voice in the hope that he could drown out the sound of Mike's laughter. Judging by the look on Caleb's face, the effort wasn't exactly successful.

[2]

"I'm all right." With each syllable, Caleb felt more pain stabbing through his face. At first he thought his jaw had been broken. Then he reached up to feel the spot with one hand and realized the pain was coming from a different source.

The barkeep was examining him as well. Although he wanted to help, he pulled his hands back before he did any more damage. "You need to see a doctor. It looks like you got some glass stuck in you."

Caleb had already figured that much out for himself. While the barkeep was being cautious, Caleb was touching his fingertips against various points along his cheek and jaw. Every touch was slick with a mixture of blood and whiskey. The blood trickled out from the numerous places he'd been cut, and the whiskey trickled into those same wounds to make it feel like fire was being pumped straight beneath his skin.

"Watch you don't pass out now," the barkeep said. "I'm

not sure I can catch you. Carrying you to the doctor is right out of the question."

Seeing the genuine concern on the barkeep's face brought a bit of a smirk to Caleb's. The smaller man seemed just as concerned that Caleb might be hurt as he was concerned for himself if Caleb happened to fall on top of him. While they were close in height, Caleb outweighed the barkeep by at least sixty pounds of muscle.

"Don't worry, Hank," Caleb said to the barkeep. "I should be able to stay awake long enough to keep from crushing you."

"That's not what I meant. Well, not entirely. I just figured that you should—"

"I know. I was just kidding."

The relief on Hank's face was just as evident to Caleb as it was to the few customers who'd made their way back to the bar in Mike's wake. One of those customers was the old miner who'd only moved to make certain his drink didn't get knocked over.

The miner grinned wide enough to display a set of teeth that looked like a crooked row of tombstones. His skin was weathered as an old saddle and sat just as comfortably over the frame of his face. "Take a lickin' like that and still got it in ya to kid? That's a hell of a thing." Lifting his drink, he said, "Here's to ya, boy!"

Caleb lowered his eyes and started to smile but found it too painful. His hands were busy picking pieces of the bottle out of his face. The pieces that were just stuck to his skin came off easily enough. Some of the others were wedged in like splinters, and the remaining chunks of glass were stuck in much deeper.

Even though Caleb was the actual owner of the Busted Flush, it was times like these that he truly felt like the kid everyone said he was. Fresh out of his teens, Caleb had been living a workingman's life for so long that he felt twice his age.

"What do you think you're doing, boy?" the miner asked. "You need to get to the doctor for that. You're just makin' it worse."

Caleb rolled his eyes. Not only did doctors cost money that he didn't have, but he saw it as a way of admitting that Mike Abel had won the fight.

"You ain't any less of a man for going to a doctor," the miner said as if reading Caleb's mind. "Of course, if you want to put on a show, I'll sure as hell watch. I ain't never seen nobody tear their own face off before."

Settling in against the bar, the miner took hold of his drink and fixed his gaze upon Caleb as though he was watching a song and dance revue.

Caleb looked back at him with his hand poised over the damaged side of his face until the old man's words finally sank in.

"Can you watch the place for a while, Hank?" Caleb asked. "I guess I'll be going to the doctor."

Hank nodded and looked more than a little relieved. "Sure I can. If Mike comes anywhere near here, I'll crack his head open like an egg."

While the barkeep patted the club that still lay in arm's reach, Caleb found himself glancing more toward the shotgun, which was a little farther under the bar. As if to pull his thoughts from where they were headed, Caleb felt a stab of pain from the side of his face.

"You able to walk, boy?" the miner asked.

Caleb nodded. "I can make it, Orville. Thanks."

"Then you'd probably be better off going to a dentist. A doctor'd bandage up them cuts and maybe give you some tonic, but you'll need something more than that unless you fancy losing more'n the glass from that jaw of yours. Trust me," the old man added, leaning forward as if to draw more attention to his crooked smile. "I know what I'm talking about."

"A dentist," Caleb moaned. "This just keeps getting better." Before he could protest more vehemently, Caleb realized his face was already swelling, and it was getting more difficult to form his words. "Where th dentis?" he asked, finding that it hurt a bit less if he kept his jaw still.

Hank walked behind Caleb to make sure he got around the bar and to the door. "There's a few places I know of, but the closest one is on Elm Street between Market and Austin."

"Wha his name?"

"It'd be Doctor Seegar you're after. My aunt had to go to him a while back to get some teeth pulled, and he did a fine job. She's been back to him since to get some false teeth made, and he did a fine job there, too."

"I'll be bag," Caleb mumbled.

Hank nodded at first, then furrowed his brow and then finally asked, "Huh?"

"I'll . . . be . . . back," Caleb repeated, this time pronouncing each word painfully.

Nodding furiously, Hank all but pushed Caleb through the front door. "Take your time, take your time. I'll make sure the Flush is here when you get back."

As he stepped outside, Caleb took a moment to clear his head and pull in as much fresh air as he could comfortably manage. Even on the days when he didn't get smashed in the face with a bottle, staying inside the saloon had a way of making him dizzy. Perhaps it was the combined scents of cigar smoke and liquor that sent his head to spinning. Then again, there was also the fact that when he looked at all those dented tables, battered chairs, chipped glasses, and rotting floorboards, he saw a pile of money that he would never get back again.

When he started thinking along those lines, it made the knock from the bottle a lot less painful.

As he started walking down the street, Caleb did his best to get his mind off the fact that his face looked like a porcupine's backside. His mouth hung open a bit and he had to suck in the occasional strand of bloody saliva dangling from his lip. Even so, he still managed to try to nod at the people he passed along the way.

Dallas was a good place to be for someone like Caleb. It was also a good place to be for someone like Mike Abel or the gambler who'd hung him out to dry the night before. There were plenty of people who wanted to make fortunes and plenty more willing to take them.

For Caleb, Dallas had been one opportunity after another. It was the place he'd wanted to go ever since he was old enough to realize that the world stretched beyond the boundaries of his father's ranch. It was the first place he'd gone when what had seemed like a small fortune had been dumped into his lap after a fever had culled some of the members of his family.

Dallas was alive and breathing. It teemed with folks who moved along its streets like blood pumping through a giant's body. It had noises and sights all its own. But as much as Caleb loved it there, he wondered if there wasn't even more that he was allowing to pass him by.

He got that way when the receipts for his saloon didn't come out right or if a liquor salesman gouged him in a particularly creative way. Thoughts of selling the Busted Flush to the highest bidder or just burning it to the ground had entered his mind more than once. But thoughts like that came to any businessman every now and then, so Caleb just put his nose right back against the grindstone and kept pushing forward.

After all, he was a businessman now.

Right and proper.

Straight and narrow.

His father was proud of him, and the rest of his family loved to puff out their chests when they talked about how Caleb had made a name for himself as a prosperous businessman in the wilds of Dallas.

Then again, proper businessmen didn't normally get their faces split apart and punctured by a liquor bottle.

It wasn't a long walk to Elm Street. The journey took him into a busier section of town where it was easy to just keep his head down and blend into the churning crowd. There were folks of all shapes and sizes going about their business. Most of them seemed to be making a lot of noise as they haggled over the price of salt or made predictions for the date of the next thunderstorm.

Before too long, Caleb found himself staggering up to a narrow building that was just tall enough to blend in with most of its neighbors. The lower portion of it was marked as A. M. Cochrane's Drug Store. Caleb walked around to a set of stairs leading to the upper floor marked by a simple painted sign that read J. A. Seegar and J. H. Holliday. Dentists. Satisfaction Guaranteed.

The door at the top of those stairs opened into a small yet comfortable waiting area. At the moment, however, the only place he truly would have been comfortable was somewhere about a hundred miles from the spot he was in.

"Can I help you?" asked a girl who was only slightly younger than Caleb. "Do you have an appointment?"

Before Caleb could make a noise or even attempt to put an answer together, he saw the girl's eyes become wide as saucers as she covered her mouth with one hand.

"Oh my goodness," she said. "Of course you don't have an appointment. Did you fall down?"

"No. I wa hi." Even though it hadn't been long since the last time he'd tried to speak out loud, Caleb felt as if his jaw had rusted shut. He winced partially from the pain and partially from the knowledge that he was going to have to repeat himself at least one more time.

"You were hit?" the girl asked. "That's terrible. Is your jaw broken?"

Still a little stunned that he'd been understood at all, Caleb shook his head. "No. There jus the glass in—"

The girl stopped him with a quickly raised hand. "That's good enough. You probably shouldn't try talking any more."

"Id Docto Seegar in?" Caleb asked against the girl's orders.

"Dr. Seegar is with a patient right now and he'll probably be busy for a while. His partner is available, though."

Caleb's eyes wandered over to a nameplate propped up on the edge of the desk in the reception area. The words on it were the same as the ones painted upon the shingle hanging outside the office.

The girl stood up as one of the doors leading farther into the office was pulled open. "Dr. Holliday," she said, "there's someone here who needs to see you."

[**3**]

Caleb leaned back in a chair that allowed him to stretch out as though he was meant to take a nap. His feet were propped up off the floor, while his upper body leaned back far enough for the inside of his mouth to be examined by the slender man who sat beside him.

Actually *slender* wasn't exactly a proper word to describe Dr. Holliday. He was so thin that his skin hung on him like a sheet draped over a skeleton. His cheeks were pale and sunken, but his eyes glimmered with an inner light. Even with all of this, Holliday still kept from looking weak. It was a hell of a feat, but he pulled it off all the same.

The dentist sat on a stool next to Caleb's chair and was just finishing up his preparations when he looked over and gave his patient a personable smile. "Not exactly the most comfortable accommodations," he said in a smooth, southern drawl. "But considering the scrape you got yourself into, I doubt a feather mattress would make much difference."

Caleb nodded, knowing better than to try to speak unless it was absolutely necessary.

"I assume it's safe to say this wasn't self-inflicted?" Holliday asked.

After waiting long enough to see that the dentist was truly expecting a response, Caleb shook his head. "I go hi wi a bo—le."

"A bottle? I usually prefer to keep the bottle on the outside and the liquor in, wouldn't you agree?"

Caleb couldn't help but smirk at Holliday's easy manner.

Reaching out with both hands, Holliday eased open Caleb's mouth and leaned forward for a better look inside. Short, blond hair was parted evenly upon the dentist's head. A thin mustache covered most of his upper lip, and the closer he got, the more gaunt he looked. His skin was pasty, yet his hands were strong and unwavering. As he leaned in to examine Caleb's jaw, a subtle wheeze could be heard under every one of Holliday's breaths.

"I do believe I've seen you before," Holliday said while he reached for a pair of pliers and began tugging at the shards of glass embedded in Caleb's jaw.

Although Caleb couldn't respond, the questioning look in his eyes was picked up immediately by Holliday.

"You run the Busted Flush, don't you?"

The moment Caleb's expression shifted, Holliday plucked one of the glass pieces from where it had been lodged. The pain came in a sharp jolt but faded quickly since the glass had only been wedged into skin rather than bone.

The sound of glass clattering against the inside of a tin cup rattled through the small room, followed by the sound of Holliday coughing twice into the back of his hand.

"One down," Holliday said. "Half a bottle to go. Normally, that statement makes me so much happier. Of course, I'm usually referring to emptying the bottle glass by glass." His thick southern accent colored every word, lending to his speech a smooth, rounded texture.

Sitting in that chair, Caleb did everything he could to get his mind away from what was being done. That left only the dentist himself to occupy his thoughts, since that pale, sunken face was practically the only thing he could see. Fortunately, Holliday seemed more than happy to fill the air with the sound of his own voice.

"I've been to the Flush more than once," Holliday continued as another chunk of glass was plucked free and dropped into the cup. "Rough place. There are some good games held there, though."

Pain stabbed close to Caleb's chin.

Next came the light rattle of glass against tin.

"I enjoy a good game or two, myself, now and then."

Not much pain this time. Caleb's face was starting to numb.

Another chip of glass fell on top of the bigger pieces.

"From what I've heard, most of your games are fair enough."

A bit of pain that felt like a small insect bite.

Another chip fell into the cup.

"I'm sure you're aware," Holliday added, "that you've got a few cheaters in the mix."

Caleb reflexively turned to look directly into the dentist's eyes. He was stopped by a firm hand that came up quickly to clamp onto Caleb's chin.

"Wha?" Caleb asked.

Still holding onto Caleb's jaw with his fingers splayed so as not to disturb any of the remaining glass shards, Holliday nodded and kept talking. "Oh, it's true. I know at least one of them well enough. I was even tossing around the notion of trying to cut myself in on his action, but since you came to me first . . ."

Trailing off, Holliday pulled at one more piece of glass. This time, the pain that shot through Caleb's face was like a spike being twisted through the bottom half of his skull. The glass didn't come free, since it was wedged into the jawbone itself rather than the flesh surrounding it.

Holliday patted Caleb on the chest as he leaned back to reach for his rack of instruments. When he leaned forward again, Holliday smiled reassuringly down at Caleb. "Now don't you move," he said, holding up a pair of larger metal tongs, "or this might sting. The good news is that I should be able to work around the teeth you've got left. You do a fine job of maintaining them, by the way."

Before Caleb could say anything, he felt the dentist's grip tighten on his head and then heard the distinct sound of metal clamping around glass. There was a crunch, which filled his head like a shotgun blast as the shard was pulled free.

Caleb squirmed in the chair. His hands gripped onto the wooden arms, and his eyes became so wide that he could barely even see through them anymore. There was some pressure, a tug, and then the warm flow of blood. The sensation that followed was warm as well and would have been agonizing if it hadn't already been eclipsed by the pain that soaked through every inch of his skull.

When he was a kid, Caleb had loved to climb fence posts and walk along the rails surrounding his father's land. One time, he'd slipped from the fence and landed the wrong way upon his left leg. The moment he hit the ground, he knew his leg was misaligned. When he reached down, he felt the bones in his knee poking out at odd angles.

A doctor had tugged on his leg to set the bones right again. Any other time, and the thought of wrenching his knee like that would have seemed awful. Compared to the way it had felt when they were misaligned, however, that lesser pain was a blessing. At least things were being set right again in the process.

Sitting in that uncomfortable chair with Holliday

wrenching the glass out of his jaw, Caleb felt that same kind of pain. It hurt, but it hurt a whole lot less than how it had been hurting before. And when it was over, at least he would be set right again.

Another glass shard dropped into a cup that was so full, the glass no longer rattled inside of it.

"All right, then," Holliday said. "Unless my eyes are failing me, I'd say that about does it. All you need is some glue, and you might be able to put that bottle back together again. Ever hear of Humpty Dumpty?"

Caleb's vision was blurred, and he felt like he was falling through murky water. All of that made Holliday's comments seem even more ludicrous. "Wha?" he asked. It didn't hurt so much to talk anymore. "What?"

Just as his fingertips grazed against his jaw, Caleb felt that steady, almost skeletal hand reach out to stop him.

"Leave it be," Holliday said. "For now, anyway. It needs time to heal, but you should be right as rain before too long."

Sitting up, Caleb pulled in a few breaths to clear his head. Moving his jaw didn't exactly feel good, but the pain was nothing compared to how it had been not too long ago.

"I can stitch up some of those cuts if you still have it in you," Holliday said.

Caleb looked over to the dentist and found that sitting up and seeing Holliday at an equal level was something of a new perspective. Holliday still looked pale and gaunt. His eyes, which had seemed a cool blue before, now seemed gray. Sweat had broken out across his forehead and slicked his dark blond hair against his scalp. The perspiration seemed to come from something else besides the heat that filled the room as it did the entire state of Texas at that time of year.

Before too long, Holliday picked up on Caleb's careful inspection of him. "You strike me as a fighting man," Holliday said.

Once more taken off his guard, Caleb replied, "What's that supposed to mean?"

"The way you're sizing me up. I've seen wild dogs with less fire in their eyes."

Now it was Caleb's turn to smile. Even though the gesture hurt, it was good to be able to do it again. "I've heard about you, Holliday. You're more than just a dentist around here."

Holliday's eyes showed a glint of amusement. When he smiled, he showed a set of well-maintained if slightly bloodied teeth. "Is that a fact, now?"

Caleb saw the bloodstains on the dentist's teeth and reacted just enough for Holliday to pick up on it. In one motion, Holliday had turned away from Caleb and pulled a handkerchief from his pocket to dab at his mouth. He cleared his throat a few times, but that soon degenerated into a series of hacking coughs.

One after another, the coughs came. They started shaking Holliday like a pair of rough, invisible hands as the sound he made became gritty and wet. And just as quickly as they'd overtaken him, the coughs were forced back down. Holliday wiped his mouth, pulled in a breath, and once again set his eyes upon Caleb.

Oddly enough, Caleb had to admit that Holliday looked even stronger than before.

"You said I had some cheaters in my place," Caleb reminded the dentist. "From what I hear, you could be one of them."

"And who told you that? Someone who bet too much and lost is what I'd wager."

"Yeah. They lost, all right."

"And let me guess. They didn't take it up with the law, either?"

"No. They didn't." Caleb nodded at the way Holliday composed himself. He liked to think he had instinct to spare when it came to judging men. Even so, it was hard to get a read on the dentist before him. "So who is this cheater, then? Will you tell me?"

"First things first," Holliday said. "How about you settle up with the girl out front for this service before I provide you with another one?"

A knot formed in Caleb's stomach. "I don't have any money with me. At least, probably not enough to pay for this."

"Are you happy with my work?"

Caleb took a moment to mull the question and found no ulterior motives behind it. Holliday's expression was genuine as he perched on the edge of his stool waiting for the response. Reaching up to feel his jaw, he found plenty of bloody gaps but no more glass. "Feels a whole lot better than when I came in."

"Then that can hold me over until you can pay me. Now, how about those cuts? Shall I see to them, or would you prefer to go to another doctor?"

"Since I'm already here, you might as well do it. If I'm going to run up a bill, I'd just as soon just run up one big one than a few smaller ones."

"Now that is what I call sound reasoning. Care for something to help with the pain?"

Fully expecting a tonic or some kind of ointment, Caleb nodded. What he got instead was something that made him look down just to make sure he was guessing correctly about what the dentist had given him. Sure enough, it was a dented metal flask. The initials JHH were engraved onto its front. A quick shake told him the flask was about half-full.

"That might sting a bit going down," Holliday said with a wink. "But it'll be worth it."

Steeling himself with a deep breath, Caleb twisted open the flask and lifted it to his mouth. When he tossed back some of the contents, he made sure to keep as much of it as possible on the less damaged half of his mouth. The whiskey was smooth and potent, with a bit of a smoky aftertaste. That wasn't enough, however, to dull the flash of pain that filled Caleb's skull like billowing smoke.

Swallowing the liquor, Caleb handed back the flask. "Tastes expensive," he said.

Holliday nodded while accepting the flask. When he took a pull for himself, he didn't so much as flinch. "Feel better?"

"No, but let's get this over with."

"What's the matter? You don't trust Hank to watch your place while you're away?"

Caleb squinted through the slight haze that had rolled in behind his eyes from the combination of pain and whiskey. "Why do you say that? And how do you know so much about my business?"

Holliday's features lightened a bit as he shrugged. "Maybe I should be asking you why you don't recognize the face of one of your customers?" After another second ticked by, Holliday smirked. "Relax, Caleb. I make it my business to know as much as I can about the person who runs a place where I play cards. It helps me avoid the money pits."

"Money pits?"

"Sure. Places where the only ones who win are the cheats and the owners who let them operate. Everyone else might as well be tossing their money into a pit."

"Clever. You think up that one on your own?"

"Not hardly." After one more pull from the flask, Holliday offered it back to Caleb. It was refused, so Holliday took Caleb's portion for himself. "Now then, let's see what we can do about that face of yours."

Caleb's first impulse was to vacate that uncomfortable chair until some of the whiskey had been purged from the dentist's system. He stayed put when he saw that Holliday's hands were just as steady now as when he'd started.

The whiskey gave Holliday's skin a rosy hue and made the smile on his face a bit more personable. Anyone else would have looked like a drunkard. For a man who appeared to be a few steps over a corpse, any bit of color was a welcome change, no matter where it came from.

Only a few of the cuts on Caleb's jaw were deep enough to need stitches. The rest only required bandaging so they could close up on their own. Now that the broken glass was out, the damage to his jaw didn't seem half as bad as it had first seemed.

"You'll be fine," Holliday said, his southern accent polishing up the words like varnish on a knife's handle. "You want some advice?"

"Sure."

"Next time you see a bottle coming your way . . . duck."

Caleb started to smile but held back when he realized that one of his cuts was still in the process of being stitched. He didn't have to wait long, however, until the dentist had completed his task and was leaning back to clean his hands with a towel.

"There you go," Holliday said in a somewhat thicker drawl. "All clean and good as new."

Sitting up, Caleb ran his hand over the lines of his face. The glass was gone, and the blood was no longer slick upon his cheek. "Much obliged. You do good work. Now, about settling the bill."

Holliday was already tipping his flask against his mouth while waving off Caleb's statement with his free hand. "Worry about that later. We still have that other matter to discuss. How about we settle both things at once?"

"Fine by me," Caleb said. Whether due to the pain or the whiskey he'd drunk to deal with it, he was having a hard time getting himself too worked up about the possibility of cheaters in his midst. Come to think of it, considering the crowd his place usually drew, having cheaters among them was no surprise. Still, rooting one or two out could go a long way in drawing better players.

"Splendid," Holliday said. "It's been a while since I've had a good game. I'll stop by the Flush tonight."

"I'll have enough to pay you for the work you did, and I'll even top off that flask of yours."

Lifting the flask in a toast. Holliday seemed to be happier about that than anything else so far. "Mind those stitches, now."

With that, Holliday got up from his stool and walked to the door. Before he could make it through the door, Holliday stopped and was taken over by another fit of coughing. He got it under control quickly enough, dabbed his mouth with his handkerchief, and then continued down the narrow hall.

On his way out, Caleb started to say something to the girl at the front of the office.

"Don't worry about a thing," she said cheerily. "Everything's taken care of."

He waved to the girl and left the dentist's office. With the whiskey's comforting haze already starting to fade, Caleb gripped the handrail and took the stairs one at a time.

[4]

The day wound up being quiet enough for Caleb to spend most of it relaxing in his office. Sitting in the room that looked to be more of a large closet than anything made to hold a desk and chair, he shook his head as he often did and wondered what the hell he was doing there.

The first answer that came to mind was the habitual one. He was there because he'd wanted to own a saloon. He'd saved his money and bided his time until he could eventually afford to put a payment down on a building that had come up for sale. With a little help from an investor or two, a few generous family members, plus no small amount of luck, the Busted Flush had been born.

Along the way, he'd also picked up a pain at the back of his skull, which hadn't lessened since he'd scratched his name upon the papers putting the saloon under his management.

Things could have gone a whole lot worse. After all, he was still in business and had managed to pick up a small group of customers. There was even talk that the Flush might make it onto the gambler's circuit. Being included on that informal list, which got circulated among the country's best players, was a hell of a boon to a man in Caleb's business.

As Caleb's mind shifted to the other side of that same coin, he felt a massive sigh work its way up to the top of his lungs. The deeper his roots sank into the business he'd so desperately wanted, the more he felt like he was getting buried underneath it all. The walls of his office closed in like the sides of a coffin. Every noise he made rattled around in there with him.

His breathing sounded like a grating rasp.

The shifting of his boots against the floor echoed in his ears. The movement of his hands over the top of his little desk was like desert rocks being scraped together.

Even the noises that came in from the main room echoed so loudly that he wanted to tear his ears off the sides of his head.

Caleb practically jumped up from his desk and stormed out of his office. When the door swung open, Hank jumped out of the way before taking a hit square in the nose.

"What's the rush, Caleb?" Hank asked as the customers leaning against the bar laughed at his near fall.

"No rush. I just needed to get some fresh air."

The old miner was still in his spot. From there, he seemed to see and hear everything that happened in the place. "No fresh air in here," he said. "At least, not when ol' Thirsty is in the room."

Everyone within earshot laughed at that. Everyone, that is, except for Thirsty.

The middle-aged man was dressed in a sloppy, rumpled suit. His face had the permanent, rosy hue of someone with just as much liquor flowing through his veins as there was blood. "Aw, to hell with ya, Orville," Thirsty grunted.

Raising his glass, the old miner shot back with, "You first, you drunk bastard."

That got another round of insults started. Some of the others chimed in like children pitching their marbles into a schoolyard game. Caleb watched the bawdy exchanges with a smile as the knot in his stomach started to loosen. The air within the saloon might have been far from fresh, but it was exactly what he'd needed.

And, using the sixth sense that his sort always seemed to have, Loco Mike Abel picked that moment to make his entrance.

Before Mike had even stepped all the way through the front door, Caleb had spotted him and was searching for the darkly dressed man Mike was there to see. It was easy enough to spot the gambler, since his face was already turning toward the door.

Placing his hand upon Hank's shoulder, Caleb walked past the barkeep and whispered, "Stay on your toes."

The barkeep didn't know how to take that until he finally spotted Mike swaggering into the saloon like he owned the place. Nodding, Hank stepped aside so Caleb could walk around the bar.

"Hell of a crowd tonight," Mike said as Caleb approached him. "Word must'a gotten out about my big game."

Caleb stepped right up to him, stopped, and took a look around for himself. "I've seen bigger."

"Yeah? Well you won't see a bigger game."

"If that's all you're here for, then go have your game. I'm more than happy to provide the table. If it's trouble you're after, then you'd best move along."

After ignoring Caleb for another moment or two, Mike finally shifted his eyes back to him and smirked. "Didn't I already deal with you?" He reached out to take hold of Caleb's chin so he could move his head from side to side. "Yeah. Looks like I did. How about you tend to your bar before I tear that face up some more?"

Caleb slapped Mike's hand aside. He could feel his nostrils flaring as every muscle in his body tensed.

Mike's smirk became even more maddening as he said, "Ohh, don't get all riled up. I didn't mean anything by it." He then put his back to Caleb and moved forward as if he'd forgotten the other man had even existed. "Now where's that dandy who thinks he can play cards?"

"That'd be me," came a voice from a table toward the back of the room.

The gambler didn't bother getting up from his seat. He was still dressed in his black suit, but his tie was loosened and his jacket was draped over the back of his chair. Some of the others at his table took a moment to acknowledge Mike's presence, but only with a quick glance over their shoulder.

Mike didn't seem to notice that nearly everyone else in the saloon had gotten back to their own business. Assuming he was the center of attention, he glanced around from one side to another, nodded and smiled to an audience that he didn't even have.

As much as he wanted to do otherwise, Caleb let Mike pass. The words that had passed between them still burned inside his ears.

Stopping once he got up to the gambler's table, Mike pulled out a chair and dropped himself into it. He kept his eyes glued to the well-dressed man as he reached into his pocket and removed a wad of folded money. "Here's my stake," he said with a snarl. "Think you can match it?"

So far, the gambler's face hadn't gone through more than half a change, which took it from casual blankness to amused blankness. Without breaking Mike's stare, he let his hand wander over the stack of chips in front of him. A few glances toward Mike's cash were all he needed before the gambler measured out the proper amount of chips and shoved them forward. It was about a quarter of his total.

"That ought to do it," the gambler said.

Mike's eyes flicked back and forth between his cash and all of the gambler's chips. Seeing the difference between the two was enough to wipe away some of his previous smugness, but not all of it. Finally, Mike stopped acting like he was on display.

"Just because we're playing against each other," the gambler said, "doesn't make us enemies."

"The hell it don't. I plan on soaking you for all you got. If I do win, you'll give me back what you cheated off me before. That's the deal, and you better have enough to honor it."

"Of course."

"Then that's all I need to hear. Oh, and one more thing." Mike lowered his voice to a deadly serious tone. That intensity cut through all of his previous swagger the way flames cut through a wall of smoke. "If'n I catch you cheating," he said, motioning toward the gun at his hip, "I'll burn you down right here in front of God and everybody. You hear me?"

"Oh, I hear you," came a voice that didn't belong to Mike or any of the other players at that table. "Come to think of it, I'd say this whole saloon heard you. That is, of course, if anyone were actually listening."

Mike's brow furrowed, and he twisted around to get a look at who'd just spoken. There wasn't anyone standing behind him or on either side. Caleb was still glaring at him from near the bar, but it hadn't been his voice. Then Mike spotted another face that matched the voice and was looking right back at him.

It was a pale, gaunt face wearing a smile that would have been more comfortable on a skull rather than any living man's head.

"Who the hell invited you to this game, Holliday?"

Caleb's eyes snapped open wide, and he didn't even bother to hide the surprised confusion that had showed up on his face. Sure enough, after a bit of sidestepping and craning his neck, Caleb was able to spot the dentist sitting at a table next to the one that he'd been watching this whole time. Holliday's cold blue eyes shifted in their sunken sockets as if to say hello.

Ignoring Mike's question, Holliday glanced over to the gambler dressed in the black suit. "Evenin', Virgil."

Holliday's drawl seemed especially thick at the moment. It was almost as if his voice had become as relaxed as the rest of him, which was currently lounging in a straightbacked chair as though it was a throne.

Dressed in his dark suit and sitting behind a healthy stack of chips, Virgil Ellis nodded politely at the dentist. "Evening, Doc. I was wondering if you were going to join us."

Feeling like the odd man out, Caleb wheeled around to get a look at Hank. "How long's he been there?" he asked, pointing out Holliday to the bartender.

Hank shrugged and shook his head.

Having already gotten up from his seat, Holliday stepped over to Virgil's table. "I thought I'd warm up until the real action got here," he said, smirking toward Mike.

Although Mike certainly wasn't the sharpest knife in the drawer, he knew well enough when he was being ridiculed. "Damn right the real action's here," Mike huffed, doing a piss-poor job of maintaining his bravado. "Now how about you just go off and hack up a lung somewhere else?"

Holliday's chest twitched with a suppressed cough. His face, however, showed no visible reaction. He was wearing clothes that were just as dark, if not quite as expensive, as Virgil's. With one hand, he reached under his jacket in a way that gave the men at the table a glimpse at the holster strapped around his shoulders.

Mike's hand twitched toward his gun, but not close enough to set anyone off. His eyes widened in nervous anticipation as he asked, "What the hell are you doing, Holliday?"

After a slight pause, the dentist eased his hand out from under his jacket. He was holding a leather pouch, leaving the pistol holstered under his arm. He hefted the pouch in his hand, allowing the clink of money from within to be heard. With a flourish, he tossed the pouch onto the middle of the table. Silver dollars spilled from it. Even the glitter of some gold could be seen within the leather container.

"I've got no objections to him sitting in," Virgil said.

Still nervous, Mike clenched his jaw and looked around at the others seated at the table. When he didn't get any support from the rest of the gamblers, he looked down to the money Holliday had offered. Mike let out a breath and licked his lips before finally forcing himself to relax. "Fine by me. I don't mind winning this one's money along with everyone else's."

"That's the spirit," Holliday said as he took a seat at the table. A few of the other players had to scoot to one side, but they let him have his spot between Virgil and Mike. "A positive attitude does wonders in poker. That is, if we are playing poker?"

Virgil nodded. "What else is there?"

"Poker's a man's game," Mike grunted. "I don't play nothing else."

"Even with the double negative, I agree wholeheartedly," Holliday said.

Mike's nostrils flared. "You got a smart mouth, you skinny little rat. Guess that's why you need to be heeled at a friendly game."

"Oh, this?" Holliday's hand drifted toward his gun, but only to tap the handle lovingly. "This is my good luck charm. And by the way, you can call me Doc."

"Yeah, I know all about you. I seen you play a few games not too long ago." Leaning forward until his belly tilted his side of the table, Mike added, "I guess since you

ain't lucky in nothing else, you're bound to get lucky at
cards every now and then." Mike leaned back and
shrugged. "Odds are damn good that you'll keel over before the night's out anyhow."

If Doc was rattled by anything that had come from
Mike's mouth, he gave no indication. Instead, he merely
nodded and signaled toward the bar for a drink. "All right
then. Let's play some cards."

{ 5 }

In the time it took a round of drinks to arrive at the table and for money to be traded for chips, the occupants of the chairs had done a bit of shuffling. While the three principal players of the game stayed where they were, some of the others who'd been gambling either moved to another spot or cashed themselves out altogether.

The ones who left did so with a cordial word and tip of their hat, scooping up whatever money they had and leaving as quickly as they could. That left two others besides Virgil, Mike, and Doc at the table. One of those was a young cowboy who still had fresh dust in his hair and the other was Orville, the old miner who practically lived at the Busted Flush. Going by the look on Orville's face, he wasn't about to miss one second of the game, no matter how many guns were present.

Virgil played the part of gracious host, engaging in small talk with anyone who cared to return the favor while rolling a silver dollar back and forth over his knuckles.

Doc quickly suppressed a coughing fit before removing

the handkerchief from his breast pocket. While he did exchange a few pleasantries with Virgil, he seemed to be more concerned with getting his flask refilled and then sampling the whiskey brought to him in a separate glass. Once a few sips of liquor were in his system, the dentist eased back into his chair and got comfortable. His eyes had taken on a grayer hue and somehow seemed clearer than before he'd had his drinks.

Mike sat on the edge of his chair with his hands folded upon the table. His eyes snapped back and forth between Virgil and Doc while he nervously licked his lips. When the drinks came, he pounded back a swig of whiskey before slapping down the empty glass and refilling it. "If all I wanted was a drink, I'd be standin' at the bar," he grunted.

"Hear, hear," Doc said, tapping his own glass against the table. "Since it doesn't look like anyone else wants to join us, let's get this show under way."

Caleb stepped up and delivered a fresh deck of cards to the table. He spread them out and made sure everyone had a chance to count them before giving them a shuffle and stepping back. Although some players got a little impatient having to wait through that little ritual, Caleb found that enough fights were avoided that way to make it worth everyone's while.

"Care to do the honors?" Doc asked while glancing toward Mike.

Mike's lips curled a bit, but when he saw that Doc was pointing toward the deck of cards, he quickly brightened up. "Don't mind if I do," he said while reaching out to snatch the cards and deal them out. One at a time, he flipped five cards to each person at the table.

Doc accepted his cards as though he was already disappointed, picking them up and searching through them one by one. "So many choices," he said.

The old miner beside Doc fanned out his cards and shook his head. "Wish I had that problem."

Going by Virgil's expression, he might as well have been looking at empty space.

The cowboy's frown grew with every card he saw. When he'd managed to get a look at all of them, the twitch at the corner of his mouth was enough to alert anyone watching that he was less than happy with what he saw.

Mike smirked a bit when he saw his first two cards but lost his enthusiasm when he saw the other three.

Although he wasn't making a big show of it, Doc watched everything everyone else was doing. He let his eyes stay on Mike, however, as he shook his head and said, "Two high cards but no pair? I hate when that happens."

"What'd you do, Holliday? Mark these cards? You workin' with that Injun saloon owner?"

"He doesn't have to be working with anyone," Virgil said. "Not so long as you're willing to air out your business for everyone to see. Why don't you just save a step and hold your cards the other way around?"

Before Mike could say another word, he was distracted by the sound of laughter coming from his right. When he looked over, he found the cowboy snickering while trying to keep his eyes on his cards.

"You think that's funny?"

Saving the cowboy from having to dig himself out of a hole, Doc tossed in a chip and was immediately raised by the miner next to him.

"Got a hold of a hand, Orville?" Doc asked.

The miner shrugged, seeming to get a kick out of Doc's banter while also trying not to respond to it. Apparently, Holliday saw something in the other man's demeanor, since he nodded to himself and watched as the others tossed in enough to match the bet.

"I suppose I'll call," Doc sighed. "I'll also take two more cards." He flipped his discards over to Mike and sipped his whiskey.

Following suit, the miner grunted, "Three for me."

"I'll take the same," said Virgil.

After suppressing the rest of his laughter, the cowboy flipped away two of his cards and waited for the replacements.

"Dealer takes two," Mike said, stressing the last word and glaring over at Doc.

The dentist shrugged without even looking over to Mike. "No need to keep hold of that third card on my account."

Doc hardly even looked at his two new cards before reaching for his chips and tossing a handful into the pot.

"Ten dollars?" the cowboy asked.

The miner was the one to respond first. "I'll cover that."

"Me, too," Virgil said. "And another five just to make it interesting." Both he and Doc looked over to the cowboy.

The cowboy pulled in a breath and took a look at his cards. Although the first one met with his satisfaction, the final one caused his face to drop almost to the floor. "Aw hell. I fold."

Mike's expression was smug, and his grin was about as convincing as a wooden nickel. "I'll see the bet . . . and raise it twenty."

Doc made a show out of studying the pile of chips at the center of the table. Every so often, he would check the cards in his hand and then lay them facedown in front of him before taking another pull from his whiskey.

"Come on, Holliday," Mike said impatiently. "You in or out?"

Finally, after fretting a little while longer, Doc asked, "So that's sixty to me?"

Mike looked confused and added the numbers in his head one more time.

Before Mike's arithmetic was complete, Virgil laughed and said, "Not quite, Doc."

"Oh," Holliday replied. "Then that'll be sixty to you,"

he said to the miner while shoving in the proper amount of chips.

The old man sifted through his cards, weighed the options in his mind and then let out a pained grunt. "The missus will kill me, but I can't lay these beauties down just yet." He matched the bet and looked over to Virgil. "Besides," he said while tapping some papers folded in his shirt pocket, "I got enough collateral to have some fun tonight."

The gambler leaned back in his chair and studied his opponents one at a time. His left hand lay on the table, rolling the silver dollar across his knuckles while he took his time deliberating. All around him, the air was filled with voices, smoke, and some music that was being played by a man with a banjo over in one corner.

Caleb watched the scene as well. While he wasn't involved with the game, he was ready to step in if the need arose. So far, it seemed as though it was the gambler's show, and he was handling it like a professional.

"Sixty?" Virgil asked.

Mike slapped the table to let out some of the frustration that had been building inside of him like steam in a piston. "You know it is! Get on with it!"

Without reacting in the least to Mike's outburst, Virgil fixed his eyes upon the man currently acting as dealer and held them there. He watched as Mike started to shift and twitch as if a campfire had been built under his chair. "Tell you what," Virgil finally said. "Make it a hundred."

Even though the cowboy was no longer in the hand, he slapped his hands together and snapped around to see what Mike would do. By the look on his face, the cowboy thought that whatever money he may have lost was more than enough to pay for the show he was getting.

Mike nodded slowly and let out the breath he'd been holding. "You think I'm stupid? I've played with you before, and I know you're full of shit."

"One way to find out," the gambler said.

"Yeah. There is. I raise it to one fifty. You want to bluff me? You'd best be willing to do it with more than what you got." He threw in his money as though the pot was already his and then leaned back to throw a sideways glance toward Doc. "You still in this, Holliday? Or do you need to go lay down for a while?"

Doc didn't touch his cards. Leaving them where they lay on the table, he took a slow pull from his whiskey and let it trickle down his throat. Thankfully, the breath he let out was nowhere near an open flame. "Tell you the truth, I'm amazed the rest of you are still in this. Especially since I'd bet my practice that Orville here has at least two pair, which should be more'n enough to beat the pair each of us wound up with."

"You think you know so much, Holliday?" Mike asked in a steady tone. "Then make yer move."

Although Doc kept his eyes on Mike, there was no threat in his gaze. Instead, there was a bit of amusement as he shrugged and went for his chips. "I bet another two fifty. Consider it a donation to the fine art of tin-panning," he said, with a glance over toward the old miner next to him.

Orville had to laugh. "I'll be damned before I get shoved out of this game." Reluctantly, he reached for one of the papers in his pocket. He brought it out, unfolded it and then dropped it onto the table. "That's the deed to a hell of a good claim. You've got my word on it."

"Tell you what. If it doesn't pan out to cover your bet in a month, I'll be back to have a word with you. Anything after that goes to me no matter what."

The miner thought about it and nodded. "Fair enough, I guess."

"That's the spirit!" Doc said while lifting his glass. "I must say, you truly surprise me. Your drinks are on me tonight, especially since I shouldn't have any trouble paying for them after this hand."

Virgil was still shaking his head while watching Doc in action. He seemed more than a little uneasy however, when he saw the way Mike's hand was inching closer to his gun. "I've seen you make some bold plays, Doc. Is this another one of those, or do you really have what it takes?"

"One way to find out."

After pausing long enough to riffle through his chips, Virgil shrugged and pushed most of them forward. "No problem here. Most of this money used to be Mike's anyway."

"Care for a little side bet between us?" Doc asked.

Virgil shrugged. "What do you have in mind?"

"First one to make Mike cry wins a dollar."

A smile broke across Virgil's face as he shook his head at the same time. Glancing over to Mike, he said, "Doc's just being Doc. He doesn't mean anything by it."

"Fuck that," Mike spat. "And fuck you, Holliday."

Mike looked back and forth between the other men so quickly that he got dizzy. The miner wasn't giving him anything to work with besides his stubbornness to fold. Doc was taunting him openly, and Virgil merely looked back at him while trying not to laugh. Those last two fed the fire in Mike's belly so much that he couldn't even begin to hide it. Looking over at the grinning cowboy just made things worse. "What the hell is so funny?" Mike asked, while all but lunging toward the youngest man at the table.

The cowboy recoiled slightly but couldn't stop smirking. "Just watching," he said while holding his hands up. "Don't mind me."

"Yeah? Well let's see how you all like this." Mike shoved his chips into the middle. "I got you covered, plus another fifty."

Doc's expression didn't shift. His steely gray eyes locked onto Mike as if he was the only other living soul in town. In the moments that he held that stare, every other sound in the saloon seemed to fade away. Finally, knowing when the other man was just about to snap, Doc pulled out a wad of folded bills from his jacket pocket and said, "I raise. Five hundred."

The miner let out a low whistle.

"Well, old-timer," Doc said. "You have anything else to bet? Or do you really have that much confidence in two pair?"

The miner shook his head and sighed. "I know better than to gamble with what I don't have. Besides," he added, glancing at the gun in Doc's holster, "I wouldn't want to make those claims sound like they're worth enough to cover this. Take 'em." With that, he dropped his cards faceup onto the table. He had two pair: aces and threes.

After a few coughs into the back of his hand, Doc asked, "What about you, Virgil?"

Virgil's face could have been made from stone. Although he wasn't outright mad, he obviously wasn't laughing anymore. The smile on his face wasn't fooling anyone, and when he dropped his cards onto the table, it seemed like he was cutting off five of his own fingers. "You got something, Doc. I don't know what it is, but my guess is it beats my two ladies."

Doc's nod was almost imperceptible. His eyes remained firmly trained upon Virgil in a way that was strangely comforting to the gambler.

"What'd you say you had?" Mike grunted. "Queens?" Although the subtle shrug he got from Virgil widened the grin on his face, that celebration didn't last long once he looked over to Doc. Bit by bit, Mike's grin dried up and finally blew away. The mention of queens didn't rattle the dentist in the slightest. Glancing down at his own cards, Mike felt as if his innards were being squeezed in a clamp.

"I heard you was lucky," Mike said to Doc. "I also heard you was a cheat. What I know for damn sure you want me to call so bad you can taste it." Without another word, he pitched his cards onto the table so roughly that they flipped over to reveal a pair of kings. "I'll get you next time."

Doc turned his cards over and set them down. There was plenty of paint to be found, but none of it matched.

"Ace high?" Mike snarled.

The cowboy gaped at the cards as if they'd come alive and started to dance.

Virgil let out a disgusted sigh but tipped his hat to the dentist. "You got me, Doc. You'd have a hell of a career in theater."

"Possibly," Doc replied. The southern drawl in his voice lent it even more of an amused tone. "But I'd rather be up close to my audience. More fun that way." He reached out and pulled in a portion of the chips while looking over to Mike.

The miner laughed under his breath at first, but then out loud. It was a sad, regretful laugh that was directed more at himself than the situation. "Good game, Doc. Next time, I'll know to listen to my gut."

"And next time, I'll try to draw better cards."

Mike was seething. His fingers curled around the edge of the table with such power that his knuckles turned white. "You . . . bluffed me . . . with an . . . *ace high*?"

"The night's young, Mike," Doc drawled. "And you've got to admit it was a hell of a ride."

Letting out a breath that was like steam coming from a bull's nostrils, Mike stood up and lifted his side of the table with him. Chips scattered and cards fluttered through the air as the heavy table knocked into both Virgil and the miner. By the time the edge of the table slammed against the floor, Mike was reaching for his gun.

"Aww hell," Caleb grunted as he jumped behind the bar. "Here we go."

[6]

Caleb jumped onto the bar, slid a few inches over the polished surface, and then dropped down on the other side. He could already hear hell breaking loose behind him, and the money needed to fix the damages rang up like there was a cash register in his head. Glasses were breaking, and chairs were surely to follow, making the stitches in his face the least of Caleb's pains.

"What's happening?" Hank asked as he crouched down to try to help Caleb to his feet.

But Caleb was already upright and searching the saloon around him. When he saw the first glint of bared iron, he grabbed hold of the barkeep's shirt and pulled him down behind the bar. A gunshot barked through the air as the table that had played host to Mike's game rolled lazily on the floor.

"Just what I thought would happen, that's what," Caleb snarled.

"You knew there was gonna be a fight?"

"I had a real good suspicion."

"Should I call the law?"

"No," Caleb said as he began searching behind the bar. Finding what he was after, he grabbed hold of the sawed-off shotgun and made sure it was loaded. "I'll take care of this myself."

∼∼∼

The first gunshot had come from another table not too far from where Doc was sitting. Even though there wasn't actually a table in front of him any longer, he remained in his seat and looked around as though he was merely sampling a passing breeze. Apparently, someone had tried to take advantage of the sudden turmoil by grabbing the money from another table.

It didn't seem as though they were going to get away with it.

"You're dead, Holliday," Mike said as he kicked his chair onto the floor behind him.

"It was a fair hand," Doc said while calmly getting to his feet. "Grousing about it won't help."

Virgil dusted himself off as he got back onto his feet. While he'd managed to avoid getting hit by too much of the overturned table, the miner sitting next to him had caught the brunt of it. Orville was holding his side but still managing to scoop up as many of his claims as he could hold with his free hand before making a run for it.

"Doc's right," Virgil said. "You lost fair and square. We both did."

Mike's lips curled back into an animal's snarl. "Fair, my ass. He either agrees to hand my money back, or I put him out of his goddamn misery."

Doc's eyes were even colder than when he'd bet everything he had on an ace high. The hand he was betting on at the moment, however, was the one hovering within a few inches of the pistol holstered beneath his left arm. "You already made a mess," Doc said in his smooth, southern manner. "Don't make it any worse."

As the players at the nearby table still struggled among themselves for the money in their own game, the flaring tempers seemed to spread like wildfire throughout the rest of the saloon. People who'd turned away from their games to see what was happening found their stacks of money depleted or another player peeking at cards that weren't their own.

Standing in the eye of the hurricane, Mike, Doc, and Virgil stared each other down as if nothing else existed.

Suddenly, thunder filled the Busted Flush as the air exploded with the sound of a shotgun being fired into the ceiling.

"Enough of this!" Caleb shouted from where he stood in the middle of the main room. "Everyone step back, put your guns on the floor, and take a breath! If we can settle up and get on with our night, there won't be any need to get the law."

Doc's voice drifted toward Mike like a stiletto wrapped in silk. "I know how we can settle this. Let's flip a coin for it. Maybe you'll have an easier time at that than trying to figure out how to play poker."

A string of unintelligible curses spewed from Mike's mouth as his hand snapped toward his gun.

With a flicker of motion and a subtle lean forward, Doc had drawn his own pistol and stuck the barrel underneath Mike's chin.

Mike froze in his place; his hand still wrapped around a pistol that was almost clear of its holster. After a bit of pressure from the gun against his chin and a devilish tilt of Doc's head, Mike loosened his grip and allowed the pistol to drop back into its holster.

"That's better," Doc said, ignoring the chaos swirling around him.

"Goddammit, Doc," came a grumbling, familiar voice. "Why couldn't you just leave well enough alone?"

Doc's eyes flickered in the direction of that question and found Virgil standing up and shoving aside a drunk who'd decided to try his hand at brawling. As he looked back toward Mike, Doc made a couple of sideways steps so he could watch both men without having to look away from either one.

"That miner had more deeds in his pocket. Deeds that were actually worth something," Virgil said. "He was about to wager every last one of them before you stepped in and spoiled the whole thing."

"Well then," Doc said. "I suppose you had every intention of splitting your share with me?"

Virgil glanced over to the miner, who was busy scrambling toward the front door while doing his best to avoid the incoming punches, kicks, or bottles flying through the air. While the brawl wasn't the biggest the Busted Flush had ever seen, it was doing a fair amount of damage.

"Damn. He's headed out the door," Virgil said.

"He's a gambler," Doc pointed out. "Not to mention the fact that he came out ahead today. He'll be back, and he won't mind playing with us. It's this one he's gonna be wary of." With that last part, Doc pushed his gun underneath Mike's chin just enough to point the other man's head upward a few more degrees.

But Virgil didn't even seem to take notice of Mike squirming and cursing at the end of Doc's arm. Instead, he shook his head and slowly lowered his arm until it was within drawing distance of his pistol. "He's not the one that worries me, Doc. At least he knows his place."

For a moment, Doc looked surprised. That moment passed quickly, only to be replaced by a subtle shaking of his head. "That truly is a shame, then. We could have made some real money together."

"Partners need to trust each other, Doc. At least a little."

Virgil's hand flashed toward his gun while his eyes remained locked upon his target. He cleared leather, certain that he would get his shot off before Doc could shift his own gun from where it was wedged beneath Mike's chin. There was a mix of regret and victory in Virgil's heart, soon to be joined by a chunk of hot lead.

Doc's right hand snapped to aim his pistol at Virgil. Without blinking an eye, he squeezed his trigger and rocked Virgil back a few steps.

The gambler's eyes were wide as the pain started to flood through his chest. His instinct was to aim and take his shot anyway, but he no longer even had the strength to hold his gun. The pistol slipped through his fingers as it and its owner both dropped to the floor.

At that moment, Doc felt some pain of his own. It was a jab in his ribs followed by a sharp stab when he tried to breathe.

Mike's elbow had pounded into his side while his other hand came up to try and knock the gun from Doc's hand. The next move he made was to draw his own pistol and thumb back the hammer.

"You cheatin' son of a b—"

Mike's insult was cut off by the roar of a shotgun at close range. The blast took a chunk out of his torso and spun him around. The pistol in his hand went off but sent its round into the mirror behind the bar.

Stepping forward with the shotgun still smoking in his hands, Caleb looked down as though he expected Mike to take another swing at him. Not only was Mike dead, but the pistol he'd been holding had been knocked clear from his hand.

Although a single shot had sparked the fighting to begin with, the shotgun blast had been more than enough to end it. Everybody in that saloon stopped what they were doing. Every face turned to stare at Caleb, who stood over the messy remains of Loco Mike Abel.

For a few seconds, the roar of the shotgun was the only thing Caleb could hear. The echo of that shot rumbled through him like a smaller tremor after an earthquake had passed.

Then, after what felt like an eternity of standing there with that gun in his hands, Caleb was able to lower the weapon and take in some of what was going on around him.

Although the saloon was considerably less full than it had been moments ago, it was far from empty. The faces that gaped back at him were mostly familiar. Every last one of them, however, seemed to be in shock.

"Jesus Christ," came one voice from near the bar. "He shot him."

"He shot him dead," agreed another. "I saw it."

"I saw it, too. Damn near cut him in half."

"I think I'm gonna be sick."

As Caleb glanced around at the people he thought he'd been protecting, he soon came to realize that every last one of them was talking about him. The bottom of his stomach dropped out, and soon the floor seemed to tilt beneath his feet. Almost immediately, he felt a steadying hand on his shoulder.

"It's all right," Doc said in a low, soothing voice. "It's all over. You did good."

But Doc's voice swam with all the others in the confusing swirl of Caleb's thoughts.

"Give me that shotgun," Doc said.

Still working on instinct, Caleb's grip tightened around the shotgun so he could pull it closer to himself.

"I'm not the one you need to worry about," Doc said. "You should probably get rid of that gun before things get worse."

"What happened?" Caleb asked while looking around at the bodies of Virgil and Mike, which lay sprawled on the floor.

"I told you there was a cheater in your place," Doc explained. "Virgil was the one. He's been lining up that old miner for a week or so. Damn near had him ready to fall, too." Shaking his head, Doc said, "That would have been a hell of a haul."

"But he was going to shoot you."

"I should have known better than to step in without thinking it through."

As the smoke was clearing and people were getting their wits about them, the air within the saloon grew heavy. The only person who seemed unaffected by that change was Doc. Unlike the others, who milled around or beat a quick path to the door, Doc pulled up his chair and dropped himself down onto it.

"Actually, you were set to fall as well," Doc said. "Virgil would have stirred up all kinds of hell, and this place would have been marked as a money pit for years. That's why I stepped in. I was hoping Virgil would just move his game to another place. Lord knows that miner would have followed him."

"I don't know how I'm going to fix this," Caleb said, looking around at his broken, bloodied saloon.

"I think you've got bigger problems than the mess."

Before Caleb could ask Doc to clarify, his answer came stomping through the front door.

Four men poured through that door. Two of them jabbed their fingers toward Caleb and Doc. The other two were not only armed but wearing badges.

"That's the man," one of the pointers shouted. "He gunned down Loco Mike, and Mike was already being held up by that other one there!"

The second pointer nodded furiously. "I saw it, too. Caleb killed Mike for callin' him an Injun. I heard all about it, an' I seen him kill Mike with my own eyes! I seen it all!"

Doc shook his head while taking a drink from his flask. "I told you to get rid of that shotgun."

"Aw Jesus," Caleb said, dropping the shotgun as both lawmen stepped forward to point their guns at him.

"Caleb Wayfinder," the first lawman snarled. "You're under arrest. You, too, Doc."

[7]

The law in Dallas was a mixed bag of volunteers and Texas Rangers passing through to keep the peace. There were a few constant faces, but Caleb had learned real quickly to enforce his own rules rather than rely upon anyone wearing a badge. It was a fairly good arrangement, since the law had never seemed too interested in doing anything but drinking inside the Busted Flush.

For the time being, a Texas Ranger by the name of Ben Mays had pulled the duty of keeping the peace in Dallas. There were other lawmen in town, but Mays seemed to be the one who was at the center of them all. It could change before too long, or it could stay the same for years. Caleb didn't care either way. All he wanted at the moment was for that damn snoring to stop.

A simple ride down any of Dallas's streets would display walls of stucco, wood, or even brick. The fact of the matter was that a lot of those walls had been crafted in factories out East, shipped by the newly laid railroad tracks, and put together by anyone with a strong back and some simple tools. Dallas had plenty of promise, but a long way to go before being strong enough to withstand a nasty gust of wind.

Unfortunately, Caleb Wayfinder's current accommodations had withstood plenty more than wind. Judging by the chips in the walls and the dents in the iron bars covering the door and windows, more than one man had tested their strength and failed. At the moment, Caleb wasn't much interested in testing his strength.

He wasn't even interested in getting up from the cot, which was the only thing besides himself inside that six-by-three cell.

All he wanted was some peace and quiet after a hard night. His jaw was still giving him hell, every muscle ached, and his head was throbbing. With the sun's rays slicing into his cell through the square window near the ceiling, it seemed as though Loco Mike Abel had been dead for years already.

In fact, the only thing that seemed real to Caleb just then was the stench of the cell and the constant thumping of the guards' feet as they walked back and forth to check on him before thumping back to a nearby desk. Caleb sat upon his cot, which was actually an old, broken door covered in a horse blanket. One leg was stretched out in front of him, while the other dangled off the edge to rest upon the floor. His back was propped against the wall, and his eyes remained partially open as they had for the entire night.

He hadn't said a word since he'd been tossed into that cell, which had done a world of good for his jaw. Having only been able to sleep for a couple hours, he'd spent the remainder of his time behind bars flicking at his stitches with the tip of his tongue. The little jabs of pain gave him something to focus on instead of the constant noise coming from his neighbor.

Dr. Holliday was in the cell next door, and when he

hadn't been talking to Caleb over the last ten hours, his coughing fits had filled the air with a wet, hacking sound that was impossible to ignore. More recently, Holliday hadn't uttered a word. His coughs had died down and were soon replaced by another sound that was just as bad for Caleb's nerves: snoring.

As Holliday's snoring continued, it started to feel like a dull saw being dragged across Caleb's eardrums. Part of that irritation came from the situation, while another part came from jealousy, since Caleb would have traded a few of his own fingers to get a couple hours of such restful sleep.

Just thinking about it made Caleb clench his eyes shut so he could try to will himself into oblivion. His back ached, his eyes were burning, and every bone in his body was crying for mercy. Every breath was a hardship, and Caleb knew for a fact that he couldn't have gotten up from his cot without a whole lot of strenuous work. Even with all of that, sleep would not come.

Holliday kept snoring like a well-fed mutt, while Caleb was forced to watch the sunlight grow brighter against a wall as his eyelids slowly pasted themselves into haggard slits. Caleb opened and closed his mouth, only to wince at the pain those simple motions caused.

The same set of boots thumped against the floor, just as they had every half hour or so since the arrival of the fresh-faced guard at dawn. The guard couldn't have weighed more than a hundred and ten pounds soaking wet but walked as if he was punishing the floor. More than a little of that confidence surely came from the gun at his hip and the stout club in his hand.

Strutting past Caleb's cell, the guard looked in through the bars with a scowl on his face. He nodded approvingly when Caleb stayed in his place and kept on walking for a few more paces. Straightening up to his full five feet eleven inches, the guard took hold of the bars of the neighboring cell and rattled the door noisily.

There was so little space in the cramped hallway connecting the cells that Caleb could still see half of the skinny guard's frame from where he was sitting.

"Rise and shine, Holliday," the guard said.

The snoring was interrupted for a moment as Caleb heard the sound of something shifting upon a board similar to the broken door beneath his own smelly blanket.

The guard fidgeted with a ring of keys hanging from his belt, and when he looked up from that, he started smacking the bars impatiently with his club. "Come on! I said get up!"

Hearing the guard's overeager voice echo through his aching head, Caleb pinched his eyelids together and let out a groan.

"I won't hear nothing from you," the guard said as he leaned a bit to one side so he could peer in at Caleb.

"What the hell?" Holliday croaked.

After finding the key he'd been looking for, the guard fit it into the cell door's lock and turned it. "Get on out of there. Ben says you can go."

Caleb only had to tilt his head to one side and press his ear to the wall for him to hear the dentist struggling to get up in the cell next to him. Holliday's movements sounded as if they were coming from one of the oafs who passed out nightly at the Busted Flush. There was a lot of scraping of limbs against the cot's edges, followed by the drop of heavy feet against the floor.

"That was the best sleep Ah've had in weeks," Holliday said in a voice that barely seemed human. His words were still thick with his southern drawl but now were rougher than tree bark and punctuated with a rasping cough that hurt just to hear it.

The guard winced at the sound of Holliday's desperate hacking. That expression changed considerably after the dentist spat a juicy wad onto the floor. "Jesus Christ, are you all right?"

"Ah'm fine and dandy," Holliday replied in a drawl that was thicker than ever. "Now what time is it?"

"Just past ten in the morning."

"And you're here to tuhn me loose?"

The guard nodded. "Yes, sir."

"And why is that?"

"Ben talked to some folks at that saloon who said you were defending yourself when that other fellow tried to shoot you."

"You mean Virgil?"

Shrugging, the guard replied, "I don't recall the name, but he was a known card cheat, and there were witnesses who said you were justified in that shooting. Since Dr. Seegar spoke up for you as well, Ben said there was no harm in letting you out. Just be sure to stay around so's we can find you if we need to ask anything else about the shooting."

Holliday's feet shuffled against the floor, and he pulled in a few tired breaths. "What about my friend in the next cell?" he asked. "When is he to be released?"

His eyes nervously twitching in Caleb's direction, the guard shrugged his shoulders. "Can't say. That's Ben's call."

Caleb felt a groan work its way up into the back of his throat, but he was too tired to push it any farther than that. His eyes had come open a bit more, which allowed him to get a good look at Holliday the moment the dentist stepped into view.

Wiping at his mouth with the back of his hand, Holliday looked into Caleb's cell just long enough to meet the other man's wary stare. No matter how badly Caleb had been feeling before, he felt better when he got a look at Holliday's waxy, blood-smeared face.

The dentist's blond hair was a tussled mess, and there

were dark circles under his eyes, which were still an odd mix of gray and blue. Of course, that could have simply been the sunlight reflecting from his pale skin. Looking away from Caleb, Holliday pulled himself upright and choked back another series of coughs that threatened to overtake him.

Turning to face the guard once more, Holliday leaned against the bars of Caleb's cell for support. In that instant, from his spot behind the dentist, Caleb thought he was going to see the dentist keel over completely. Despite the pain in his own body, Caleb jumped to his feet and reached out to slip an arm through the bars and hold Doc upright before he crumpled to the floor.

To Caleb's surprise, Holliday wasn't about to let himself drop. He also wasn't about to accept any help from anyone else. Twisting away from the support Caleb offered, Holliday took a few steps down the hall. Unfortunately, that allowed the guard a real good look at Caleb reaching out from his cell.

"Get away from there!" the guard shouted as he swung at Caleb's arm. "I said you're not to be released, and I meant it!"

The guard's club slammed against the bars, crushing Caleb's elbow in the process. Even as Caleb pulled his arm back in, the guard was reaching for the gun holstered at his hip. In the same instant the young man's hand found the pistol's grip, he realized that he couldn't move his arm enough to get that weapon out of its leather resting place.

Even though Caleb had been right there the whole time, he hadn't spotted Holliday's movement as the gaunt dentist had reached out and slapped his hand down on top of the guard's to trap the lawman's gun before it could clear leather.

Confused and rattled, the guard looked at Caleb and his own holster a few times before realizing that it was Holliday who prevented him from drawing.

"Keep this up, Doc, and I might reconsider letting you go," said a man from the other end of the hall.

Caleb tried to get a look at who'd spoken, but couldn't see much of anything besides the two men standing directly in front of his cell. Pressing his face against the bars allowed him to spot the Texas Ranger making his way to the scuffle between Holliday and the young guard.

Ben Mays was a handsome fellow with light brown hair and a glimmer in his eyes that seemed to welcome whatever trouble he saw. Plain, battered clothes hung over his muscular frame, and a well-worn hat rested a ways back on his head. As he stepped up to Holliday, he kept his hand on the grip of his gun without drawing it. Even so, the threat was easy enough to read in his face.

"You're an upstanding member of this community, which is why I don't mind cutting you a little slack," Mays said. "But if you don't step away from that boy, I'll have to toss you back into your cell."

Holliday sucked in a breath and took a step back. Holding both hands up, he leaned against the wall opposite Caleb's cell and nodded.

Mays nodded as well as he reached out to pat the guard on the shoulder. After a few good-natured slaps, he practically shoved the kid back down the hall to where the rest of the lawmen conducted their business. "Go on and collect Doc's things," Mays said. "That is, unless he intends to stay for a while longer?"

"I believe I shall be excusing myself," Holliday said in a voice that was much more familiar to Caleb. "I was hoping my associate here could join me as well."

Without looking at Caleb, the Texas Ranger shook his head. "Not right now, he won't."

"And why is that?"

"Because he killed Mike Abel."

"You mean Loco Mike Abel?" Holliday asked. At first, the sound he made was a cough. That cough shifted into a laugh. "Surely the man's name speaks for itself. If I was defending myself in there, then surely my friend in the next cell was doing the same."

"I'll be needing to check on that."

"And he's supposed to sit in there and wait?"

"That's how it works, Doc. You should know that by now. I hear you've had to sleep off a hard night's drinking in every one of these cells at one time or another."

"Hardly," the dentist replied, sounding more like a southern gentleman now that he'd had a chance to collect himself.

Glancing over at Caleb, Mays took in the sight of the other man as if he was looking at a dog standing up on its hind legs. "Witnesses say this one here gunned down Mike after the fight was over. That's murder in anyone's book."

"He was going for a gun," Caleb said in a voice that was even rougher than Holliday's. After clearing his throat and straightening up, Caleb added, "Mike was stirring up shit since the first time he walked into my place. He lost at cards and then started shooting. He's not the first asshole to get himself killed like that."

"No," Mays said as he squared his shoulders with Caleb and stepped up to the bars, "but he's the first asshole that you gunned down in front of a dozen witnesses. Doc here gets to leave because he's an upstanding fellow with even more upstanding fellows to vouch for him."

"And what does that make me?" Caleb asked.

"It makes you the fellow sitting in that cell waiting for me to do my job."

"And if I don't have enough upstanding folks to vouch for me?"

Mays narrowed his eyes and said, "Then you'll be the fellow who hangs for committing murder."

If Caleb's cell had been a respite from the chaos of the Busted Flush, it was a sanctuary after Holliday's coughing and snoring were taken out of the mix. After the dentist was released, Caleb managed to get back to his cot and catch some well-deserved sleep. His arm was aching, and the stitches in his jaw were still hurting, but the quiet of that cell was enough to beat it all.

Caleb was yanked from his sleep by the pounding of boots against iron bars. This time, it wasn't the young guard who'd fetched Holliday earlier but another guard with long gray hair gathered up by a leather strap behind his head.

"Do I finally get something to eat?" Caleb asked.

The guard shook his head and grumbled in a voice soaked in gin. "You can get something to eat fer yerself," he grumbled as he unlocked and opened the door.

Caleb got up from the cot, walked right up to the bars,

and stopped just short of leaving the cell. "What's going on?"

"You're free to go."

"But Mays said I had to stay."

"I guess he spoke to enough folks to convince him you could leave. Anyways, I suggest you do just that before anyone changes their mind."

It was hard for Caleb to argue with that logic, so he walked out of the cell and headed down the vaguely familiar hallway. The last time he'd walked through there, he'd been kicking and screaming with the blood pumping like a torrent through his head. Now that he was calmed down again, he barely even recognized the inside of the Texas Ranger's office.

There wasn't anyone else inside the place apart from the one, older guard. A clock on the wall said it was getting close to eleven at night, and the shadows outside the office's windows verified that nicely. Caleb could already hear the rowdy voices that marked practically every night in Dallas, drawing his next thoughts immediately back to his saloon.

"I wouldn't leave town if I was you," the guard said as he lowered himself onto a chair behind one of the office's three desks. "Until this clears up, you should stay where we can find you. Otherways, Ben will come looking for you."

"Well, he knows where to find me."

The guard let out a snorting laugh and said, "Sure he does. We can round you up quick enough if you step out of line."

"Will I need to talk to a judge?"

"I reckon so."

Caleb stood there for a moment. waiting to see if anything else would happen. With the threat of being hung still lurking in his mind, he half expected to be shot in the back as he walked out through the front door of the office. But nothing so dramatic happened as Caleb stepped out of the building and back onto the street.

It was a hot, sticky evening, and the crickets were almost chirping loud enough to drown out the voices and music coming from the entertainment district. Normally, Caleb heard those sounds and smiled at the thought of all the money that would be flowing through the Busted Flush.

Tonight, however, it was just noise.

"I believe I owe you a drink," said a voice from the nearby shadows.

Caleb turned to look and found a narrow silhouette leaning against a post in front of the storefront across the street. Recognizing the figure immediately, Caleb crossed the street and approached the man who'd been waiting for him.

Holliday's skin was even paler in the moonlight, and the darkness made his cheeks appear to be even more sunken. Even with all that, the dentist looked better than he had earlier in the day. His eyes weren't so cold, and the angles of his face weren't as sharp as they had been before.

As he got closer to the dentist, Caleb began to pick up on the reason for Holliday's better mood. "You've already been drinking," he said.

Straightening up, Holliday took a step forward and tugged on the lapels of his black waistcoat. Beneath the waistcoat, he wore a dark gray shirt and a black string tie. His black pants matched the rest of the outfit, making Caleb look like a vagrant in comparison. On his right lapel, he wore a gold and diamond stickpin that glittered like a star that had been plucked from the collection overhead.

"And here I thought I was going to be civil," Holliday said.

"Too late for that, Dr. Holliday."

The dentist furrowed his brow and took a step forward. "You did save my life, so I figure I ought to pay you back in kind." He extended a hand and put on a smile that was too bright to be anything but genuine. "And please, call me Doc."

Before he could think about anything else, Caleb found himself shaking Doc's hand. The other man's grip was strong and steady, which didn't seem to match the aroma of whiskey that hung like a thick cloud around his head.

"You have a last name, Caleb?" Doc asked.

"Yeah. Wayfinder."

Doc took back his hand and snapped his fingers. "That's right. After all the confusion over the last day or so, that slipped my mind. Now, how about that drink you promised me?"

"Wait a second," Caleb said after catching a glimpse of the Texas Ranger's office. "I need to find Ben Mays. I don't even know why the hell I got out so quickly. And besides, you're the one that owes me a drink."

"Semantics. Besides, there's no need to worry about Mays."

"What do you mean?"

"You're out because you don't deserve to be inside that miserable cage. That's the beauty of our divine justice system." When he said that last sentence, Doc didn't even try to mask the sarcasm in his voice.

"Last time I heard, it sounded like Mays was gonna use that divine system to string me up and hang me out to dry."

"Possibly," Doc said with a shrug. "But there was no way he could do that after so many witnesses came forward to give their accounts of what happened."

"Witnesses came forward?"

Doc was walking down the boardwalk, heading straight for the loudest part of town. "Of course they did. All it took was a little organization to get them together and set their stories straight."

Although Caleb had been walking at Doc's side, he came to a halt the moment he heard those last few words.

When he saw that Doc had no intention of stopping, Caleb reached out and dropped his hand onto Doc's shoulder. It took a good amount of effort to turn Doc around.

"You got some people to lie to Ben Mays?" Caleb asked.

Knocking Caleb's hand away, Doc replied, "There was no lying involved, thank you very much. There were folks in that saloon who saw what truly happened, and all I did was gather them up and point them in the right direction."

Caleb's eyes narrowed. "And what about setting their stories straight? What, exactly did that involve?"

Doc looked back without reacting in the least to Caleb's frustration. In fact, the more Doc studied Caleb's face, the more he nodded. "All right, so maybe I suggested a few things they should say, but not a bit of it was a lie."

"Great," Caleb snarled as he turned and pressed his fingers against his forehead to try to soothe the ache that was growing inside his skull. "How long do you figure it'll be before Mays finds out about this and hauls me back into that cell to rot?"

"You know what your problem is?" Doc asked in his easy southern drawl. "You worry too much. You didn't do anything wrong besides put down that mad dog before he killed someone. If it wasn't you, someone else would have killed that son of a bitch, and Mays knows it. All he needed to hear was verification from someone else to that effect."

Oddly enough, the more Caleb thought about it, the more sense Doc's words seemed to make. "Who did you get to speak for me?"

"Just half a dozen or so people that were there when everything happened. Mays showed up like clockwork asking around about what happened. Besides the barkeep at your saloon, those others just said what happened."

"And what about the ones that were saying I killed Mike Abel in cold blood?" Just mentioning that caused those accusations to echo through Caleb's mind just as they had been ever since the shooting had stopped.

Doc waved off that question like it was a gnat buzzing around his head. "Forget about them. They didn't bother showing up while Mays was poking his nose about."

"So I'm really free?"

"You're out here walking around, aren't you?"

"Yeah. I suppose I am."

"Then let's get that drink and stop fussing about the past."

"Sounds good, Doc. I know just the place."

～～～

It was the busiest time of the night for any saloon, but the Busted Flush was even busier than usual. The moment Caleb walked in, the entire place exploded with cheers and joyous hollers, which died down just before shots got fired into the rafters.

Caleb waded through the people, most of which he recognized, and made his way to the bar. Hank was all smiles as he reached across to slap Caleb on the shoulder like a proud father on graduation day.

"Glad to have you back, Caleb!" Hank said. "I knew you wouldn't be gone for long!"

Caleb's head was spinning as he looked around at the folks who were already getting back to their own revelry. "Jesus, I didn't know so many people cared about what happened to saloon owners around here."

As if on cue, one of the less familiar faces in the crowd shoved past Caleb and snapped his fingers to get Hank's attention. "Hey barkeep, you still handing out them free drinks?"

Hank turned and quickly poured a splash of whiskey into one of the smallest glasses. When the other man saw that he was barely getting a finger and a half of liquor, he shrugged and downed it in one gulp. After letting out a wheezing breath followed by a twitch, the man dropped the glass and headed for the door.

"Ah," Caleb said as he looked around at everyone crammed into the Busted Flush. "Now it makes sense."

"We are happy to have you back, Caleb," Hank said. "I just thought a party would brighten your spirits."

"It did, Hank. Thanks."

Suddenly, Hank's eyes widened, and he put on another grin. "Is that you, Dr. Holliday?"

"It certainly is. Did I hear mention of free drinks?"

"Well, one free drink anyway. For the party. Here you go." Hank poured the splash of whiskey into a clean glass and set it onto the bar.

Doc scooped up the glass and downed the whiskey in a fluid, practiced motion. Reacting as if he'd taken a sip of milk, Doc set the glass down and nudged it forward. "Just one, you said?"

Before Hank could respond, Caleb hopped over the bar and said, "Doc's drinks are on the house. Every last one of them."

Although Hank smiled amiably, he shot more than a few wary glances in Caleb's direction. "Are you . . . uh . . . sure about that?"

"Yep." Snapping his eyes in Doc's direction, he added, "But just for tonight."

"Fair enough," the dentist replied. Then he nudged the empty glass a bit more in Hank's direction.

Fretting to himself, Hank reached to the shelf behind the bar for one of the bottles of whiskey. After lingering for a moment, he shifted his hand toward one of the less expensive selections and placed it in front of Doc.

With the bottle in one hand and his glass in the other, Doc poured himself a generous portion and downed it in much the same way as he did the first time around. As before, he barely even flinched as the firewater burned its way through his system. Lifting his empty glass to the barkeep, Doc said, "Hank, my friend, you and I are going to get along marvelously."

Seeing that Doc was doing just fine on his own, Hank walked toward the office in the back and motioned for Caleb to follow him. After fixing himself a drink of his own, Caleb went along happily as one of the other barkeeps stepped in to take his place.

"When did you and Dr. Holliday get so close?" Hank asked in a quick, hurried whisper.

"We're not blood brothers or anything, but he's a good enough sort."

"I've only seen him about town a few times, but I've never seen him get involved as much as he did earlier tonight when he came around here."

"What happened?"

Taking a quick glance behind him, Hank put his back to where Doc was sitting and explained, "He asked every last soul in here about what they saw the other night and if they knew where to find the others that were here. He even came to me and asked what I'd be telling Ben Mays when he came calling."

"I hope you intended on making me look good."

"Of course I did," Hank said dismissively. "But some of those others seemed more inclined to call you a murderer than anything else."

"That's just not true, Hank."

"I know you're not a killer, but some folks around here don't like the things they've heard about you. Some of them point to the rougher days in your youth and say you're a bad influence on this town."

"Good Lord, all I ever did was get into some fights and pull some stupid shit when I was a kid. Whatever they heard about me must be a bunch of gossip. I've done nothing but run the Flush since I first made it to Dallas."

Patting the air to soothe Caleb's nerves, Hank said, "I know, I know. All I'm saying is that I was mighty surprised to hear some of them folks sing your praises to the law after they were pointing fingers at you when Loco Mike was bleeding out on the floor."

Once again, Caleb could feel his face getting warmer. The pounding in his ears made a throbbing rhythm in his head that was almost enough to drown out the sound of his teeth grinding together. After a few breaths, Caleb looked around at the festivities around him.

"You say Doc told those people to lie?" Caleb asked.

Hank shrugged his shoulders. "I don't know what they told that ranger, exactly. It was just odd to have so many people backing me up when I told what happened between you and Mike."

"And you told the truth?"

"Sure I did."

"Then I guess there's no problem. After the night I had, I'm willing to take what I can get and move on from there."

Even though Caleb was doing his best to put some feeling into the smile he was wearing, Hank wasn't faring so well. Instead, the barkeep looked more like he'd just discovered a splinter wedged in his nether regions.

"I'm glad you're out of jail and all," Hank said. "But there's been some folks asking around for you since Mays came and went."

"One of those witnesses you were concerned about?"

Hank nodded.

Just then, the sound of the front door slamming against the wall rattled over the rest of the noise inside the saloon, followed by a snarling voice. "There's the man I wanted to see!"

Caleb turned and saw one man practically filling the doorway with his bulk and wearing a sloppy, shit-eating grin. Coming in behind the big fellow was a smaller man witb a grimy face followed by an old man who struck Caleb as familiar.

The first two were staring daggers across the saloon, and both of them wore guns strapped around their waists.

"Let me guess," Caleb said. "Those are the men you're talking about?"

Hank nodded sheepishly. "Yep. That'd be them."

[9]

Doc held the bottle he'd been given by the neck and dragged it along with him to a table with only one other occupied chair. The crowd inside the Busted Flush was thinning a bit, but there were more than enough people left to provide ample cover for a man who clearly wanted some time to himself.

After sitting down and putting his bottle in front of him, Doc reached for his glass. Unfortunately, the glass he was looking for was still on the bar where he'd left it. "Damn it," Doc muttered. Meeting the curious gaze of the gray-haired gentleman sitting across the table from him, Doc lifted his bottle and tipped it back to pour some whiskey straight down his throat. By the time he set the bottle down again, the other man was gone.

Letting out a satisfied sigh, Doc felt a scratch at the back of his throat and clenched for the coughing fit that he knew was closing in on him. He snatched a handkerchief from his breast pocket and draped it over the back of his hand with a well-practiced flip of his wrist. Hacking a few times into the folded linen, Doc drowned the remaining coughs with whiskey and sighed again as the fit subsided.

Lifting the bottle once more, Doc swirled the whiskey inside and took quick measure of how much was left. Before he could take another swig, he spotted a well-dressed gentleman working his way through the crowd. Doc's light blue eyes fixed upon the man with the freshly trimmed beard and fashionable, navy blue suit.

"Good evening, Henry."

Doc smirked at that and replied, "Evening, John."

John Seegar was one of the few people who called Doc by his middle name. It seemed to be appropriate since the fifty-year-old dentist shared Doc's first name and cut down on some confusion since both men also shared the same dental practice on Elm Street.

After settling himself into the chair, Seegar pulled in a breath and then winced as if he'd instantly regretted it. "Normally you spend your nights at the St. Charles."

"They do host better games over there."

"Yes. Indeed."

A few awkward moments passed as Seegar squirmed and stared down at his hands, which were picking at a stray splinter on the table in front of him. Finally, the older dentist looked up and caught Doc taking another drink. "What the hell are you doing, Henry?"

"I'm having a drink. Care to join me?"

"Thank you, no. What I meant to ask was, what are you doing to yourself? You know I don't approve of the way you spend your nights, but surely you can see that this isn't—"

At that moment, the front door was kicked open, and the odd-looking trio of men shouted across the saloon to catch Caleb's attention. Doc's eyes went over to the bulky man and immediately picked out the miner who'd sat in on the poker game with himself, Mike Abel, and Virgil Ellis.

Although Doc started to get up, he was stopped by the stern look etched onto Seegar's face. Seeing Caleb stride through the crowd and step up to the two armed men and the older miner was enough to put Doc somewhat at ease. It seemed Caleb was confident enough talking to the men on his own.

"Are you going to answer me?" Seegar asked. Although he'd noticed the noisy entrance of the three men, he regarded it as just another vulgar display that was all too common in such places as the Busted Flush.

"I do my job," Doc replied as he sank back into his chair.

"Just barely." Softening his voice, he added, "You're a fine dentist, Henry. It's just that lately you've allowed your nightlife to interfere. I mean, do I really need to point this out to you?"

Doc's grip tightened around the neck of the bottle. "You've always stood by me, John. That's why you should know that I can't just go about like I have a nice, cheery future in front of me."

"You certainly won't have a future if you keep pouring that liquor down your throat."

"I don't know if I'll live to see next Christmas, and my nightlife doesn't have much to do with it."

Seegar nodded solemnly. "Your consumption doesn't bother you as much out here in Texas as it did in Georgia. You told me so, yourself."

"When I first got to Dallas, maybe. But that was a year ago. Besides, you don't have to be a doctor to know that the reaper will find me here just as surely as he would have found me back home. I don't see any reason why I should sit back and wait quietly for the inevitable."

"I always admired that fighting spirit. Henry. But how are you so certain what's inevitable and what isn't?"

More than any other time, Doc felt like a kid when he was in Seegar's presence. That much was clear to see in the way he sat as if deferring to the older man. His cool blue eyes were fixed upon a spot on the table, and a grim expression remained a part of his face.

"Remember when you first came to Dallas?" Seegar asked. "I met you at the train station and took you home to meet Martha and the kids. We felt like a real family right from the start. Dr. Hape in Atlanta couldn't recommend you highly enough, and I was more than happy to take on a young man like yourself with such promising credentials."

"I remember, John. It wasn't that long ago."

Seegar nodded. "No, it wasn't that long ago, but a lot has happened in the meantime. We had a great practice. An award-winning practice, no less," he added with a proud smile. "Ever since then, you've been drinking and gambling as though it's going out of season. Even though you won't come with me and the family to church, I know you were raised better than that."

"I was just raised Methodist," Doc said. "It's not a disease, you know."

Welcoming Doc's dry wit the way a starving man welcomed Thanksgiving dinner, Seegar nodded and laughed heartily. After easing back so he could take a look around the saloon, Seegar eventually let his eyes settle upon Doc. This time, Holliday had no problem meeting his gaze.

"You're slipping, Henry," Seegar said in a level voice. "I wish there was a better way to put it, but I won't insult your intelligence by skirting the issue."

"Is that what you came here for?"

"I think you already know it is."

Doc lifted the bottle partly to his lips but set it down again without tasting a drop. "I did have a notion. Your forehead wrinkles when you're worried about business. That, and when you're about to tell someone they need to get all their teeth pulled."

Seegar chuckled. "Guess I couldn't make it too well as a gambler, huh?"

Smirking, Doc replied, "I'd be more than happy to play some high-stakes games against you. Of course, I don't exactly know what I'd do after winning the practice as well as your house and life savings after a solid half hour of poker."

"It'd probably be closer to ten minutes. Speaking of that, I've heard you've become quite the professional where gambling is concerned."

"I've been known to dabble. I find that the games I played as a child around the kitchen table were twice as cutthroat as anything you're likely to find in a gaming parlor."

"Used to be that when I heard folks talking about you around here, they'd mention your professionalism as a dentist or even those imported clothes you like to wear. Anymore, I hear people discussing all-night poker games at the St. Charles Saloon or you dealing faro at the Alhambra."

"There's just as much respect to be earned being a sporting man as in pulling teeth," Doc said with a current of annoyance running beneath his tone.

This time, when Seegar spoke, he punctuated his words by knocking his fist against the table. "Dentistry is a respected profession. You went to school for it, and you've still got a commitment to your cousin where that is concerned. Or have you already forgotten about Robert?"

Doc's eyes snapped into sharp focus as they locked onto Dr. Seegar. "Robert can handle himself just fine, and if you're suggesting I would have any part in harming his future—"

"I know you wouldn't intend on hurting Robert," Seegar quickly amended. "But weren't the two of you going to open a practice once he graduated from his own studies?"

Doc nodded.

"And I understand the two of you were very close as children."

"Like brothers."

"Then how do you think he would feel about you drinking yourself into a stupor every other night and not even showing up for work more than two or three days out of the week? How would Robert feel about you taking up as a professional gambler and carrying a pistol like so many of the troublemakers that live in saloons like this?"

"I don't show up for work because there's hardly any patients showing up anymore. It's been that way all year, and it's only getting worse. And if you have the gall to say I'm to blame for slow business, then I will be forced to disagree."

Seegar lifted his hands and shook his head. "I wouldn't dream of blaming you for that. But there are ups and downs in any business. A dental practice isn't any different. Someone needs to call you out for the mess you've made of things on those other accounts."

"Mess? Whatever do you mean?"

"Don't make me repeat myself, Henry."

"I still practice dentistry when I can, and will never give up that profession. In case you haven't noticed, this lovely Texas air hasn't cured my condition, which is why I must seek comfort in the arms of this particular mistress," Doc explained while holding up the whiskey bottle. "I find spitting up blood and having dizzy spells much easier to bear after a few drinks. Besides, since most drunks already have those conditions, I might as well taste the benefits as well."

"What benefits?"

"Being able to ignore the pitying looks I receive, for one. Folks see me coming, and they give me those goddamned doe eyes like I'm some invalid that somehow managed to get up and dressed for a walk." Doc's voice had lowered almost to a hissing snarl. "They ask how I'm feeling or how the fine weather's been treating me as if they truly gave a damn. At least the men at a card table offer more by way of conversation than the hushed condolences I get otherwise."

"Folks mean well," Seegar retorted. "You know that."

"Then maybe I prefer putting the odds in my favor for a change. You ever think about that?" As if suddenly realizing the aggression in his voice, Doc took a breath and let it out calmly. "Ever since I've been born, folks have been planning my funeral. And when I manage to pull through, they say it's a miracle. Well I have news for you and everyone else. It's not a miracle. I've been fighting every day of my life, and when I was too weak to fight anymore, there have been precious few out there to help me along.

"You say I'm putting those people I care about to shame? I say that I'm still fighting tooth and nail, even though I sometimes don't see the sense in doing anything but curling up and hacking out my last breath."

Seegar listened to every word and thought carefully before responding. "Your condition isn't too far along to—"

"This is the condition that killed my mother," Doc said, "and she was one of the strongest people I ever knew. It might kill me, and it might not, but I'll be damned if I'm going to just stay quiet and keep my head bowed as some illness has its way with me! My mother as well as anyone else who truly cares for me would rather see me indulge in all seven of the deadly sins rather than roll over and give in."

"Anyone would be proud to see the things you've accomplished, Henry. All I'm asking is that you don't throw it all away. By all means, keep living life to the fullest, but don't waste away in places like this, filling yourself with liquor. You're better than that!"

Nodding, Doc looked down at the table to collect his thoughts. When he looked up again, his anger had left him completely. In fact, he barely even displayed the effects of drinking half a bottle of whiskey.

"You know what I think the problem is?" Doc asked.

Seegar's face brightened a bit. "What's that?"

"You and I have different interpretations of living life to the fullest."

And with that one sentence, Seegar knew he'd just lost the battle he'd come to fight. "Can I at least ask you to stop dealing faro? That reflects badly on a man in my . . . a man in our profession."

"Dealing cards is a profession," Doc pointed out.

"It's hardly a profession. A trade, perhaps, but definitely not an honest one."

"Well then," Doc said as he lifted his whiskey bottle, "here's to a dishonest trade."

As much as Seegar wanted to be angry, it was hard to look at the young man in front of him and hold onto his animosity for more than a few seconds. The twenty-two-year-old Holliday wasn't quite the anxious youth he'd been when he'd stepped off that train a year ago, but he still possessed an undeniable spark in his eyes. That spark hadn't dimmed once, even when Doc had been in the grips of the roughest days his consumptive disorder had to offer.

Seegar motioned toward the bar and had a glass brought over to him. All he needed to do from there was hold the glass out for it to be filled by Doc's steady hand. "To a dishonest trade," he said somberly.

Both men knocked back their drinks without saying a word.

There was plenty more that Seegar wanted to say and there was always a storm brewing behind Doc's eyes, but they both managed to just sit back and enjoy their whiskey. It wasn't a stony silence that formed between them, but more of a quiet contemplation. Each of them sifted through the memories that had been stirred during the conversation, knowing full well that both trains of thought were no longer on similar tracks.

It took Seegar a few more sips to empty his shot glass

and when he was done, he set it down in front of him. Turning the glass between his fingers, he looked at Doc and said, "I'm sorry for coming in here and speaking to you the way I did."

"And I'm sorry for listening," Doc replied with a smirk.

Laughing a bit, Seegar kept rolling the shot glass between his fingers as if he was hoping there was just a bit more whiskey in there. "You've got plenty of promise, Henry, but I hope you understand that I can't have a partner that would rather be somewhere else instead of at our practice. I'd say the same thing even if you'd taken up ranching or any other activity that occupied you as much as playing cards."

"I understand."

"I hope there's no hard feelings," Seegar said, even though the look on his face showed that he wasn't expecting any good feelings. "This is just the way it needs to be." When he managed to take another look in Doc's direction, however, he found the younger man extending a hand across the table.

"No hard feelings, John," Doc said. "Although I will take exception if I stop getting Martha's invitations to dinner."

"You don't have to worry about that. Whenever you're in Dallas, there's a spot for you at our table."

No matter how much Seegar wanted another shot of whiskey, he got up while shaking Doc's hand. After that, he turned and worked his way through the crowd until he could find his way out the front door. Once outside, Seegar let out a slow, sorrowful breath.

{10}

Caleb had walked out of the Busted Flush without taking much notice of the table where the two dentists were sharing drinks. He was too concerned with the bad intentions scrawled all over the faces of the men who were waiting for him at the front door. And though the old man standing there with those other two wasn't anything close to threatening, he couldn't have been there to wish Caleb good luck after being released from jail. The elderly miner was shifting and squirming way too much on his feet to be pondering anything good.

"What's this about?" Caleb asked once he was practically toe-to-toe with the biggest of the three.

The man taking up the most of Caleb's field of vision was slightly shorter than Caleb and had a gut that hung like a sack of lard over his belt. Although the top of his head was shiny bald, the hair on the sides and back of his head hung down like a thick, greasy curtain. Thick arms hung out at an angle from his shoulders, and sausagelike fingers dangled like meaty fringe at the ends. When he spoke, a brushy mustache curled in to scrape his teeth and collect saliva at the ends of each whisker. "You remember my uncle?"

Caleb didn't need another look at the miner. Instead, he took a moment to examine the third member of the group. That one might have been of a similar height to Caleb but was stooped over at an odd, sideways angle, thanks to the way his left shoulder was gnarled and twisted into something of a hump.

The humpback's face was crusted as though he hadn't bathed in a month, and he had the pungent stench to go along with it. Dirty clothes hung on his narrow frame, making the gun belt around his waist look more like a rope tied around the middle of a scarecrow.

"I asked you a question," the fat man said, his intrusive mustache lending an odd sound to some of his words. "You remember my uncle or not?"

"Sure, I recognize him," Caleb said. "That just leaves me wondering who the hell you other two are."

Digging his thumb into his chest, the fat man said, "I'm Kyle, and this here is Jim."

The humpback gave a short, upward nod when he heard that last word.

"We're Orville's kin, and we got a problem with you."

Already, Caleb could see a few people outside trying to get a look into the Flush. When they realized they couldn't see through Kyle's girth, they moved along toward some of the other saloons down the street. That sight made Caleb feel like he'd just tossed some money from his own pocket into the gutter.

"I've had a real bad couple of days," Caleb said angrily. "So how about you roll your asses away from the door so folks can get in?"

For a moment, Kyle looked stunned. He glanced from one side to another as if he was waiting to see the person that Caleb was really talking to. When he didn't find any likely candidates in the vicinity, he grabbed hold of Caleb's shirt and dragged him outside.

Kyle's strength was a bit more than Caleb had been expecting. Before anyone could do anything about it, all three of the younger men were outside the saloon with the miner not too far behind.

With his face twisted in an ugly snarl, Kyle slammed Caleb against the closest wall he could find. "You see that old man, there?" he asked, jabbing a finger toward the miner. "That's Orville Deagle."

"Orville Deagle is both of our uncle," the humpback said as he leaned in so close that Caleb could smell the rot in his teeth.

"Yeah," Caleb said with a grimace. "Why the hell should I care?"

"I know all about the shit stains you cater to in that saloon of yours. It's men like Virgil Ellis and that Doc Holliday that took damn near everything my uncle had in this world."

After waiting this long, Caleb figured that he'd seen the best that these men had to offer. If there were any more armed assholes waiting for him outside, they would have surely made themselves known just to put some more bite into Kyle's bark. Caleb met Kyle's stare and snapped both arms up and out to knock the fat man's hands away.

"I asked you once already," Caleb growled. "Why the hell should I care? The last I saw of your uncle, he was running out of my place without leaving behind what he rightfully lost. If you've got a problem with Virgil, then you're in luck, because he's already been fitted for his coffin. If you've got a problem with Doc, you can mention it to him in person, because he's right inside."

Jim reached over Kyle's shoulder and pushed Caleb toward the wall. "My uncle got out with some claims, but they weren't worth half as much as the money he got cheated out of before any of that trouble started. Our problem's with the asshole that set up them crooked games. We know damn well you get a cut from every—"

The humpback was cut off as Caleb shot both arms out in a quick snap of motion. His left arm caught Kyle right under the chin, and the right extended to take hold of Jim by the collar. Shocked by the way Kyle was suddenly staggering back, Jim let out a pitiful groan when he realized that he wasn't able to get away from Caleb.

Hauling Jim toward the wall, Caleb pivoted at the last second to clear a path for the humpback to stumble past him and run face-first into the front of the Busted Flush. Jim's face hit with a dull crack and left a bloody stain upon the wood panels.

By this time, Kyle had worked through the pain shooting through his mouth and was working himself into a real lather. The taste of blood trickled into the back of his throat, causing the fat man to ball up his fists and start swinging. Even though his first wild punch clipped the back of Caleb's head, his next punch gave him nothing but more pain as it slammed into the wall not too far from where Jim had landed moments ago.

As Caleb twisted around to deliver a punch to Kyle's ribs, he was wearing a wide grin. "I don't know what you were thinking coming back here," he said while tossing a right hook into Kyle's face. "But I'm kind of glad you did."

The fat man reeled from the punch but quickly recovered. Before he could respond in any way, he saw Jim hop up with his arms splayed out to either side. The humpback let out a crazy shriek as he wrapped his arms around Caleb's neck and hung onto his back like a tick.

"You boys obviously don't come to my place too much," Caleb continued with just a little bit of a wheeze thanks to the added weight hanging off his back. "Because, if you did, you'd know that I'm used to this sort of thing." Rather than try to shake free of Jim or the humpback's flailing punches, Caleb reached up and grabbed hold of both of Jim's arms.

As Caleb turned to put Jim directly between himself and the saloon's wall, he said, "In fact, this is doing me a bit of good." He then pushed back off of both legs to smash Jim against the wall. "This might even serve as some advertising to show just how much I care to keep the bad element out of my saloon," Caleb said as he slammed Jim once more against the wall.

When Caleb let go and stepped forward, he left Jim stuck there like a swatted fly.

"I don't even care what you two assholes were after anymore," Caleb said.

Now Kyle was standing directly in front of Caleb wearing a murderous look on his face. Fortunately, he seemed to have forgotten about the gun at his side and instead swung his fist with every ounce of his muscle behind it.

Waiting until the last moment, Caleb ducked and moved to one side. That way, Kyle got a clear shot at Jim, who was still peeling himself off the side of the saloon. Caleb almost felt sorry for the humpback as the fat man's knuckles buried themselves into the poor bastard's face.

Jim slid to the ground in an unconscious heap.

"All right, fat man," Caleb said as his blood still pounded through his veins, "you can either collect your friend and leave, or we can keep dancing."

Kyle's eyes flashed, and he started to accept the challenge with his fists. The moment his hand brushed past his holster, his smile took on a whole new level of ferocity; and he began to skin the gun with a clumsy draw. Before he could clear leather, he was stopped by a wavering voice from a few feet away.

"Hold up, Kyle," Orville said from where he was standing. "There's not to be any shooting. We agreed on that."

Neither Kyle nor Caleb would take their eyes off of

each other, since doing so would only prompt the other to make a move.

"I know what we agreed," Kyle said. "But it looks like this asshole wants to keep fighting."

"Put the gun away," Orville insisted. "Maybe then I'll put mine away, too."

That caused Kyle to swivel and get a look at the old man for himself. Sure enough, Orville was holding a revolver that looked like something of an antique. Still, the weapon seemed to be in working order, which was enough to earn a bit of respect.

"You wanna shoot this one?" Kyle asked. "Go ahead."

Orville looked scared; there was no denying that. He also looked ready to fire at a moment's notice. "I'll shoot the leg of the first man who tries to make this any uglier than it needs to be. That means all three of you."

By this time, the humpback had cleared the fog in his head just in time to see Orville point the revolver at him.

"Now, are you boys gonna act like we discussed?" Orville asked.

"Yes, sir," both Kyle and Jim answered in unison.

Turning his eyes and his gun toward Caleb, the old man asked "What about you?"

"I'm not the one who started this," Caleb replied.

"That's not what I'm asking. Are you gonna come along and hear us out, or are you gonna start swinging again?"

After a few seconds of deliberation, Caleb shrugged and nodded. "What the hell? I'll hear what you have to say. But we could have all been talking real civil right now over a drink if these two hadn't dragged me out here the way they did."

"Maybe," Orville said as he tucked his outdated revolver back under his belt and covered it with his jacket. "Maybe not. Let's just see how it goes."

"All right, then. How about we head back into my saloon so we can have that drink?"

"No," Jim snapped. "My uncle's already been attacked once in there! Lord only knows what you got inside if'n he sticks his face in there."

"He wasn't attacked. He didn't even—" Caleb stopped himself, took a breath, and said. "Fine. We can talk somewhere else. But I'm not stupid enough to follow you three into some alley after getting bushwhacked once already."

"Where'd you rather go?" Orville asked.

"What about the Alhambra? It's just one street down."

Orville and his two nephews started walking down Main Street to where it intersected with Houston. Caleb, on the other hand, remained rooted to his spot. Kyle was the one to stop and wheel around like a bull that was about to charge.

"Come on, then!" the fat man grunted.

"First I want to know what this is about," Caleb demanded. "I've been through too much lately to waste my time with senseless bullshit from the likes of you fellas."

This time, the nephews glanced over to their uncle before saying another word.

Nodding. Orville said, "It's about an arrangement that needs to be struck between us. After what I been through and what I done already, I deserve something by way of payment."

Caleb let out a choppy, humorless laugh. "Look, everyone in the Flush last night got a scare, and from what I saw, you skinned out of there quicker than most."

"Yeah, but I heard about what them gamblers said. They meant to cheat me out of my money and my claims. Them things is my bread and butter."

"Well, they didn't get anything from you they didn't win fair and square. Two of those men are dead. I'd say that settles things between you fellas."

"That still doesn't settle up between us."

"How so?"

"It's because of me that you're not sitting in that jail cell right now."

That struck a nerve inside Caleb's chest that had been itching ever since his backside had left that old, smelly horse blanket. "What do you mean?"

"You're either going to make this right," Orville said, "or I'll rethink the story I told to Ben Mays and see to it that you get tossed right back into jail. I can also add a few more things to my story that will more than likely get you strung up."

Caleb let out a sigh. Even as he started walking down Main Street, he felt like his boots were sinking in quicksand. "All right," he grunted. "Let's have that talk."

{11}

The Alhambra was one of the finest-looking buildings in sight. Unlike many of the other structures, this one hadn't been slapped together from a kit. A fire that had swept through town the previous autumn had taken out a good number of businesses, including the Alhambra's previous location. In fact, many gamblers said the place was better than ever now that it was in a prime location on the corner of Main and Houston Streets.

Caleb had only just been feeling the bite of having such a competitor so close to his own establishment. That bite sank in a little deeper when he walked into the Alhambra to spot plenty of faces that had only left the Busted Flush less than twenty minutes ago. Rather than find some other place to have this talk, Caleb ignored the smarmy waves thrown to him by the Alhambra's barkeep and picked out a table in the corner next to the piano. He sat down with his back to the bar and hoped nobody else had seen him walk in.

"Hello there, Caleb," said a petite waitress with her

shoulder-length blonde hair tied back with a black ribbon. "Did you run out of good bourbon at the Flush?"

"Maybe I just came to sample this beer," he offered. "You ever think of that, Sarah?"

The blonde stared down at him with an amused smile and said, "You must really be in the mood for our special brew since I hear there's a party being served in your honor down at—"

"Just get me a beer," Caleb interrupted. "Please."

Letting him off the hook with a squeeze on the shoulder, Sarah leaned down to plant a quick kiss on Caleb's forehead. "Anything you say. What about your friends, here?"

Since he'd been more than happy to be distracted by the brush of Sarah's hair against his face, Caleb was reluctant to acknowledge the "friends" she'd spotted. Even so, there was no mistaking the pungent odor of the humpback's breath or the loud creak of Kyle's chair as it squealed for mercy when the fat man sat down upon it.

"Bring them beers, too, I guess," Caleb said grudgingly.

Sarah nodded, tossed a flirtatious grin at the other three men, and turned to walk away amid the rustle of her bright red skirts.

"Appreciate the drinks," Orville said. "That's right friendly, considering the circumstances."

Caleb smiled amiably. "Great, then why don't we just consider us squared up?"

Orville shook his head. "I'm afraid not."

"All right, then. Let's get this over with as quickly as we can. How about we start off with how you think you're responsible for me getting out of jail?"

The old man pulled in a breath and steeled himself. "That's the God's honest truth, mister."

"The name's Caleb Wayfinder."

Hearing that caused Kyle to chuckle. Under his breath, he muttered, "Goddamn Injun."

Seeing the glare on Caleb's face was enough to cause both Kyle and Jim to start reaching for their guns.

"Why don't I just call you Caleb?" Orville offered. "Like I was going to say, me and my nephews helped get you out of that jail."

"How do you figure?"

"Because I showed up at the request of Dr. Holliday to offer my version of what happened when Mike Abel was killed."

"Were you the only one that showed?"

"We was there, too," Jim said. "And we talked you up real nice."

Nobody at the table seemed to have even noticed that the humpback had opened his mouth.

"There were others," Orville said. "Dr. Holliday saw to it that plenty showed up. Some of them didn't even know Mike was dead. I think it was the first time a few of them had even stepped foot in your saloon."

"That'd account for most of Dallas," Sarah said as she stepped up and set mugs of beer down in front of each man. Like most servers who made a decent living at the job, her timing was impeccable.

Caleb waved off the sarcastic comment, but Sarah wasn't going anywhere. "I can settle the bill later," he told her.

"I'm to collect it now. Manager's orders."

Twisting in his seat, Caleb spotted the well-dressed manager of the Alhambra who was waving at him from across the room. "What ever happened to professional courtesy?" Caleb asked.

Sarah shrugged.

Even though he knew Sarah and the manager were just needling him, it couldn't have been a worse time to look for a laugh. Caleb slapped some money into Sarah's waiting hand and quickly turned his back to her. Only then did the blonde study the table with concern.

"Is everything all right with you boys?" she asked.

Kyle had yet to take his eyes off of her. More specifically, he had yet to take his eyes off the plunging neckline of her dress. "We're just fine, darlin'. Don't you worry."

Dealing with the likes of Kyle and his equally leering cousin was just another part of Sarah's job. She bent down to whisper in Caleb's ear, ignoring the way Kyle and Jim's eyes widened at the extra bit of cleavage she showed them.

"You just let us know if there's going to be trouble," she said.

"I think you'll know the moment anything starts," Caleb replied. "I haven't been attracting trouble of the quiet variety lately." He felt a pat on his shoulder, and then Sarah moved away to check on some other tables.

"Ben Mays came by to ask what went on at your saloon," Orville said as if Sarah hadn't even stopped by the table. "He listened to plenty of stories and found plenty of witnesses to tell them. That was enough to clear you of them charges."

"That's because I didn't murder Loco Mike. He was going to kill Doc, so I shot him down."

"And that's what I told Ben Mays."

"But you weren't even there when that part happened," Caleb pointed out. Orville shrugged. "Even so, I was the only one in that card game that wasn't directly involved in the shooting. My testimony held plenty of weight, just like Dr. Holliday said it would. The only thing is that I think I deserve some compensation for what I did."

"Since you weren't there when the last shot was fired, for all you know, you were lying to a Texas Ranger," Caleb pointed out. "Putting that aside, what you told Ben Mays was the truth. However you cut it, you don't deserve much more than my thanks."

Pulling in another breath, Orville straightened in his chair and looked over to both his nephews. Seeing that fat man and the humpback somehow gave the miner enough courage to put some grit into his voice. "If that's how you feel, then I can go over right now and tell Ben Mays the truth.

"I can also tell him about how Dr. Holliday set it up so you were shown in a real good light so you could escape. Then I can tell him how Dr. Holliday and that other one meant to cheat me out of my mining claims. That dentist friend of yours is becoming more known for his drinking and gambling than pulling teeth, so I don't think Mays will have any trouble believing what I tell him. In fact, I think he was disappointed that he didn't hear as much the first time around."

Even though Caleb tried to avoid the law when he could, he knew Ben Mays well enough to know that Orville wasn't just spitting out idle threats. The Texas Ranger might not have had it out for him, but he would have preferred to have a definite culprit to Mike Abel's shooting rather than admit to locking up the wrong man. Texas Rangers were known for plenty of things. Admitting they were wrong wasn't exactly one of them.

"So you're blackmailing me?" Caleb asked. "I mean, we might as well just put all the cards on the table here."

"It's a fair exchange. If I didn't say what I did, you probably wouldn't be out of that cell."

"Probably. But you could be wrong."

"I could. Care to try your luck?"

Caleb fought back the urge to jump across that table and make the old miner sorry for even starting this conversation. Instead, he lifted his mug and took a sip of the Alhambra's house brew. To add insult to injury, that beer was at least twice as good as the stuff Hank whipped up to serve at the Busted Flush.

"What kind of compensation are you talking about?" Caleb asked.

"I want twenty percent of the house take on the games

you run, including the high-stakes games that come through there when professional gamblers come to town."

"My place isn't on the gambling circuit. If I was, I'd be in a lot better shape than I am right now. Take a look around," Caleb said while holding up his hands to indicate the plush surroundings of the Alhambra. "This is the type of place that's on the circuit."

"I play enough cards in the Flush to know that some big names come through there every now and then. There have been a few games I seen with more money in one pot than I'll ever see in a lifetime of sifting through dirt."

"Those are the exceptions. Not the rule."

"Well, even if you get one big game a year, I think a share of it would do wonders for me and my kin."

Caleb gritted his teeth and took another sip of beer. Even though he knew he was being gouged, he also knew that the miner wasn't completely misinformed. Orville was about to get his lifeblood drained out of him by Virgil Ellis. And, being a businessman himself, Caleb couldn't exactly fault the old man for grabbing onto an opportunity when it presented itself. The man did, after all, play a big part of getting Caleb out of that damned cell.

Then again, the more he thought about the miner's deal, the better that cell seemed.

"Tell you what," Caleb said. "You did go a long way in helping to clear my name. And though I had no part of you getting cheated, I did hear something mentioned along those lines taking place in my saloon. So how about I pay you a reward for damages done?"

Despite the wariness in Caleb's voice, his words did seem to have an impact upon the old miner.

Before Orville could confer with his nephews, Caleb added, "How about something to the tune of . . . a hundred dollars?"

It didn't take a skilled poker player to notice the hungry flinch in the corner of Orville's eye. There was a bit of a tremor in the miner's voice when he said, "I don't know. I mean . . . the deal was for—"

"All right," Caleb interrupted. Letting out a defeated sigh, he dug his fingers through his roughly cut hair and brought himself a little closer to the real amount he was willing to pay to get this miner and his family out of his sight. "How about three hundred? And that's going to set me back for quite a while."

"Three hundred?"

"I can't make it much more than that, Orville. I've got to eat, too, you know."

Now that he had something else to think about, Orville didn't bother looking over to either of his nephews. On either side of him, Kyle and Jim fretted and let out dissatisfied grunts like a couple of kids who weren't getting enough attention.

Caleb's fingers worked their way over the top of his scalp as he watched every move Orville made. He could feel the old man coming around to his way of thinking and with every second that passed, Caleb felt the ache in his temples start to recede. The Busted Flush wasn't much, but it was all he had. He'd built the place from the ground up and seen it flourish, and in a town like Dallas, that was no small accomplishment.

"It's a good deal," Caleb said. "Taking any more than that, I'd be better off sitting in that cell. At least that way I'd have a roof over my head."

When Caleb saw the contemplative look on the miner's face, he actually felt some hope take root inside of him. The fact that Orville was considering what he heard and seeing the sense in Caleb's words spoke volumes. It showed that folks might not be as greedy as Caleb had assumed. Perhaps a man could listen to something else besides his own love of money.

"Fork over what we asked for," Kyle grunted, completely shattering what little goodwill might have been festering inside Caleb's heart. "You're just trying to sweet-talk us, and we ain't gonna listen no more."

Orville looked over to the fat man. "Kyle, maybe we should—"

"No!" Jim spat. "Kyle's right. This here is our show, and we make the decisions. Ain't no way this cheatin' bartender is gonna run things. He needs to listen to us, and that's all there is to it."

Caleb didn't need to study the old man any longer. He could already see the battle was lost.

"You hear that, Injun?" Kyle asked with the smuggest of grins on his face. "It ain't your place to name the price. It's your place to pay up or face the law. My bet is that if Ben Mays and the rangers don't string you up for running a crooked place like that shit hole of yours, the town law will. What do you think of that?"

At that moment, Caleb's first impulse was to slam both Kyle and Jim face-first into the table. Although Orville wasn't high on Caleb's list, the fact that the miner was willing to roll over and not do anything to stop his two asshole nephews from spouting off said plenty about the old man.

Just as Caleb was about to give in and let his fists do what they were aching to do, he looked around and spotted another familiar face. Standing at the end of the bar closest to the front door, taking casual interest in the conversation at Caleb's table, was one of the local deputies.

The town law might not have had as wide a jurisdiction as the Texas Rangers, but they could make Caleb's life just as miserable. Now, it made a little more sense why Kyle was trying so desperately to push Caleb over the edge.

"You want me to throw a punch right here in front of that deputy?" Caleb asked. "Then you're shit out of luck. You want a piece of my saloon? You'll have to come and get it. You want the reward I offered? Say yes right now, and we can be done."

Caleb waited for a few moments before standing up. He took his beer and finished it in one long swig. When he put the glass down without hearing another word from any of the three men, Caleb took some money from his pocket and tossed it onto the table.

"That's for the beers," Caleb said. "If you want one more cent out of me, you can kiss my ass."

Caleb turned and nearly walked straight into the blonde waitress, who'd been approaching the table with another round of drinks.

"Anything else they drink doesn't go on my tab," Caleb announced. "They can pay for their own damn beers."

Sarah nodded and smiled. "I hear you."

There was a spark in Sarah's eyes as she looked Caleb up and down. Judging by the smirk on her face, she'd heard most or all of Caleb's final words to the other three.

Orville was shaking his head and muttering something to himself while his nephews were practically steaming as they got to their feet.

"So what's it gonna be, fat man?" Caleb snarled. "You want to take a shot at me or just stand there looking stupid?"

Kyle managed to hold Caleb's stare for a full second before blinking and looking away. Jim didn't even make it half that long.

Caleb felt good when he turned his back to those men. He felt so good, in fact, that he put one hand on Sarah's waist and pulled her in for a quick kiss on the lips. She was too stunned to say a word, but the smile on her face had doubled in size.

From there, Caleb left the Alhambra and headed back to his party.

It had been almost two full days since the last time Caleb had caught sight of Orville Deagle or either of the miner's nephews. Granted, Caleb wasn't exactly turning over every stone to find those three, but he hadn't expected his exit from the Alhambra to work out quite so well.

In the time that had passed, Caleb had been enjoying the quiet and taking care of the Busted Flush. There was a poker tournament scheduled for the following month and plenty of details went along with it. There was liquor to buy, gamblers to invite, entertainment to arrange, and supplies to purchase. The main drawback that quickly sprouted up, however, was the lack of money to do any of those things.

Caleb sat in his office, poring through countless ledgers and sifting through so many papers that they all slowly began to turn his brain into mush. When he closed his eyes, Caleb heard the familiar sounds of folks talking and laughing, but all of that seemed to be too far away for him to consider. It was something like looking up at the stars and knowing better than to try and reach up to touch one of them.

Rather than stare at the same spot on his desk or gaze longingly at the door, Caleb shifted in his seat to get a look at a section of wall he hadn't recently committed to memory. What he found there wasn't anything new, but the simple wooden frame had been there for so long that it might as well have melted into the shoddy wood paneling.

Caleb didn't have to stretch too far to reach out and brush off a few layers of dust that had settled upon the frame, which hung from a rusty nail. The first thing his fingers uncovered was a slightly faded image of his own smiling face. When he saw that, Caleb couldn't help but smile once again.

Getting up, he started looking for a cloth of any sort that he could use to clean off the rest of the picture. Since he couldn't find anything suited to that purpose, he took the picture off the wall and pulled the bottom of his shirt out from behind his belt to swipe away the thick layers of dust and cobwebs.

When he was finished, Caleb looked down proudly at the photograph that had been taken what felt like a lifetime ago. The picture was of Caleb, Hank, and Sarah standing in front of the Busted Flush. Strung across the front of the saloon was a colorful banner that read, Grand Opening.

Hank had been a modest investor as well as the first bartender to work at the Flush. Serving drinks at the new saloon had been Sarah's first job. All three of them were smiling proudly, but Caleb's grin eclipsed them all. Looking at that picture now, Caleb shook his head at how young and eager he looked with that dopey smile plastered across the front of his head.

Normally, Caleb didn't care to sit for photographers. But on the day that picture had been taken, Caleb would have stood for hours if it meant preserving that proud moment forever.

Hank still worked the bar and was working the kinks out of his brewing skills. Sarah was the best server Caleb could have asked for as well as a decent cook. Ever since she left to work at the Alhambra, things just weren't the same.

Even after he hung the framed photograph back upon its nail, Caleb found himself staring at those faces and smiling right back at them. That smile faded more than a little the moment he shifted his eyes from the past to take in the cluttered office and stack of paperwork that represented his present.

Hank's steps weren't loud, but the bartender's feet sent a familiar series of creaks through the floor, which told Caleb to expect the door to open in about a second or two. A second and a half later, there was a quick knock before the door was pushed open.

"You still in here?" Hank asked.

Caleb dropped back down into his chair and said, "Looks like it."

"Well, I thought I'd let you know that one of them Deagles came and went just now."

"Which one?"

"I don't recall their names."

"The fat one, the old one, or the humpback?"

Chuckling a bit, Hank replied, "I guess it was the third, but I can't say as I spotted a hump. He was here with Sheriff Hopper."

"What?"

"Sheriff Hopper was with him."

Caleb felt his heart jump a little toward the back of his throat. "What did the sheriff want?"

Hank shrugged and looked around at the clutter which practically filled the office. "Hell if I know. By the looks of it, he sure as hell didn't want to be with that Deagle kid."

Thinking it over for a moment, Caleb let out the breath

he'd been holding and asked, "They're not still here, are they?"

"Nope. The sheriff paid his respects and took off."

"Good."

"The Deagle kid left a little bit later."

"Even better."

"Why don't you come join the rest of us, Caleb? There's plenty that needs done out front, and it'd be good for you to get out of this closet for a while."

Caleb got to his feet but didn't make a move toward the door. Instead, he found himself drawn back to where the picture was hanging. Standing in that same spot again, he crossed his arms and stared at the photograph. "You remember when this was taken?"

Grudgingly, Hank stepped farther into the office. Not only did he take exception to the mess in there, but his wide shoulders and barrel chest made it difficult for the barkeep to maneuver without knocking into something or other with every step. He didn't quite make it to Caleb's side, but he got close enough to get a look at what was hanging on the wall.

"Sure, I remember that," Hank said. "Nobody could've wiped that grin off your face. Hell of a day."

"Yeah. It was."

"You don't sound too convinced."

Glancing over to the barkeep like a man that had been caught, Caleb turned his back to the picture and trudged back to drop into his chair. "Guess I was wondering what the hell I was thinking back then."

Hank's head snapped back, and he blinked as if flash powder had just been ignited. "What's that supposed to mean? You were thinking that you just opened your own saloon and hoping you'd still be in business farther down the road. You did just that, Caleb. Here you are. Here we all are." Glancing at the picture, Hank shrugged and added, "Well, most of us anyway."

"Sarah's still working at the Alhambra," Caleb said in response to Hank's unspoken question. "My guess is that she's helping balance the books a whole lot more than she serves drinks."

"She always did have a knack for numbers. Couldn't take being cooped up for very long, though."

"Maybe I've got that same problem."

"Is that what all this moping is all about?"

Hank didn't need to be told that he'd struck a nerve. He could see that much written on Caleb's face. Reaching out, he patted Caleb's shoulder just roughly enough to make the chair squeak beneath him. "I don't know how you spend so much time in this damn office without losing your mind as it is. If it's getting to you, then why don't you work up front for a bit."

"I don't think I'd be much of a replacement for Holly."

"Not unless you sprout red hair and learn how to properly fill out a corset," Hank said.

"Yeah, well the last thing the Flush needs is another man behind the bar."

"Who's to make that decision? The owner? Oh, wait a second, that'd be you." Hank smirked when he saw Caleb chuckle at that. "Look here, now. You've worked hard to get this place off the ground, and I know you don't want to give it up. I also know you deserve a change of scenery. You used to like working out front before we hired them others, so why not come back out from behind this desk for a while? It may just remind you of why you wanted to own a saloon in the first place."

"Well, there is the tournament coming up. I guess it wouldn't hurt for me to be up front for all of that."

"There you go."

Caleb nodded, feeling less like a kid that wanted to skip school and more like a man who was taking the reins back for himself. "All right, you talked me into it. When do you want me to start?"

Hank was already untying the apron from around his waist and handing it over. "How's now strike you? I could use a breather."

Caleb reached out for the stained apron but stopped short.

"I recognize that look," Hank said. "Don't go changing your mind on me so quickly, now."

"Not changing my mind, but I do need to take care of something before starting my shift behind the bar."

Hank smiled and leaned in to nudge Caleb in the side. "You want to head to the Alhambra and ask Sarah to find her way back here?"

"Not exactly. I need to pay another visit to my dentist."

[13]

The stitches in Caleb's jaw had become nothing more than a nuisance bothering the side of his tongue. Spending more than his share of time in a saloon, he was plenty used to the aches and pains that came along with a fight. On his way down Jefferson and heading toward Elm, Caleb came up with plenty to say to Dr. Holliday that had nothing at all to do with stitches.

When he reached A. M. Cochrane's Drug Store, Caleb didn't even bother looking at the shingle marking the dental practice upstairs. He instead climbed those stairs and walked up to the girl in the front office. As before, there was nobody else waiting to get in.

"I need to get my stitches removed," Caleb said. "Can I do that now, or do I need to come back?"

The girl looked eager to see another human face and was already scrambling to knock on the door behind her. "Oh, there's nobody else ahead of you. Dr. Seegar can take you right now."

"Actually, I need to see Dr. Holliday. He's the one that saw me before."

The door swung open as Caleb had been talking, and Seegar stepped outside. "Dr. Holliday is no longer practicing at this location," he announced in a dry, formal tone. "But I'd be happy to finish any work he might have started."

Caleb didn't try to hide the shocked expression on his face. "Doc's not here? Where did he go?"

"I'm not certain right now. Would you like me to see to those stitches?"

Caleb nodded, wanting more than anything to get that blasted string out of him before he ripped it out himself.

Seegar led him past the little room where Caleb had met Doc the first time. Seegar's work space wasn't much bigger, but it was plain to see that he cared for it a lot more than Doc had tended to his own area. The chair was polished and covered with fresh linen, and each piece of equipment sparkled like it was new.

Even the air smelled cleaner as Caleb lowered himself onto a cushier chair and leaned back. "What happened to Doc?"

Collecting the tools he needed, Seegar spoke as if he was talking to himself. His voice sounded vaguely distracted as he sat down next to Caleb's chair and reached for his instruments. "Nothing happened to him. He simply no longer works out of this office."

"Is he all right?"

Blinking and studying Caleb's face as if for the first time, Seegar replied, "He's as well as he can be, considering his condition. Consumptives have a hard time of it, after all. The stresses of working in a professional capacity aren't the best for a man like him over long periods of time."

"So he's taking some time off?"

Seegar chuckled and reached into Caleb's mouth with

what appeared to be a pair of thin pliers. "I guess that's a simpler way of putting it."

Caleb couldn't feel much more than Seegar's fingers against his jaw, followed by the tugging of those stitches coming loose. It was a strange mix of stinging and tickling as the stitches were slowly dragged from his jaw and dropped into a cup beside the chair. The smell of everything Caleb had eaten for the last day or two drifted into his nose.

"Wi Dog ee ack?" Caleb asked.

Without letting go of Caleb's jaw, Seegar shook his head. "He won't be back at this location, no. Are you a regular patient of his?"

"No. Jus un tine."

"Wait a moment. You're the owner of that saloon near the Alhambra, right? What is it?"

"The Nusted Lush."

"Right, the Busted Flush. If Henry owes you any money, I might be able to settle his account."

"No," Caleb said as the last stitch was pulled out of his jaw. When he saw Seegar scoot back, Caleb sat up and dabbed at his chin with the napkin he'd been handed. "No, it's nothing like that. I just need to talk to Doc about something I heard."

"Is it important?"

"Actually, I'd like to thank him. Also, there is something he probably needs to know."

Seegar thought about that for a moment. Although he seemed suspicious at first, he eventually eased up and said, "I understand Henry was looking at a place on the corner of Main and Lamar. It's over the bank. Maybe you can find him there."

Dr. Seegar didn't feel like talking much after that. While he wasn't rude about it, he did seem to rush Caleb out of his office as quickly as he could. The stitches had been removed without a hitch, so Caleb paid what he owed and moved along.

It was about a two-block walk for Caleb to get to Lamar. At the corner, there was a tall building holding the Dallas County Bank. Since it was such a walk from the Busted Flush, that bank wasn't the one that Caleb frequented. As he stood on the street and looked up at the building, he started to wonder if he'd stopped at the right place.

After taking a look up and down the street, Caleb decided that he was either overlooking something, or Dr. Seegar had intentionally misled him. The Dallas County Bank was the only one on that corner, and Seegar didn't seem like the type to lie when he was so contented to stay quiet only moments before. Caleb pulled open the door and stepped inside.

"Can I help you?" asked a bald man with a monocle dangling from a ribbon threaded through his lapel. He wore a dark suit that labeled him as a banker more than if he had that word stitched across his chest.

Putting a businesslike tone in his voice, Caleb said, "I'm looking for Dr. Holliday. I was told that—"

"Oh, yes," the man said somewhat distastefully. "He's been inquiring about renting the space over this bank. I believe his practice won't be ready for customers for a little while, yet."

"Do you know where I can find him?"

The man in the suit let out a sigh and started glancing around for somewhere else to be. "I don't handle his affairs. If you'd like to leave a message for him, I can see that he gets it."

Caleb may not have liked it, but he did know what was going through the banker's mind. While he'd been going through the process of buying property down the street and getting the financing required to set up and maintain a saloon, Caleb had dealt with plenty of bankers. It had been a while, but he soon found himself easing back into that frame of mind. All he needed to do was to reduce everything around him into potential profits and losses while also imagining that his shoes were three sizes too small.

"I know you've got plenty to do," Caleb said in a dreary, defeated tone that was almost a dead ringer for the banker's, "but I need to talk to Mr. Holliday about a payout from one of his old partners. I have a large sum of money that Mr. Holliday requested and he seemed to want it pretty quick."

The banker's ears perked up at the sound of that, confirming Caleb's suspicion that the man did have something to do with renting out the space that Doc was after. Still, there was a little bit of suspicion in the banker's eyes that might not have been there if Caleb had been wearing a matching suit.

"Mr. Holliday mentioned something about putting down a deposit on some property," Caleb added, hoping he wasn't going a little too far.

Judging by the accommodating smile that appeared on the banker's face, Caleb had gone just far enough.

"The address he gave me was Dr. Seegar's house," the banker said in a low voice. Turning to one of the nearby counters, he found a deposit slip and scribbled something on the back of it. Handing the slip over to Caleb, he said, "I believe it's just under a mile along Ross Street."

Caleb read what the banker had written and found an address.

"That's where I was supposed to send any inquiries or papers regarding the space upstairs. Do you think he'll be completing the process?"

"Of renting that space?" Caleb asked. "Of course. I wouldn't be surprised if he put down a bigger deposit after he gets the money I'm delivering."

If the banker seemed at all concerned about the information he'd given, that went away once he heard those words spoken in Caleb's confident tone. "Splendid! I'll start getting the final contracts drawn up."

Tapping the slip to his temple in a quick salute, Caleb said, "I'll tell him the good news. Good day to you, sir."

"And to you."

{14}

The Seegar home was easy enough to find. Unfortunately, when Caleb knocked on the door, nobody answered. After knocking a few more times, he peeked into the closest window and swore under his breath at the utter stillness inside the well-maintained house. Just as he was about to give up, Caleb heard a shot crack through the air. His first instinct was to duck and look around for who'd fired at him. When he heard the next shot, he realized that nobody at all was firing at him. In fact, the shots were coming from somewhere behind the house.

Doing his best to step as lightly as possible. Caleb climbed down from the Seegars' porch and worked his way around the house. Out back, there was a little patch of land containing a few trees and a small garden. One of the trees was big enough to hold a swing from a thick branch as well as the first traces of a tree house.

Standing amid the domestic trappings, Doc looked more than a little out of place with his sleeves rolled up and a smoking pistol in his hand. His arm hung at his side as though the weight of the pistol was enough to drag it down. His back was to the house, and he looked toward the end of the property, which was sectioned off by a sturdy fence.

Casually, Doc lifted the gun, extended his arm, and pivoted around to take aim at Caleb. When he saw who was approaching, he pointed the gun away from Caleb but didn't lower his arm. "It's not proper to sneak up on a man."

"With all the gunshots going off lately," Caleb said as he held his open hands in front of him. "I wasn't too concerned with being proper."

Doc chuckled once under his breath before lowering his arm and turning away from the house. There were several bottles lined up on the fence. When Doc squeezed his trigger, one of the bottles exploded into a shower of glass shards.

"Is there something you need?" Doc asked.

Caleb walked forward and stood next to Doc. The dentist was still impeccably groomed and had his blond hair neatly parted. He was even dressed in the imported clothes that had become one of his calling cards. But there was something odd about the shoulder holster strapped around his slender frame and under his gray silk vest. The diamond stickpin was in place as well, not too far from where the holster hung against his side.

"I had a word with Orville Deagle a few nights ago," Caleb said.

"Really? I don't suppose you were spared the nastiness of meeting his two dimwitted nephews as well?"

"They were along."

In a flicker of motion, Doc's arm snapped up, and he brought his pistol up to fire. The shot cracked through the air, but only a single chip was taken from the neck of one of the bottles.

"Better you than me," Doc said.

"Actually, your name did come up in the conversation."

"Ah." Doc sighed as he lowered his arm, let it hang for a moment, and then snapped it up to take another shot. This time, the bottles remained completely untouched. "The plot thickens."

"It sure does. They told me that you rounded up witnesses to lie for me when Ben Mays came around asking about the shooting."

As Doc lowered his arm and rolled his head about to work a kink from his neck, he said, "*Lie* is such an ugly word. I prefer the term, *organizing your defense*." His arm snapped up, and the gun spat its smoke and fire. The bottle that had been chipped before now lost its upper half and wobbled on the fence before coming to a stop.

"Will you stop that and listen?" Caleb snarled. "They threatened to change their story, and I'm pretty sure Mays wouldn't mind seeing me hang once he gets a halfway decent excuse."

Doc turned to face Caleb properly while opening the cylinder of his pistol. The gun was a Navy model Colt and appeared to be in fine condition. Emptying the spent shells, Doc let his hands do their work while his eyes remained fixed on Caleb. "Mays keeps some pretty unsavory company. He also can't stand gambling and drunkards. That puts saloon owners pretty low on his list."

"Great, Doc. That makes me feel a whole lot better."

"Don't fret too much about it," Doc added with a wink. "I'm not too high on that list myself."

Despite the worries filling Caleb's mind, he couldn't help but laugh at Doc's easygoing wit. When spoken in his comforting Georgia drawl, matters just didn't seem as grave as they had been a few moments before.

"One of those nephews came by my saloon with the town law," Caleb said.

"Sheriff Hopper is in this? He doesn't have as big a problem with gambling."

"I know. He didn't seem too concerned, but that doesn't mean this is over. Somehow, that miner and those other two got it in their heads that I'm the one to solve their financial woes."

Fishing out bullets from his vest pocket, Doc fit them into the pistol and snapped the cylinder shut. He then slipped the Colt back into his shoulder holster and positioned his feet so that he was standing sideways in relation to the fence. "If you had their financial woes, you might be getting a little desperate yourself."

"What's that mean?"

"Just what you think it means. Our mutual friend the prospector isn't exactly on stable ground when it comes to his finances. Then again," Doc added as he flexed his fingers and fixed his eyes upon the bottles, "not many in that profession are."

"How do you know all this?"

"It's my business to know."

"Why? Do you fix Orville's teeth?"

Doc glanced over to Caleb and then pulled in a breath. There wasn't too much of a wheeze associated with that action today. "I'm referring to my other business."

Caleb nodded and looked out to the bottles. "Ah, that's right. You're quite the gambler. I hear you're becoming a man to keep an eye on when it comes to poker."

"Orville's new to poker. He's more inclined to buck the tiger."

"You mean faro?"

Doc nodded before drawing the pistol from his holster and taking a shot. Caleb had seen quicker draws, but Doc's aim was on the money. The bottle that had already been blasted in half now shattered into a glittering mist. "The trick is to keep everything steady," Doc recited. "Right down to the breath you take before and after you fire. Concentrating on the breath after is what pulls you through."

"How bad is Orville's debt?" Caleb asked, ignoring Doc's free shooting lesson.

"At least seven hundred, and that just covers what he owes to Champagne Charlie."

Caleb scowled when he heard that name. Champagne Charlie ran the St. Charles Saloon and was known to be one of the happiest fellows someone could meet. "I never knew Charlie was that hard on the folks who owed him money."

"He's not. It's his partner that needs to be watched."

"Partner?"

After placing the Colt back into its holster, Doc drew and fired in a motion that was slightly quicker than the time before. He took a piece from the next bottle in line and swore, even though that bottle teetered and eventually fell off the fence.

Caleb walked around to stand between Doc and the fence. Looking straight into the dentist's eyes like that made Doc seem younger somehow. His cheeks were sunken as always, but his blue eyes still had a spark that was as bright, or brighter, than anyone else in their early twenties.

"Didn't you ever learn the finer points of gun safety?" Doc asked in his normal, droll manner.

"I never knew Charlie had a partner, Doc, and that doesn't sit right with me, since I've made it my business to know such things."

"Don't feel too badly. I doubt I would have known myself if I hadn't had a few bad nights dealing faro at the St. Charles. I'd just gotten my layout, and Charlie was kind enough to let me start in on a busy night. After the house lost one too many hands, I was approached by a rather somber gentleman who didn't have too many kind words for me."

"Do you know who he was?"

Doc shook his head. "Only that he showed a bit too

much interest in Charlie's affairs to be anything but a partner or his father. Since his age doesn't fit the latter, my money would have to go to the former."

"What did he tell you?"

"That I could either become a better dealer or I'd have to repay my losses out of my own pocket. I told him what I thought of that in none too many words, and he promptly threatened to eviscerate me with my newly purchased Will & Finck shears."

"Card-trimming shears, Doc?" Caleb asked with a grin. "You should know better than that."

"They came with the rest of the layout. Anyhow. I assured him my dealing would improve, and I haven't seen him since."

"He must have put a fright into you."

"Hardly," Doc replied as he drew his pistol and fired three shots in quick succession, causing three more bottles to pop. "I intended on improving without being so rudely commanded."

"Well that doesn't help answer my original question."

"And what was that again?"

"Why you handed over one hell of a bargaining chip to a man in desperate need of money? *My* money!"

Doc smiled and extended his arm. After using the pistol to nudge Caleb to one side, Doc sighted down the barrel and then let his arm drop to his side. "Do you know the root of all evil?"

"Yeah. Money."

"No. The love of money is the root of all evil, and there seems to be plenty of roots squirming around just beneath the surface here."

Caleb's frustration was becoming difficult to contain. "I've got a saloon to maintain, Doc. I can't afford to have someone coming after it that's got some real ammunition to use against me. If things get too bad, I might just find myself broke or dangling from a noose before I know what went wrong."

"Now you're just working yourself into a tizzy."

"That's easy enough for you to say. You're not the one with his head on the block. You're the one that handed the ammunition to them Deagles in the first place."

Doc wasn't shaken by Caleb's accusations in the least. Instead, he seemed to be chewing on something in the back of his mind, which soon brought a smile to his face. "You recall those roots I was mentioning before?"

"Huh? Oh, yeah. I guess." The more he stood there, the more Caleb realized it was useless to try and steer Doc's mind anywhere it didn't want to go.

Holding his Colt at arm's length, Doc sighted down the barrel but didn't pull the trigger. "With all these folks scrambling so desperately for their money, we might be able to treat ourselves to our own nice little payday."

"We?"

"Yes. As in, you and I."

"All I want is to get my saloon out of harm's way."

"Is it?" Doc asked.

The suddenness of that question took Caleb by surprise. "Why else would I be going through all this trouble? Why else would I come here to talk to you?"

"Maybe it's because you know we can help one another."

"All right. Since you'll just tell me anyway, I'll bite. How can we help each other?"

"By sinking a few roots of our own," Doc replied with a crafty smile.

"I'm more worried about staying alive and in business."

"Yeah, you're too worried," Doc said as he pulled his trigger.

Caleb didn't flinch at the gunshot. Instead, he felt the hackles rising along the back of his neck. "What the hell's that supposed to mean?"

When Doc opened the cylinder of his Colt this time, he did it with a snap of his wrist and dumped the spent shells quickly. "You spend your life worrying too much about the worst, and you miss out on everything else. Believe me, Caleb," he added while reloading the pistol. "I know all about that." Snapping the pistol shut, he added, "Take how you found me as an example. That took something else than just being worried."

Caleb laughed and said, "Oh, well I asked around a bit. That's all."

"It would take more than just asking, I hope."

"Well, I talked to Dr. Seegar and then had a chat with a man at the Dallas County Bank. Once I made him think I might put some money in your pockets to pay your rent, he was more than willing to lend a hand."

"Very enterprising," Doc said with a nod. "That's the spirit I'm talking about. Between the two of us, we have no need of fussing about with things like pennies for profits every month and sweet-talking customers just so they can remember us the next time they feel a thirst or a pain in their mouth. There's plenty more out there besides just that. Haven't you ever thought about that?"

"Sure I have, but there comes a time when a man has to think about little things like settling down or running a business."

Doc flipped the pistol around his finger with a flourish. "And why is that?"

"Because . . . that's just the way things go!"

But Doc was still staring at Caleb, spinning the pistol as though the weapon was just something to keep his finger busy. "You know who you sound like?"

"No, but I'll bet you're gonna tell me."

"You sound like me, right before I got fed up and started doing what made me happy rather than what I set myself up for when I didn't know any better."

"Running my saloon makes me plenty happy. I'd just

like to keep it open instead of having it taken away by some dumb-shit miner."

Doc shook his head. "That's not it. If you were just worried about that saloon, that's where you'd be right now. I may not be a businessman, but I know that you have to have angry drunks spitting threats at you on a daily basis. It just comes along with the territory."

"Yeah, it does. But that's not—"

Doc cut in after quickly raising his hand. ""It seems to me that you're more upset at the very notion that these loudmouths have the power to step in and make such a mess out of the quaint little garden you planted for yourself."

"Jesus, you've been drinking again. That explains all this chatter."

Spinning the pistol once more, Doc dropped it into his holster and turned to stand toe-to-toe with Caleb. "Sure I have, but I've also been thinking about things. Some of us may look the part more than others, but we're all dying. Either one of us could get trampled by a runaway bull, get struck by lightning, or perish from any one of a long list of things that folks can die from. Does that mean we need to sit in a cramped little office and just wait for it to happen?"

Hearing those last few words practically slapped Caleb across the face. "What did you say?"

"You heard me. I sat in a smelly office yanking rotten teeth from people's heads. Hell, I went to school for it! How absurd is that? But I feel more alive when I'm out there doing what makes me happy than when I'm keeping my mouth shut and doing what I'm told. We may not have crossed paths too many times just yet, but I can see that same thing buzzing around inside of you. Am I wrong?"

Caleb knew the quickest way out of that conversation was to tell Doc that he was wrong. Dead wrong. Unfortunately, he couldn't shake the thoughts of sitting in his own dirty little office, longing for the escape of working behind a bar. Compared to that paper-filled, dusty office stuck within those thick walls, Ben Mays's jail cell hadn't seemed too bad.

"I'm not wrong," Doc said to fill the silence. "I can see that."

"So what? This ain't nothing new. Practically every man that comes into my saloon gripes about what he does for a living. Either that, or he gripes about not being able to make a living. All men gripe. So what?"

"But how many men do something about it?"

Caleb shook his head quickly and backed away. "Don't do anything to put my place at risk, Doc. That's what I came to say."

"All right then. How about we work to make sure that the Busted Flush not only stays in business but also gets out of any financial woes you may have?"

"And how would you suggest we do that?"

"Well, the first step would be to put your place on the circuit."

Caleb's eyes lit up. Being on the gambler's circuit meant being in the loop for every big game when the real professionals came to town. Big-league players meant bigger house takes, and even when those gamblers had bad streaks of luck, others would come to fill their shoes or get in line to take one of those players down. In the end, it was the saloons that came out ahead, and only saloons on the circuit even made it into those games.

"I've tried to get on the circuit for years," Caleb said.

Nodding, Doc said, "I've been doing some gambling myself and have come to appreciate the fineries of that profession. I believe all you need is to expand your gaming repertoire and allow someone with similar interests to take an active role."

Caleb couldn't help but laugh. "You've got a hell of a way of saying a little thing like you want to work at my saloon."

"Seeing as how I'd rather pull my own teeth out rather than grow old in my current profession, I think a steady job dealing faro might be a welcome change."

"I never did see the sense in faro."

"That's because playing it is a step above tossing your money into the street. Not everyone thinks along those lines, which is why *dealing* faro can be quite lucrative."

"And how will that get me on the gambling circuit?"

"It's a first step in bringing your saloon up to snuff. What do you say? Are you willing to take on a new dealer?"

Caleb pondered that for a few moments before nodding. What put it all together for him was the notion that it would be so much easier to keep an eye on Doc in the Flush than having to track him down whenever something went wrong. "All right. But if the law comes snooping around, just keep your mouth shut. Sound good?"

"That sounds marvelous," Doc replied, extending his hand.

Caleb shook Doc's hand, finding himself once again surprised at the strength in the dentist's bony grasp.

"You keep in mind everything else we talked about," Doc said. "I'm not one to wax philosophic with just anyone, you know."

"In order for the Flush to last the week, I'll need to find a way to get those goddamn Deagles away from me for good."

"I am so glad you mentioned that. I've been entertaining some intriguing notions regarding that very topic."

"I hope you don't intend on shooting up my place," Caleb said with a nod toward the fence. There were only a few more bottles lined up, and when Caleb shifted his eyes back to Doc, he found the Navy model Colt being handed over to him.

"Actually, things may get a little rough before they get better," Doc said. "Are you up for it?"

Caleb took the gun from Doc's hand and let his finger settle over the trigger. From there, he extended his arm, took aim, and fired enough times to empty the cylinder. When the smoke cleared, all but one of the six remaining bottles had been shattered.

"I think I can handle myself just fine," Caleb said while handing the gun back to its owner.

It was just past nine that night when Doc came back into the Busted Flush. The suit he wore was freshly pressed and so black that it made his diamond stickpin stand out like a single star in an otherwise barren night sky. A large, flat case was tucked under one arm, and the smile on his face was wide enough to light up the room. Tipping his hat to everyone he met, Doc made his way to the bar where Hank was waiting.

"I'd like to have a word with Caleb, if you please," Doc said in his cordial southern drawl.

Hank nodded and took in the sight before him. "I hear you're to be dealing faro."

"That is correct, sir."

"That's an awful big change from dentistry, ain't it?"

"Every man is allowed his distractions, and with the annoying trend in which people have been maintaining their oral hygiene, I find that the added income is all too welcome."

Although it had been Hank's intention to put Doc through the same paces that he put every gambler, he soon found himself sharing the same high spirits that had gotten into the young dentist. "Caleb's set to come out here and work behind the bar. I'll have him check in on you before I leave, since it's bound to get busy in here tonight."

"Ah yes, the big poker tournament."

"Well, we hope it'll be big. I just hope it'll be bigger than the last few."

"Perhaps I can sit in for a few hands."

"Why don't you worry about dealing faro for now," Hank said. "Your table's right over there."

Looking in the direction where Hank was pointing, Doc spotted a table against the far wall that was sectioned off with rope.

"Holly's to be your lookout," Hank said.

"Fine. Hopefully she'll be able to keep her eyes on the cards instead of the dealer."

"That's what she gets paid for," Hank replied. After Doc had turned and walked through the room, the barkeep shook his head and stepped up to the door leading into Caleb's office. He knocked and stepped inside to find Caleb already jumping out of his seat. "Dr. Holliday is here."

Caleb smiled and stepped around his desk. "Great. Did you show him to his table?"

"Yep. He brought his own setup and is getting situated now."

"Perfect."

"I don't know about all this, Caleb. I mean, Holliday has a reputation around Dallas that don't have a thing to do with his dental practice."

"In case you haven't heard, I've been getting a reputation myself after Mike Abel got himself killed in here."

"How about a little respect? You were the one that killed him, after all."

"Don't start preaching to me," Caleb grunted. "What the hell's wrong with you, anyway?"

"Just what I said. Something about having Holliday in here don't set well."

"You're just hungry. Go have some supper and leave the Flush to me. You've earned a night off. Besides," Caleb added, "you always get nervous when we hold poker tournaments."

"I guess it's the gamblers. They all wear guns and don't mind using them."

Caleb waved off those words and walked past Hank. "Then you chose the wrong line of work, my friend. Spend a night alone with your wife, and maybe you'll feel better come the morning."

Hank nodded and grinned. "You may be right about that. Just be sure to let Holly know all that goes into watching over a faro game."

"She's done it a few times. Now will you get out of here before a rush comes in and you're forced to stay?"

"I'm leaving, I'm leaving. See you tomorrow."

But Caleb seemed to have already forgotten about the barkeep in his rush to get up front. It always got busy on tournament nights. Although the rush usually petered out after most of the locals realized just how unlucky they were, Caleb never missed those first few hours.

Nights like those were the ones that had gotten Caleb into the saloon business in the first place. There simply wasn't anything to compare with the feeling of gambling for more money than most folks saw in months of back-breaking work. The whiskey tasted better when it was poured between shuffles by a smiling woman leaning over your shoulder. The same old songs from the same piano sounded better when that music drifted through the smoky air and mingled with all those raised voices.

Anything could happen on nights like those. Fortunes could be won or lost. Bullets could fly. Romance could bloom. All of that and more seemed possible when Caleb tied that apron around his waist and stepped up to his bar. The only way for it to get any better was if he was the one sitting at a table, planning his next bluff or testing his luck against the tricky turns of fate.

"Gimme another!" shouted Thirsty from his spot at the end of the bar.

Caleb looked over to the regular and asked, "What're you drinking tonight? Beer or whiskey?"

"W . . . whis . . ." Rather than complete his order, Thirsty opened his mouth, leaned over, and dumped his last two meals onto the floor. "Whiskey!" he shouted after swiping his mouth with the back of his hand. From there, he wobbled on his feet and slumped forward to use the bar as his pillow.

So much for the bright side of saloon ownership.

Caleb dropped some rags onto the floor to stop the pungent fluids from spreading while one of the other bartenders went to fetch a bucket and mop.

"While you're down there," came a voice from the other side of the bar, "why don't you shine my boots?"

Caleb looked up with his toe still pressing a rag into the puke when he got a look at a very unwelcome sight. The humpback leaned against the bar with a leering grin upon his ugly face and a full week's worth of uneven stubble around his crooked mouth.

"If you're here to talk some more trash to me about paying off your uncle, you can turn right around and leave," Caleb said.

Jim shook his head. "Too late for that. And it's too late for no more of yer reward offers, too."

"Good, because that offer's not good anymore."

"Deal's changed, asshole. Me'n my cousin got some real backing now, so you'd best step in line before you end up dead."

Caleb straightened up and leaned forward. Although

that put him close enough to choke on Jim's stench, it also put him within easy reach of the polished club nestled just under the bar. "What did you just say?"

"You heard me, cocksucker. You either hand over the shares of this here place, or you won't have it no more."

"Get out of here before you're tossed out."

"Oh? And who's gonna do that? Y—"

Jim was unable to finish his sentence because he was already being dragged over the bar and tossed into the chunky puddle that Thirsty had spewed onto the floor.

Keeping one hand firmly clenched around the front of Jim's shirt, Caleb shoved the humpback down until he'd dipped every bit of his face into the puke. "You need to learn what happens when you push a man too many times, Jim."

Caleb pounded Jim's face into the puke once more.

"It's an ugly thing. Wouldn't you agree?"

As soon as Jim had a moment to suck in a dry breath, he squirmed and struggled to break Caleb's grip. "You son of a bitch! My uncle helped you out, and this is how you—"

Instead of being shoved into the vomit, Jim was flipped onto his back and slammed down just hard enough for the breath to be forced from his lungs. He was then dragged across the floor, kicking and swearing the entire way.

Ignoring the words that flew from Jim's mouth, Caleb hauled the humpback to the back door and kicked it open. Jim's shirt was starting to tear, so Caleb grabbed hold with both hands to make sure the humpback felt every wooden step as he was pulled out of the Busted Flush and dumped into the lot behind it.

"You asshole!" Jim snarled.

After shutting the door and making sure nobody was in the immediate area, Caleb clamped one hand around a fresh section of Jim's shirt and his other hand around the humpback's throat. He then lifted Jim to his feet and shoved him against the wall.

"What did you say to me?" Caleb asked. "You'd best think before answering, because you don't have your lard-ass cousin here with you."

Jim steadied himself and quickly tugged his shirt back into line. "You heard me, Injun. I said you need to sign over them shares, or you'll wind up dead. After that, I called you an asshole."

Caleb tightened his hand into a fist and buried it into Jim's gut. The humpback folded around Caleb's arm, and a loud groan filled the night air.

"Get the hell out of here, Jimmy. There's no more business between me and your uncle. If you leave now, there won't even be anything between you and me."

Although Jim started to walk away, he was moving too slowly to be seriously considering Caleb's offer. Sure enough, he reached behind him for something under his shirt at the small of his back. When his hand reappeared, it was wrapped around a slender boot knife.

Jim wore a gnarled smile as he hunkered down and lunged forward with his knife. Turning to one side, Caleb swatted at the humpback's wrist and diverted the blade before it got anywhere close to grazing him.

"Fucking Injun!" Jim spat as he staggered for a step and then collected himself to take another swing. This time, Jim lashed out with a backhanded swipe that was surprisingly quick compared to his first attempt.

Caleb managed to hop back but wasn't fast enough to get out unscathed. He felt the blade tear through the front of his shirt as well as a few layers of skin as it raked over his belly and sent a fine, bloody mist onto the saloon's door.

Looking down, Caleb pressed his hand against his midsection and looked at the blood for himself. With his heart slamming in his chest and his ears filled with the pounding noise of every thump, he didn't feel the first hit of pain. Instead, there was an icy calm that came over him and prodded Caleb onward, despite the blade that Jim was swinging at him for a third time.

Rather than trying to dodge the blade, Caleb reached out for it and felt the steel chew into the side of his hand. Jim smirked wider at the sight of blood and pressed on with even more resolve.

"Yer dead now," Jim snarled as he took a few quick stabs at Caleb. "We can just take what we want after yer in the ground."

Caleb stepped back quickly, avoiding the next few stabs. It didn't take much for him to read the pattern in Jim's strikes, and Caleb prepared for another lunge. Since most beginning fighters went for the spot they'd already wounded, Caleb reached down with both hands to catch Jim in the very same act.

Leaning in, Jim reached out to sink the blade into Caleb's belly. Instead, he was stopped short and unable to pull his arm back. Both of Caleb's hands enclosed Jim's wrist and then twisted sharply. Jim let out a pained holler and let go of the knife as if it had suddenly become red-hot.

While keeping hold of Jim's wrist, Caleb swept the knife away with the side of his boot. "You ain't the first to swing a blade at me," Caleb said. "But I'll see that this is the last time you try it."

With that, Caleb twisted Jim's hand against the wrist until he heard bones crunching and grinding together. The humpback was staring at him with his mouth agape but in too much pain to make a sound. That way, he could hear the sound of the bones in his wrist as they finally snapped like wet twigs beneath his skin.

There was no more resistance in Jim's wrist, so Caleb let it go. He then took hold of Jim's shoulders and pushed him away from the saloon. "Stay out of my sight," Caleb growled. "Or the next thing I'll break is your neck."

Jim might have tried to say something, but his words became tangled up in a series of labored breaths and whimpers. He managed to keep moving through the lot behind the Busted Flush and all the way to Commerce Street before shouting a few more halfhearted insults over his shoulder.

Caleb couldn't have cared less what Jim said. He didn't even care too much about the blood trickling down his belly and soaking into the front of his shirt. A few quick touches and a glance was all he needed to be sure that the wound wasn't much more than a scrape. When he looked up again, he saw the door swinging open and a pale face looking out at him.

"Having a bit of trouble out here?"

"Better late than never, huh, Doc?" Caleb replied.

"Well, I did manage to look up in time to see Jim's legs kicking over the side of the bar. By the time I realized he wasn't going after a free drink, I decided to come a check on you."

Letting out a breath, Caleb nodded and said, "I'm doing fine, Doc."

"Then I suppose that cut across your stomach is a fashion statement?"

"Not exactly, but it's nothing serious."

Doc extended a finger and pulled down the flap of Caleb's shirt that had been cut open. After a quick examination of his own, he nodded. "Did he say anything interesting, or was he too busy scampering off?"

"Actually, he mentioned something about having someone else backing him." Caleb didn't care too much for the way Doc pondered that possibility. "Do you think he was bluffing?"

Doc shrugged and replied, "I didn't see his face, so I couldn't say for sure. I do know that these Deagles are pressing awfully hard for something that is more or less out of their reach. I admire a man for taking a shot at something, but this is above and beyond what one might expect."

"You admire these assholes for trying to carve off a piece of my saloon?" Caleb asked.

"No. I admire the effort." Seeing the unapprecialtive scowl on Caleb's face, Doc patted him on the shoulder and started walking back into the saloon. "Looks like you've discouraged any further efforts."

"And what about this backing?"

"If that was a bluff, nothing will come of it. If there really is someone else behind this, then all we'll need to do is sit back and wait for the next shoe to drop. Either way, there's no reason for us to stand out here when all the real fun is inside."

And just like that, Doc was done with the matter. Although he still had his doubts, Caleb couldn't argue with Doc's logic. Judging by the noise coming from inside the Flush, there was more than enough in there to keep him busy for a while.

[16]

After stumbling onto Commerce Street, Jim broke into a run and made a straight line for Market. Along the way, he spat out an endless string of obscenities that had as much to do with Caleb Wayfinder as it had to do with the stabbing pain that shot from his wrist all the way up to his shoulder and back down into the pit of his stomach. The hand above his broken wrist had already gone numb, allowing Jim to see straight just long enough to find the St. Charles Saloon.

As one of the more respected saloons in Dallas, the St. Charles was also one of the most fortunate, since it had survived one fire that had claimed the lives of two establishments on the other side of the block. It was also known as a friendly place to gamble, which was more of a testament to Champagne Charlie Austin, who ran the place wearing an ever-present smile on his wide face.

Charlie was known as a good fellow and a straight shooter, which brought a hell of a lot of players to his card tables and tournaments. Charlie was just as likely to buy a man a drink as he was to pour one, and he did his best to greet folks as they walked into his saloon. This night was no exception.

"Hello there," Charlie said even before he saw who'd kicked open the St. Charles's front door. Once he got a look at the weary humpback, Charlie rushed forward, grasping the bar rag that hung from his back pocket. "You're hurt, Jimmy!"

Jim's first instinct was to slap away Charlie's helping hand. His next was to grit his teeth and snarl in pain since he did the swatting with his newly broken wrist. "Just get the fuck away from me," Jim spat. "And get me something to drink."

Although Charlie didn't appreciate Jim's brusque manner, it wasn't in his nature to return such ugly behavior. Instead, he backed up and went to the bar before he said something he might regret.

The St. Charles was as full as it was on any other night, meaning that nearly every table in the place was playing host to card games of various sizes. Smaller, narrow tables were situated around the edge of the main room, which were reserved for faro. A small stage was currently being used by a dark-haired woman singing along with a moderately talented guitar player.

At one of the faro tables closer to the door, Kyle's bulbous head poked up when he heard his cousin's venomous cursing. He then rushed up to the front of the saloon as quickly as his stout legs would carry him.

"What the hell happened to you?" Kyle asked the moment he got a look at Jim.

Snatching the shot of whiskey Charlie handed to him, Jim downed the liquor before replying, "That goddamn Injun jumped me behind his saloon."

"Son of a bitch!"

"What are you two going on about?"

Both Jim and Kyle jumped a bit since they hadn't even noticed the other man step up and join their conversation. The new arrival was average in height and build, allowing him to blend into the crowd within the saloon. What made him stick out a bit was the seriousness in his face and a darkness in his eyes, which plenty of gunfighters had worked years to perfect.

"Oh, uh, nothing, Bret," Kyle stammered.

Jim grabbed his wrist and let out a labored groan as another stab of pain lanced through that side of his body. "Nothing, my ass. My goddamn hand is busted!"

Bret took another step forward to examine Jim's hand. His bald head sported a few long scars, but nothing to make him look half as ugly as the humpback. A narrow face and bony features were accented by a thin mustache that looked as if it had been sketched under his nose using a pencil and ruler.

"You should see a doctor about that," Bret said.

"I don't like doctors."

"Then quit crying like a woman and tell me what happened."

Although he immediately regretted his refusal of treatment, Jim stuck by his posturing and proceeded to lay out a quick account of his recent visit to the Busted Flush. "And when I tried to have a word with that Injun, he pulled me over the bar and took me outside to threaten my life."

"All without merit, I suppose?"

"Yeah, Bret. I was just meaning to talk."

Bret looked Jim up and down before nodding. "I see you're not wearing a gun. What about that pig sticker you keep under your shirt?"

"Huh?"

"The knife," Bret said in a tone of voice that cut just as well as the weapon in question. "What about the knife you're so fond of carrying?"

"You told us not to go in there with weapons, so—"

Without another word, Bret reached out to grab hold of Jim by the hump on his back. When Jim started to protest, Bret's other hand flashed out to wrap around Jim's broken wrist so he could give it a quick squeeze. Whatever Jim was going to do or say was quickly eclipsed by the pain that engulfed him. After the humpback had dropped to one knee, Bret pushed him over and pulled the back of Jim's shirt up enough to see the empty scabbard tucked under his belt.

"You brought that knife in with you?" Bret asked in a cool, detached voice.

"I didn't . . . carry any weapon!"

"If that's the case, the scabbard wouldn't be here. Where's the knife?" When he didn't get an answer as quickly as he would have liked, Bret placed one boot against Jim's broken wrist and pressed down as if he was mashing out a cigarette. "Where's the knife, Jim?"

"The Injun took it from me!" Jim squealed.

"Did you pull it when he hauled you out of the Flush?"

"Yeah! I cut him, too, but he got the knife from me!"

"Is that how your hand got busted?"

Tears were welling up in Jim's eyes, and he hung his head even lower when he saw how many people were turning to get a look at what was going on. "Y . . . yeah. That's how it happened."

And, just like that, Bret's boot was no longer pushing down against Jim's broken bones. In fact, Bret was helping the humpback to his feet and dusting him off. Smiling more to the customers that were looking on, he motioned for Charlie to come closer. "Get this man another drink."

Leaning in so only Jim and Kyle could hear him, Bret whispered, "You see how much easier things go when you're straight with me?"

Since he was in too much pain and too embarrassed to speak, Jim merely nodded.

"Yes, sir, Mr. Weeks," Kyle said.

Bret helped Jim over to the door and even assisted in getting the humpback's arm draped over his cousin's shoulders. "You'd better have something more to show for your actions tonight, and I'd better hear about it before we get to the doctor. Otherwise, I'll make the pain you're feeling now feel like a fucking siesta."

"I know you told us not to go over there," Jim wheezed. "But I couldn't just—"

"It's not too far to the doctor's," Bret warned.

After sucking in a few breaths and shaking off his cousin's efforts to help him walk, Jim pulled in his wounded arm and staggered down Main Street alongside Bret and Kyle. "There was a good turnout. Plenty of card games going on."

"There's a tournament kicking off," Bret said. "You need to do better than that."

Jim's eyes darted back and forth in their sockets as if he was frantically trying to find salvation in the boardwalk under his feet. Suddenly, his eyes grew wide, and a hopeful smile jumped onto his face. "Doc Holliday was there!"

"Holliday's been gambling plenty lately. Keep trying."

"No. Not just gambling. He was dealing faro."

Reflexively, Bret glanced back in the direction of the Busted Flush. "Is that so?"

"I saw him when I was walking in. Holliday was sitting behind a faro table getting all set up to open for business."

Bret's eyes narrowed as he shifted his stare back to the street in front of him. "Now that is interesting. Did he have any part of what happened to you?"

Jim shook his head. "No, it was all that Injun's doing."

Although he'd been fairly silent this whole time, Kyle was unable to hold his tongue any longer. "We can't let this pass, Mr. Weeks. I know we was supposed to steer clear of that place, but we can't let that Injun think that he can walk all over us like this."

"Us?" Bret asked with amusement. "The only one that

got trampled was Jim, here, and that's only because he had
to go off on his own to talk tough when he should have
kept his damn mouth shut. I've been working at this for too
long to have the likes of you two muck it up now."

"Yeah, but—"

Weeks silenced Kyle with a quickly upraised hand.
"But, since a move's already been made, there's no need to
let it end there. This didn't fit into my timetable, but it was
something that was to happen eventually."

The bald man's brow formed a sharp ridge over his eyes
that all but hid them completely from view. What little
could be seen made it obvious to anyone with eyes of their
own that Weeks was sifting through more than just the
ramblings of a humpback and his fat cousin.

"I know I messed up," Jim sputtered. "But that was only
because I was caught by surprise. The next time I go back
in there, I can clean that Injun out of that place for good,
and we can get that other bartender to fall right in line with
us."

"Tell you what," Weeks said. "Get that hand patched up,
and then we'll see about letting you go back to that saloon
to have a word with Caleb Wayfinder. Maybe this time,
you shouldn't go it alone."

Jim's eyes lit up, and he practically started to dance
right there in the street. "I know if I take some of the others with me, we won't have a lick of trouble!"

"Just don't make a move without letting me know.
There are some other preparations that need to be made."

"Yes, sir. I swear I won't."

They approached the darkened storefront rented by one
of Dallas's physicians. It wasn't the biggest or most respected place in town, but it was closest to the St. Charles,
which was all that concerned Bret Weeks. After rapping on
the side door long enough to wake the doctor who worked
and slept there, Weeks and Kyle left Jim to get his hand
seen to and then started retracing their steps down Main.

"I want to go with Jimmy next time," Kyle said. "He needs someone to watch out for him. I'll make sure he don't do anything stupid."

"What you need to do is look up a friend of mine."

"Huh? No. If Jim's going back to break up that saloon, then I want to be there, too."

"The friend I'm referring to lives a few days' ride from here," Weeks went on to say as if Kyle hadn't said a word in the meantime. "You'll just head south from town and stay on the road right until the last minute. I'll be sure to draw you a map so you don't miss it."

"But Jim will—"

"Jim will do just fine on his own," Weeks interrupted. "My boys will be right there with him to keep him in line. Our deal was that you, your cousin, and your uncle all do as I say, or none of you will see a dime. When you came to me, I told you I could make all of you prosperous men. None of that will happen unless you can take orders. You understand me?"

Reluctantly, Kyle nodded.

"Good. Speaking of your uncle, what has he been doing lately?"

Muttering like a pouting child, Kyle replied, "Still digging in the dirt. What little dust he finds just gets pissed away that same night in a poker game. Same as always."

"Good. Maybe he'll start pulling his weight before that weight pulls him down."

[17]

The Busted Flush's poker tournament was usually a large affair and accounted for a good deal of the saloon's income during the month of March. This March, however, saw a tournament that came and went without much ado. Over the week the tournament was held, Caleb saw marginal profits coming from the poker players themselves. Taking in the entire month as a whole, on the other hand, was another story.

Although the tournament itself was something of a disappointment, Caleb found that he was happier than he had any right to be. April was already looking to be a better mouth for profits, and standing behind that bar while avoiding the dreary office behind it did wonders for his constitution. He felt more alive and in higher spirits than he had in a good, long time. With Hank more than happy to take on the structured schedule that came along with keeping the books in line, he was happier as well. At least, his family was happier since they got to see him at more respectable hours.

Caleb found himself sleeping until noon and staying up until sunrise as the sole custodian of the Busted Flush during its most lucrative part of the night. And although the poker tournament hadn't panned out too well, the saloon's profits were slowly climbing to unforeseen heights. The cause of this was its new appreciation for the game of faro.

The first few nights had been slow at Doc's table. Faro wasn't exactly anything new to the Busted Flush, but it took a distant second to Caleb's personal favorite of poker. What few tables that were given to faro usually wound up being used to hold hot dishes or sandwiches meant to entice gamblers to stay put and play a few more hands of five-card draw or seven-card stud.

Once Doc laid out his kit, folks started taking notice. At first, they'd been more curious about the dealer than his game. Caleb didn't care to keep up with the rumors and gossip that floated through every saloon in every town, but it was hard to ignore the fact that the subject of a good deal of that gossip was the dentist-turned-gambler now working at the Flush.

"Will you look at that?" Caleb mused as Hank made some repairs to one of the beer taps.

Hank glanced over at Doc's faro table and shrugged. "It's not even full."

"Yeah, but that's a damn mob compared to the action faro usually gets in this place."

"We could've done better ourselves if we put some effort into it."

"What do you mean? Doc's doing a hell of a job. The man loves his work."

"You call that work?" Hank asked, answering his own question with a grunt of a laugh forced out under his breath.

"As opposed to pouring drinks into Thirsty's gullet? At least Doc doesn't have to clean puke off the floor."

"Gambling ain't no way to make a living," Hank grumbled. "You'd do well to remember that."

Doc's grasp for figuring numbers and calculating odds seemed like magic to someone who didn't know the tricks of a gambler's trade. Sometimes, Doc had such a good handle on the odds that it seemed like he had to be cheating. And as far as cheating went, that practice was so commonplace in saloon gambling that it was damn near accepted. The only thing that was truly frowned upon in that regard was getting caught.

Explaining even a piece of that to Hank was a waste of time. And besides that, Caleb was too busy enjoying his saloon to fuss about relieving the older man's pessimism. "You want to know why Doc's working out so well?" Caleb asked.

Hank pulled a pipe from beneath the tap and started pushing a rag through it to clean out the mold and sludge that had gathered in there. "Why don't you enlighten me?"

Caleb pointed to the Flush's front doors, which were being propped open by a brick instead of a drunk that refused to leave after being chucked out. Walking in, wearing a smile that practically spilled out and dripped onto the floor beneath him, was a man in his mid-thirties dressed in a rumpled brown suit. The jacket was folded and draped over one arm, and the sleeves of his white cotton shirt were rolled up just past his elbows.

Accompanying the man was an attractive woman in a dress decorated with a red flower pattern. Her long brown hair was tied back with a simple pink ribbon that matched the choker tied around her neck. To say that she wasn't as excited to be in the Busted Flush as her husband would have been an understatement.

"Are you sure about this, Steve?" she asked while taking in the sights and smells of the saloon. "I mean, I hear the Alhambra is so much nicer. Or what about the Crutchfield House? That's just across the street."

Steve took another few steps into the Flush and started nodding enthusiastically. "I won't hear any of it, Jen. This is the place I want to be." His eyes widened when he spotted the poker tables, and it was an obvious struggle for him to keep from running over there. "The man I talked to at the train station said this is the place I wanted."

"The man probably gets a dollar every time he points someone in this direction," the woman replied. "Come on. We haven't even found a hotel yet."

Caleb moseyed over to the couple and put on a smile. "I didn't mean to snoop, but I can have a room rented in your name so you can get right to business. What's your game?"

The man was slightly taller than Caleb and had a bit more bulk around his midsection. Of course, that wasn't saying much, since some posts had more bulk around their midsections than Caleb Wayfinder. When he removed his dented bowler hat, he pushed back the stray tufts of dark hair that had been set free. "Actually, I was hoping to play some poker. I hear there's a tournament?"

Caleb winced. "You just missed the tournament, but we still hold more poker games a night than you can shake a stick at."

"Perfect!"

"By the way, I'm Caleb Wayfinder. I own this place."

Extending his hand, the man said, "Steve Wright. This lovely lady is my wife Jen."

Caleb shook Steve's hand as well as Jen's. Although she smiled politely enough, she was still easing her way toward the door. Leaning in and lowering his voice to a stage whisper, Caleb said, "Actually, Mrs. Wright, Field's Opera House does put on a better variety show than we do. If you'd rather take that in, I know a girl named Sarah who would be plenty happy to accompany you."

That not only put a genuine smile on Jen's face but also

made her squeeze Caleb's hand a little tighter as she shook it. "Really? That sounds wonderful."

"My partner was just about to leave. If you'd like him to walk you over there, Hank would be more than happy to oblige."

Still gazing longingly at the poker tables, Steve nodded but wound up shaking his head. "Actually, if it's all the same to you, I think I should take her there myself."

"Should I set up a spot for you at one of our tables?"

"Sure. I guess."

Caleb spotted something familiar in the way Steve was looking at the gambling tables. It was a look in the man's eyes that reminded Caleb of a kid that just couldn't pick out the right flavor of candy stick from the selection in front of him.

"What about faro?" Caleb asked. "Doc's going to be dealing all night and he's been a favorite among those who buck the tiger."

"You host faro games, too?" Steve asked.

"Sure do."

"That sounds fine, but I'm more of a poker player."

"I think you might be able to twist Doc's arm into starting a game. He has a knack for putting together some wild ones." The more he spoke, the deeper Caleb felt the hook sink into Steve's mouth. All he needed was one last tug to land the catch for good. "How about I reserve a table for you and let Doc know you're coming? I'm sure you can pick up a few more players at the show if you drop his name."

Steve nodded and said, "I'll do that. It's been great meeting you, Caleb."

Even after Steve escorted his wife out the door, Caleb still found himself smiling. The other man's enthusiasm was like a charge that was still working its way through the air.

"What the hell are you grinning at?" Hank asked as Caleb stepped back behind the bar.

"Did you see that couple?"

"Yeah. Pretty wife."

"She wore two lovely gold rings and had a handsome cameo on that choker. Steve also had a hell of a nice watch in his vest pocket. Gold chain and all."

"Ah, so you're hoping they might plunk down that fine jewelry onto one of the poker tables?" Hank asked.

"Only if things go better than expected. Actually, I was just happy to see a man come in here who has money in his pockets and no gun around his waist. Things are looking up for the Flush, and players like Mr. Wright just proves it."

Hank patted Caleb on the shoulder. "Not to rain on your picnic, but Mr. Wright ain't even here anymore."

"He'll be back."

"You certain about that?"

Caleb nodded. "That fellow didn't have a liar's face. Either that, or he's one of the finest actors in this country. Myself, I'll put money down on him sitting right here later tonight after he gets that pretty wife of his to a show and settled in."

Hank let out a tired grunt and worked a kink out of his back. "Well, you can hope all you want, just so long as it doesn't interfere with me going home right about now."

"Go on ahead. Give my best to the kids."

Before heading to the door, Hank examined Caleb's face and nodded approvingly. "Seems like getting out of that office truly did wonders for you."

"You're better than a doctor," Caleb replied. "I feel almost like the man in that picture hanging up in my office."

"I don't know about that," Hank said as he narrowed his eyes to study Caleb even harder. "You're not so gloomy anymore, but you're far from the lad that started up this saloon with me."

"What's that supposed to mean?"

"Maybe it's just that the fellow in that picture would have been happier to be running a business that's doing well instead of luring visitors into a card game so someone like Doc could fleece them for all they're worth."

"The house take on games like that are what keep the Flush above water. Don't forget it."

"I guess. Anyway, have a good night, and try to let that nice fellow keep his wedding ring."

"I'll try, but I can't make any promises." Caleb didn't have to wait long before he got a scolding glare from Hank. When he saw that, Caleb smirked and added, "Just kidding. Get out of here before you worry yourself to death."

Hank turned his back to Caleb and shuffled toward the door. Although a good portion of the Busted Flush was alive with laughter and boisterous voices, none of that seemed to rub off on the bartender. On the contrary, Hank couldn't seem to leave the saloon fast enough and showed no signs of looking back.

A few moments after Hank left, another familiar figure rose up over those seated at the various tables scattered throughout the Flush. Doc got up from his faro table and made his way over to the bar where Caleb already had a shot of whiskey waiting for him.

Taking the liquor and tossing it back like a splash of water, Doc set the glass down and lifted a fist to his mouth. His eyes clenched shut, and a series of coughs rattled his shoulders. Although most of the hacking was muffled by his hand and tightly closed lips, Doc wasn't able to keep all the coughs inside of himself for long.

"I see . . . you're taking on the role of genial host now?" Doc asked between coughs.

Knowing that Doc didn't appreciate anyone trying to tend to him when his consumption was acting up, Caleb satisfied himself with the fact that the coughs didn't seem too serious just yet. "Yeah, well, that nice couple had a look about them."

Doc chuckled once, which turned into a grating hacking sound that made Caleb's throat hurt just hearing it. "I take it that means you set him up for a game?"

"Oh yeah."

"Splendid. By the way, there's a man over there who wants to have a word with you regarding some accusations of cheating."

"Anything I should know before I start blindly defending you?" Caleb asked.

Doc merely shrugged. "Tricks of the trade, Caleb. Nothing special."

"Is that him steaming over by your table?"

Glancing over there, Doc nodded. "That's the one."

Caleb sighed and prepared himself to deal with the angry gambler. "How much did he lose?"

"Given enough time, he was set to lose all he had." Seeing the impatience growing upon Caleb's face, Doc added, "About four hundred."

"And you couldn't handle him yourself?"

"I could handle him just fine. I just came over here for a drink."

"Then you go there and handle him, and I'll work my way over in a minute."

But Doc wasn't in any hurry to move. In fact, he hardly seemed to be paying attention to a word Caleb was saying.

"Is there something else you wanted to tell me about?" Caleb asked. "Someone who threatened to shoot you if he lost again, perhaps?"

"Have you ever seen that man before?" Doc asked.

Noticing the way Doc was intently staring into the crowd of card tables, Caleb tried to pick out the person that had just been mentioned. Surprisingly enough, there was one man in particular who stood out from all the others. "You mean that one with the blue bandanna?"

"That's him," Doc said with a nod. "He's been giving you the eye for the last hour or so, but hasn't left that table. Sometimes, he just picks a spot on the wall and stares at it for a few minutes without moving a muscle."

The man in question sat at one of the small round tables that wasn't used for cards or dice. He sat there alone, dressed in a dark jacket that looked as if it been dragged through the mud before being slapped over his shoulders. Bristly hair sprouted from his scalp at odd intervals, but not in the way that Caleb's hair grew. Instead of being the result of a bad haircut, this stranger's appearance came more from the fact that his face and scalp resembled a half-melted candle.

Now that he'd spotted the man, Caleb couldn't take his eyes off of him. The figure sat bunched over slightly with his head bowed and eyes glaring up at the rest of the world. Those eyes were so dark and so far back in their sockets that it was difficult to say which direction they were pointed.

"I don't know the man, myself," Doc said, "but I thought you might want to know that he's packing a pistol in his boot as well as the one around his waist."

"That seems to be the fashion these days."

"Only around here," Doc replied. "If you weren't so good at pulling in unlucky souls from off the street, I might consider moving my game to a more respectable establishment."

Coming from anyone else, that might have sounded like an insult. But when it was delivered in Doc's smooth voice and Georgia drawl, it sounded as good-natured as it was intended to be. It was fortunate that Caleb didn't intend on responding to Doc's comment, because he would have been speaking to empty air. Doc was already on his way back to his faro table.

"What's gonna be done about this?" griped a short,

olive-skinned man with a full beard and an unruly mustache. "I been cheated, and that's all there is to it!"

Doc settled into his chair and cleared his throat after a few hacking breaths.

The busty redhead who'd formerly been the main drink server at the Flush took her spot on lookout. Perched upon a stool behind the table and to Doc's right, she handed a deck of cards to the slender, pale-faced dealer and smiled to the players gathering around the front of the layout.

Slamming his fist down, the olive-skinned man stared straight down into Doc's eyes. "You hear me, you pasty son of a bitch? You're either paying my money back, or I'll have a word with the owner of this place."

"Don't bother with that," said someone behind the complainer. "Doc and the owner of this stink hole are in it together."

"All right then," the olive-skinned man grunted. "I'll just take my money back. Make it quick, Holliday. I hear there's some honest games over at the St. Charles."

"Put your money on the table or shut up," Doc said plainly as he placed the cards into a small, open wooden box.

The olive-skinned man blinked and looked around as if he'd just heard another language. "What was that?"

Looking up, Doc fixed a stare upon the complainer that left no room for debate. "Place a bet or step away. Those are your only two choices, since you won't be getting a refund. That's as simple as I can put it. Or would you prefer if Holly here drew you a picture?"

"Why you hustling little . . ." The rest of the olive-skinned man's threat was lost as he shoved himself back a step and fumbled for the pistol holstered at his side.

Doc's hand moved in a flicker of motion as it left the top of the table, glanced toward his shoulder and reappeared wrapped around his Navy model Colt. "Place a bet, sir," Doc drawled as he thumbed back the Colt's hammer, "or step away."

Whether he was trying to save face or trying to keep his trembling hands busy, the man did as he was told and dropped some money onto the ten of spades drawn upon the felt.

Clearing his throat without a single cough, Doc discarded the top card of the deck with his free hand and slipped another card out to be turned over. It was a ten. "Very good. You're a winner." Shifting his gun slightly so it was pointed up at the complainer's face, he added. "I suggest you enjoy your winnings before your luck turns."

The man reached out hesitantly, since doing so brought his hand closer to Doc's Colt. He then swept up his money and retracted his arm as if he'd just stolen the bait from a bear trap. "Come on, Mark," he said to his buddy behind him. "Let's head over to Thompson's."

By this time, Caleb walked over wearing a cordial grin on his face. Before he could say a word to the disgruntled gambler, the olive-skinned man and his friend were already rushing to the door. Caleb looked over and saw Doc easing his Colt back into the holster under his arm.

"You got everything under control here?" Caleb asked.

Doc merely shrugged and smiled as bets started coming in from all sides. Plenty of men were quick to fill the newly vacant spots around the table. "Right as rain," Doc replied.

When Caleb looked back to where the stranger with the blue bandanna had been sitting, all he saw was an empty chair.

Orville Deagle walked into Thompson's Varieties after having stopped in to check nearly every other saloon or gambling hall in town. Having burned down in the same fire that had claimed the Alhambra back in October, Thompson's was located within spitting distance of the St. Charles. When Orville spotted the men leaning against the short bar at the back of Thompson's main room, he thought he might have wandered into the St. Charles by mistake.

Not only were his two nephews there, but Bret Weeks was there as well, looking very much like a well-fed coyote sitting among the hounds. Weeks was the first one to spot Orville and motioned for the old miner to come over and join him. Reluctantly, Orville shuffled toward the well-dressed businessman.

"Evening, Orville," Weeks said. "What brings you by?"

"Is there someplace more private we can talk?"

Glancing around at the entire place, Weeks shrugged and replied, "What's the matter with where we're at? The

men in here are too busy with their own affairs to worry
about ours."

Although there was plenty of drinks served at
Thompson's Varieties, it was more of a place devoted to
gambling than spirits. The lighting was just enough for serious card players to read their hands, and the air was thick
with cigar smoke. Working girls made their rounds, adding
to the varieties promised in the establishment's name.

While both Kyle and Jim acknowledged their uncle's
presence, neither of them said a word to the grizzled old
man.

Orville knew better than to try to convince Weeks to go
anywhere he didn't want to go. Rather than wasting any
breath, the miner clasped his hat in both hands and muttered, "I want out."

"Out? Out of what?"

"Our arrangement," the miner said with a bit more con-
viction. "Out of the deal. Out of everything. I just want to
go back to working my claims and making an honest living."

Weeks's eyes narrowed, and he stepped up to the miner
with his arms crossed firmly across his chest. "We had a
deal."

"And nothing's come of it. I said my piece to the owner
of the Flush, but nothing happened. I didn't expect no compensation when I agreed to say what I did to that Texas
Ranger anyhow."

"But you know that you were going to be cheated in that
game," Weeks pointed out.

Orville nodded. "And the man that was gonna cheat me
is dead. Things between me an' him can't be any more settled than that."

"I don't give a rat's ass what's settled or not," Weeks
snarled. "You don't get to walk away from this. Not when
I've already put so much time into getting my hands on a

piece of that damn saloon." He softened a bit and added, "Besides, you're the one who came to me. Remember?"

"I asked for a loan to cover my losses since my claims didn't pay out. The rest was your idea."

"And it was the way we agreed for you to work off your loan. I already paid off your debts, so it's up to you to hold up your end."

"I can pay you back the old-fashioned way."

"But that won't get me controlling interest in the Busted Flush. That's what I want, and that was our deal."

"But you already own a share in nearly every saloon in town," Orville protested. "You already make more money than you know what to do with, so what's the point in going after a place like the Busted Flush?"

"Not that I need to explain myself to you, but plenty of action has been headed over to the Busted Flush lately. By the looks of it, they're set to account for a bigger piece of gambling revenue than this place or the St. Charles combined."

Weeks was approaching Orville as he spoke, not stopping until he was close enough to glare directly into the miner's eyes. "All you need to worry about is that I paid you good money to do your job, and that job ain't been done yet."

"I went and said what you told me to that Caleb fellow," Orville protested. "Nothing came of it. If I go to the law, I won't last a single day in court because what I say can't hold up."

"All right then," Weeks said. "But you haven't done nearly enough to earn the money I put out on your behalf."

"My nephews have done plenty." Hesitantly, Orville reached into his pocket and pulled out a bundle of folded bills. Some of the money looked new enough to have been freshly printed, while some of it seemed to have been washed up after a rainstorm. "I had to borrow to get some of it, but it's all there. I can't abide by this no more."

"Abide by what?" Weeks asked, refusing to even look at the cash in the miner's trembling hand.

"What you got my nephews doing, that's between them and their maker. As for me, I'm done."

Weeks looked like he was ready to explode with rage. His ears had turned beet red and his lips curled back into a threatening snarl. Before he could act on those impulses, he pulled in a breath and let it out with a measured hiss. "I know you've had to wait around since Wayfinder has proven to be a little more stubborn than expected, but my pieces are in place, and I'm set to make some moves that will put the Busted Flush in my hands.

"In case you don't realize what that means, I'll have a share of all the major gambling spots in Dallas. I'll also have effectively eliminated anyone big enough to give me any real competition. Once I sink into the Busted Flush, any place that wants to become bigger than some back-room watering hole will have to go through me."

Orville nodded while still holding out the folded money. "I understand all that, Mr. Weeks, but all that kind of thing is well over my head."

"When I win, all my partners win, Orville. That includes you and your nephews."

"But to earn my keep, I'll have to be a man that I ain't and do things that I'll never be proud of. My nephews may be right by that, but I'd rather scrape half a living out of the dirt than lie, cheat, and steal just to line my pockets."

"Every businessman lies," Weeks said without so much as a tremble showing in his smile. "It's part of the game. Just like every gambler cheats. The only trick is to keep from getting caught and believe me, we won't get caught."

"But I know what I done," Orville replied. This time, he took hold of Weeks's hand and pressed the folded money straight into it. "My nephews can do what they want, but I'm out. That's all there is to it."

Weeks closed his fist around the money and looked over

his shoulder to where Jim and Kyle were watching. Jim's arm was held straight by a wooden splint and wrapped up in tight bandages.

"You know this Caleb Wayfinder is a dangerous man," Weeks said as he looked back to Orville.

The miner nodded.

"He killed Mike Abel, and he might just kill you for the threats you already made."

"I been fine over the past month or so. If he wants to find me now, then that's the way it'll be."

"He's been asking about you," Weeks pressed. "If you're off my payroll, I won't have much reason to put myself on the line to protect you."

Orville's brow furrowed as he studied the other man's face. He hadn't heard one instance of Caleb Wayfinder asking about him. He'd even seen the owner of the Busted Flush and gotten nothing more than a tip of the hat for his troubles. But the menace in Weeks's voice was more than enough to make Orville concerned.

"I'm out," the miner said with resolve. "That's all there is to it." With that, he turned his back on Weeks, the money, and his nephews so he could head for the front doors. Orville reached out for them, wincing at the thought of a bullet drilling a hole through his back.

That bullet came after a pop of noise and the slap of lead against flesh. Orville felt a jolt of pain followed by the kick of the round which sent him face-first to the ground. Before he hit, Orville's vision was fading. He couldn't breathe. He couldn't hear. He couldn't even feel his chin slam against the wooden slats.

"Jesus Christ," someone at one of the card tables shouted.

But Weeks was already stepping forward wearing a surprised look on his face. "That old man just tried to kill me!" he said for the benefit of everyone looking on.

Although plenty of the others were surprised enough to

buy Weeks's act, Kyle and Jim knew better. Before they could do anything about what they'd just witnessed, strong arms wrapped around them and dragged them out of sight. Both cousins kicked and struggled but were unable to get free in the short amount of time it took for them to be hauled away.

Weeks strutted into the back room behind the men carrying the two cousins as the commotion in the main room grew louder and louder. Neither Kyle nor Jim could get a look at the men holding them, but that didn't much matter. Their eyes were searching for Weeks.

"What the hell was that?" Kyle grunted as the door to the back room slammed shut and Weeks stepped into view. "You just killed Uncle Orville!"

"He wanted out of our arrangement," Weeks said simply. "Now he's out. Tell you the truth, he wasn't working out too well."

Jim squirmed and kicked with such force that the bigger man holding onto him was forced to tighten his grip and lift Jim off the floor. Even as the other man's arms cinched in around his splinted arm, Jim kept right on struggling. "You didn't have to do that! Orville wouldn't hurt nobody!"

With a flicking wave of two fingers, Weeks signaled to the men holding onto Jim and Kyle. At that signal, the grip around both men shifted so a beefy hand could clamp down over both of their mouths.

"I believe things happen for a reason," Weeks stated. "Your uncle pulling this shit forced me to move away from a plan that was going nowhere and force me to put my second alternative into motion. It also allows me to see if you two are truly with me or against me."

Kyle tried to talk but found his words muffled by the hand over his mouth. After a nod from Weeks, that hand moved away, and Kyle was allowed to speak. "We're with you. We just didn't think that our uncle would have to die."

"That was his doing."

"Yeah," Kyle grunted. "I know."

After studying Kyle for a few moments, Weeks looked over the fat man's shoulder and nodded. He did the same to the man holding the humpback, and both cousins were let go. Weeks stood just in front of the door that separated the small supply room from the rest of the gambling hall. "All right," he said. "I want you to go out there and back up what I said about your uncle trying to kill me. After that, we can discuss where to go now that he's dead."

The cousins glanced at each other for half a second before they came to a silent agreement.

"Fuck you, bastard," Jim said as his hand flashed for the gun at his side.

Weeks flipped open his jacket and snatched the pistol from his fashionably tooled holster in the blink of an eye. Bringing the gun up just high enough to clear leather, his other hand crossed over to drop the hammer upon the round beneath it. The room filled with the thunder of that first shot, but Weeks wasn't done yet. His hand was already fanning the hammer back a second time. Smoke and fire spewed from the gun barrel again so quickly that it sounded more like a single, stuttering blast rather than two separate ones.

The first round caught Jim dead center and passed through to gouge the man behind him. The second bullet punched a hole through Jim's heart and knocked him against the wall as his eyes glazed over.

Kyle went for his gun as well but didn't even get his finger on the trigger before feeling an arm wrap around his neck from behind. Once more, he was lifted up as a sudden pain lanced through his stomach. That pain was soon followed by the flow of something warm over his belly and down his crotch.

Kyle was already growing weak. It was hard to take a breath, and his vision was blurred by the time he was able to make out the shape of a fist pressed against his stomach. That fist lifted slightly to reveal a bit of the blade that had been stuck into his gut. Slowly, the man behind Kyle dragged the knife across to widen the gash in Kyle's stomach.

In a quick motion, the blade was pulled free, and the man behind Kyle stepped aside to let the fat man drop. Kyle's back hit the floor, forcing more blood out of his wound. The gun dropped from Kyle's hand since he was now more interested in getting a look at the ugly face that was staring down at him.

Taking the blue bandanna from around his neck, the man used it to wipe off the bloody blade of his knife. When he smiled, it made the deep creases in his face twist into something that looked more like a vat of putty being stirred by an invisible finger. In places, the flesh seemed to hang loosely off of his skull while it stuck to other spots without moving.

Seeing that both cousins were down, Weeks spun the pistol around his finger as he dropped it back into its holster. "You all right?"

The man who'd been holding onto the humpback quickly examined his wound and started to nod. "Nothin' but a scratch."

"Go out and say that one of these two took a shot at you as they tried to head out the back," Weeks ordered. "Go on, while that blood's nice and fresh."

The other man did as he was told, marching past Weeks to pull open the door and stagger through it.

Weeks made sure to stay behind the door so he could ease it shut with the back of his boot. "What about you, Grissom?" he asked the man with the knife.

Grissom let out a breath and sheathed his knife. Turning reflexively to face Weeks with a side of his face that was less scarred than the rest, he said, "Oh, I'm just fine. This tub of shit didn't even get a gun in his hand."

It was hard for Weeks to take his eyes off of Grissom's face, even though he'd seen it plenty of times. So many layers of scar tissue were piled onto his neck and cheek that Grissom's flesh appeared to be flowing right off of his bones. "Yeah," Weeks said. "Well, I thank you for stepping in."

"That's what you pay me for. That is, unless you plan on taking back my fee as well as that miner's."

Laughing uncomfortably, Weeks said, "No, no. You've still got a job to do."

"I hope it's more along my normal line of work. I'd prefer that over gutting pigs any day."

"It is. Hopefully it will be as productive as the job you did back in October."

Grissom nodded and grinned like a man who was thinking back to a day spent in bed with a beautiful woman. "It'll be all that and more. You just let me know when to start in."

"Shouldn't be long, but you need to sit tight until I give the word. If you do have to wait a while, you'll do just that." Still seeing the gleam in Grissom's eye, Weeks took a step forward and asked, "You hear me?"

Although that snapped Grissom out of his thoughts, it didn't peel the smile off his face. "I guess I can hold off for a while longer, especially since you been taking such good care of me since I got here."

"Speaking of that, I'll need you to stop beating on my working girls. They need to stay pretty if they're gonna earn their keep."

"Well, you might have to give me a girl all my own if'n you want me to stay around here doin' nothing."

"I'll see if I can spare anyone," Weeks said. "For now, I'll need you to get these carcasses out of here. I should be able to keep the law from poking around too much, but it wouldn't look right to have this room full of blood and stinking all to hell."

Grissom looked around and quickly spotted the narrow door that was all but hidden behind a stack of crates full of liquor bottles. "That lead outside?"

"Sure does. Haul those two out of here."

Even as Grissom was squatting down to slip his arms underneath the fat man's corpse, Weeks grinned and said, "On second thought, why don't you just get out of here?"

"An' leave these two?"

"That's right. I think the skinny one's got a new knife. Check his boot."

Grissom pulled up Jim's pant leg and found the scabbard. Sure enough, there was a knife in there to replace the one he'd lost behind the Busted Flush.

"Put that knife in his hand," Weeks said as he stepped over to Kyle and dug the pistol from the fat man's holster. Reaching down with his free hand, Weeks took hold of Kyle's wrist and straightened out the dead man's arm before fitting the gun in between Kyle's pudgy fingers.

"Oh yeah," Grissom said. "Pretty as a picture."

[19]

The audience had cleared out of Field's Opera House hours ago. After drinking their cordials and saying their long-winded good-byes, the more cosmopolitan crowd tucked themselves into their beds while the more sporting among them made their way back to the saloons and gaming halls.

Like many other towns of its size, Dallas took on a second life when the sun went down. Bawdy music and the promise of easy money handed out by girls in their sparkling dresses was more than some men could resist. Most of those men never had any intention of resisting.

It wasn't much when compared to the opera house, but Jed had worked at the Busted Flush for a while and could play a mean harmonica. He could even strum a banjo before he got too much whiskey in his system. By the time Steve Wright made his way back into the Flush, the banjo was long gone and Jed was spitting his foul breath into his harp.

Caleb spotted the grinning newcomer immediately and welcomed him with a hearty handshake. "I was just about to give up on you, Steve," Caleb lied. "You finally managed to find your way back here?"

Steve nodded and shook Caleb's hand vigorously. "As soon as I could get away from the missus."

Caleb winced sympathetically. "I've been dragged to the opera house once, myself. It wasn't pleasant."

"I hear that. I've been thinking about getting back here ever since that fat lady began to sing. Is Doc around?"

"He sure is, but he's over dealing faro."

"Faro, huh? Are we still on for poker?"

"Of course," Caleb said as he draped an arm over Steve's shoulder and steered him toward the narrow table against the wall, which also just happened to have some of the house's most favorable odds. "But didn't you say you wanted to try bucking the tiger?"

Steve's eyes were already widening as he spotted the one empty seat toward Holly's end of the table. "Actually, yes. I did."

"Then tonight's your lucky night, my friend. Doc's one hell of a teacher." Standing behind Steve, Caleb showed the man to his seat and gave Doc a subtle wink. "This is the man I was telling you about, Doc. Steve Wright, this is Doc Holliday."

Doc smiled in a way that raised the cigarette clenched in the corner of his mouth. He extended a hand across the table and said, "I hear you're quite the gambler."

"Not really," Steve said. "I just like to dabble when I've got some money burning a hole in my pocket."

"Well, by all means, burn away."

Steve laughed good-naturedly enough but was unable to hide his discomfort when looking down at all the markings on the felt-covered table. "I . . . uh . . . don't exactly know what I'm doing here, so—"

"Nonsense," Doc cut in smoothly. "Don't let all this

trouble you. This here," he said, tapping the wooden box at his right hand, "holds a deck of cards." With his left hand, Doc produced a deck of cards and deftly fanned them out and in before spreading them onto the table in a perfectly symmetrical arc. "As you can see," he explained while flipping the end card to cause the arc to ripple over until each card was now faceup, "it's just a standard deck. Nothing special and nothing to be worried about."

Catching the intimidated expression on his own face, Steve chuckled and nodded. "So far, so good."

"I put the deck into this box, drain the soda . . ." After dropping the deck faceup into the box, he peeled off the first card, revealed it, and set it aside. "Top card's the soda, by the way. We have to come up with new names to keep this simple little game interesting."

That got a laugh from Steve as well as the others sitting at the table.

"I take one card off the top," Doc said, "and set it aside. That one loses. The one you see in the box wins."

Taking the cigarette from his mouth and holding it between two fingers of his left hand, Doc made a sweeping motion across the felt table. On the table were depictions of every card in the suit of spades. "You bet on a card by putting your money on which one you think will show up. Put one of those pennies on top of your bet if you think that card is a loser."

"And what if none of those cards come up?"

"Then that would make you the loser. But don't worry, the odds are about fifty-fifty since we don't mind you keeping track of which ones have already been played." As he said that, Doc pointed to the spot directly across from him where a skinny old man sat behind a contraption similar to an abacus.

The abacus was sectioned off into portions representing each of the thirteen types of cards with beads in each area to show how many of those cards had already been played.

"And just in case you don't trust me," Doc said as if such a possibility was too absurd to even be considered, "Holly stays right here to keep an eye on me."

Reflexively, Steve's eyes went to the redhead perched on a stool next to Doc. Her long, scarlet hair was pulled into a braid that hung over one shoulder. The braid stopped just short of tickling the skin above her ample cleavage, which was bared thanks to the low-cut neckline of her purple dress.

"Howdy, ma'am," Steve said with a tip of his hat.

Holly winked at him. Technically speaking, she was there to keep more of an eye on those doing the betting than the dealer, but she didn't see any need to point that out.

"You ever hear of skinning?" Doc asked as he collected the cards from the table and box so he could shuffle them all together.

Steve shook his head. "Nope. But I do play plenty of five-card stud."

Doc ignored the invitation for poker and kept shuffling. "Skinning is a wonderful game I used to play as a child. This right here isn't too much different. Faro's an easy way to make me a very poor man."

Although a few of the other players chuckled under their breath at that, most of them were just anxious for Doc to shut up and start dealing.

"Give our friend here a loan, Holly," Doc said as he cleared his throat and set aside the cards for a moment.

Leaning forward, the redhead fixed her eyes on Steve and slipped two pale fingers down into her ample cleavage. When her hand reemerged, there was a folded dollar between her fingers.

Coughing under his breath, Doc reached into his pocket, found his flask, and took a few quick sips. When he put the flask down again, his breathing was more or less normal.

"I couldn't take this," Steve said while holding the dollar. "I've got my own money."

"Pick a card," Doc said as he put the deck into the box. "Any card."

Even before Steve had made his decision, the other players at the table scrambled to put their money down on the various cards depicted upon the felt. Some of those bets had pennies on them and others were covering more than one card at a time. Eventually, Steve slapped his dollar onto the eight.

Nodding, Doc cleared his throat and slipped the first card off the top. "Here's the soda," he said as he revealed the nine of clubs.

One of the men who'd put his money on the nine to win swore and punched his knee.

Doc's hand drifted to the box and peeled off the top card, which was the king of hearts. Under that one was the eight of diamonds. "There now," he said in a southern drawl that was smooth as honey. "Wasn't that easy?"

Once again, Holly leaned forward and slid some money toward Steve. She also paid off the other two gentlemen at the table who were smart enough to follow the newcomer's lead.

"That's it?" Steve asked.

Doc nodded. "That's it. There's plenty more cards in here to go," he said while patting the box. "What's your next lucky pick?"

For a moment, Steve glanced back and forth between the felt layout in front of him and the poker games that were taking place less than five feet in almost every direction. Doc was taking another drink from his flask and wincing as the liquor made its way down his throat while Holly played with her hair in a way that seemed to tickle the uppermost curve of her breasts.

"I'm in," Steve said decidedly. "Can I bet on more than one at a time?"

"Only if you want to break my back even quicker. Holly, show the man the finer aspects of this little game."

"Glad to, Doc." With that, the redhead leaned forward again to explain where bets were placed and what each spot on the table meant. This time, every man at that table seemed more than happy to wait and watch the show as she explained what they already knew so well.

～～～

Caleb leaned on the bar with both elbows. Although he'd tossed a few drunks out for trying to fall asleep in that very same position, he figured that he'd cut himself a little slack since the sun was turning the sky a bright blue. Not that Caleb would have seen the sky, of course. At the moment, he was doing his best to keep from seeing double.

"How long's he been at it?" Caleb asked the young woman leaning against the other side of the bar.

Dolly was one of the working girls who'd been making the Flush their base of operations. Having just gotten back after putting one customer to bed, she had no trouble at all stepping away from the bar to get a look at the watch dangling from the closest drunk's pocket. "Just past nine," she reported.

"Jesus Christ, that's almost twelve hours."

Standing on her tiptoes and craning her neck to get a better look at Doc's table, she said, "Looks to me like he's doing all right."

"Which one? Doc or Steve?"

"If Steve's still in his spot after playing so long against Doc, he must be doing something right."

"Maybe. I guess I'd better go over there and have a look." With that, Caleb sucked in a breath and tried to force the cobwebs out of his head. He managed to keep his walk steady enough as he crossed through the saloon, but couldn't resist dropping into the closest of Doc's unoccupied seats.

"Why, Caleb," Doc said as if he'd just awakened from a seven-hour nap. "You're just in time to witness our friend's triumphant return."

"That's right," Steve said enthusiastically. "Ol' number eight's been my lucky number all night long, and I know she won't let me down now. Five hundred dollars. Just to be safe, I'm coppering a three-hundred-dollar bet on the ace!"

"Bucking the tiger?" Doc asked as he tapped the felt. As the phrase suggested, there was indeed a tiger painted on the picture of that ace.

"You bet your ass, Doc! Now turn over those cards and let's get this show moving!"

Caleb dragged himself out of the seat and walked over to Holly. The redhead was holding up well enough, but she was in the habit of sleeping until four in the afternoon to make sure she was on her toes.

"How much?" Caleb whispered into Holly's ear.

"He's been up as much as three thousand, but Doc's been taking it away piece by piece."

Caleb glanced at Steve's stack of chips and counted another six hundred that wasn't in play.

Pulling in a wheezing breath, Doc took a card with a trembling hand and flipped it onto the stack. The card in the box was the four of clubs, but the one on the table was the ace of hearts. "The tiger pulls through," Doc said in a cracking voice. "Well played, suh."

Hearing Doc's southern drawl become so thick set off warning bells in Caleb's head. That, combined with the trace of red on Doc's lips, made him put a hand on Doc's shoulder and bring himself down a bit closer to the dealer's level.

"Maybe it's about time to pack it in," Caleb said. Looking over to Steve, he added, "We'll be open later on. Why not pay your wife a visit and come back tonight? I think we could all use some sleep."

Steve's eye twitched as he watched the larger of his two bets get pulled toward Doc. When he saw his winnings for the smaller bet come his way, he said, "I'd hate to stop before making my money back. Jen would kill me if I came home this far behind."

"Hard times call for . . ." Doc paused and coughed into a handkerchief. After dabbing at the corner of his mouth, he managed to croak out the rest of his sentence. "Hard times call for bold moves, Steve. You know that all too well."

"I sure do, Doc. I sure do. One last play for all the marbles. Eight might have kicked me a little, but it won't do it again." Steve pushed all of his money onto the eight marked upon the felt and watched it as if he expected the pile of chips to perform a song and dance.

Still holding the handkerchief to his mouth with one hand, Doc used his free hand to peel off the top card and snap it away.

"You all right, Doc?" Caleb asked.

Doc's eyes went to Holly at first and then to the man sitting behind the abacus. When he spotted Caleb, he seemed surprised to find someone else at the table. After a few quick blinks, Doc nodded. That movement alone was enough to shake a few beads of sweat loose from his blond hair to trickle along his sunken cheek.

"There's a bet in progress," Doc rasped.

Steve watched the cards as if he was about to jump out of his skin. Every time Doc's hand trembled over the box of cards, he twitched expectantly. Just when he was about to bust, he saw a card get pulled from the box and set down next to it in the losing position. It was the jack of hearts.

The only one who wasn't chomping at the bit to see the next card was Doc himself. When he forced back another cough and managed to lift his hand to reveal the card in the top of the box, it was to search for the nearby flask.

"It's an eight," Steve said in disbelief. "Good Lord, it's an eight! I love this game!"

Caleb moved forward before Steve could reach for more chips or Doc could reach for another card. "Holly, pay our friend here what he's owed. Lester, can you pack away this table?"

The man at the abacus nodded and started going through the motions of collecting the cards and the rest of the faro setup.

"Time for me to close up," Caleb said.

Once he had his fists full of winnings, Steve managed to find his voice again. "This is the best night of my life. Jen's not going to believe this."

"Bring her along later, and I'll buy the champagne," Caleb said in a rush. "But I need to clear this place out right now."

Finally getting up from his seat, Steve stuffed his money into his pockets and clasped Caleb's hand to shake it vigorously. "I'll take you up on that. In fact, I'll buy the drinks when I come back tonight." Looking over to Doc, he said, "I'll be looking forward to another game. Maybe later we can play some poker."

Doc nodded, but it was all he could do to keep himself upright.

After escorting Steve to the door and locking up, Caleb rushed back to Doc's table. "You all right?" he asked. "I've never seen you this bad. Should I fetch a doctor?"

"I . . . am a doctor," Doc wheezed. "Just fill up my flask."

"You've had plenty," Caleb said. "I don't want you to die in my place. There's already been too much of that around here lately."

Doc grinned to reveal the blood that was inside his mouth and smeared over his teeth. "I guess I could . . . use some . . . rest."

That was all Caleb needed to hear. Lifting the dentist

out of his chair was like lifting a scarecrow. "I'll take you back to your place, and if I see you try to come in here anytime soon, I'll toss you out myself."

"I hooked that . . . player for you real good," Doc said.

"You mean Steve?"

Doc nodded. The glazed look in his eyes made it difficult to tell if he even knew he was being taken through the front door and into the street. When the fresh air hit his face, he responded just a little bit. "He's a friendly enough . . . sort."

"Yeah, and it looks like he'll be coming back no matter what. You don't have to be here for it."

"All I need is a bit of rest," Doc said.

Caleb and Doc were walking down Main Street. The sun hadn't been up long enough for its rays to become cruel, and the early morning air still had a bit of refreshing dampness just beneath its surface. Surprisingly enough, Doc was responding to every step they took. Caleb could practically feel the dentist's inner fire coming to life like a glowing ember inside a furnace.

"Do I need to load you onto a horse?" Caleb asked.

Doc shook his head. "I'm staying over the bank on Lamar."

"You mean that storefront over the Dallas County Bank?"

"That's the one. A man's . . . got to make an honest living when he's not . . . playing cards."

Caleb laughed and felt Doc start to pull away from him. "You all right to walk?"

Pausing for a moment, Doc pulled in a breath and glanced over at him as if just realizing where he was and what was happening. That fog cleared quickly enough as Doc said, "I appreciate your help, Caleb, but I can make it on my own from here."

"That's all right, Doc. I don't mind."

"I won't be carried like some invalid. I'm sure you've got plenty to do."

"First of all, I'm not carrying you. Secondly, the only thing I've got to do is have some breakfast, and there's plenty of fine restaurants down Main Street. Now, are you going to make me wait for you to run on ahead, or do you mind taking a stroll with me?"

Although Doc's pale, blood-stained face looked imposing enough, his eyes carried a fiery anger of their own. After a few seconds had passed, he simply looked tired. "Maybe I could show you my new practice. After all, it was thanks to your pull with that bank manager that I got enough time to put down the deposit."

"You've actually got a practice going?"

"I'm not exactly fighting off the customers, but there's a cot in the back, and the quiet is good for me."

"You know any places to eat around there?"

"A few."

"Good," Caleb said. "Because I need to discus that loss I took thanks to your friend Steve Wright."

"He's going to be in town for at least a few weeks. Maybe longer."

"And how do you know that?"

"We were at that table for the better part of twelve hours," Doc said. "You tend to learn an awful lot about someone in that time. Speaking of which, I owe you my thanks."

"Why?"

"Because I've found myself shoved out of plenty of saloons, and I was lucky to still have my hat when I hit the street. Not many people take the time to point me in the right direction."

"Earn back my losses, and we'll be even."

Doc smirked and nodded. "The wheels are in motion, Caleb. Just stand back and let them turn."

[20]

Doc was back in his seat after a day's absence from the Busted Flush. In the weeks that followed, Steve Wright became something of a permanent fixture in the saloon as well. He played poker and faro, holding his own like most of the other gamblers in the place. It wasn't until May that Caleb found out Steve was taking a commuter train into Dallas every week just to maintain his games. It seemed that the Busted Flush was finally on the map.

Standing behind the bar, he glanced over his shoulder as the office door swung open and Hank wandered outside. Although the older man looked tired, he was in better spirits than when it had been Caleb pulling that same duty.

"Quitting time already?" Caleb asked.

"Already?" Hank groused. "It's damn near seven o'clock!"

"You sure you don't mind fussing with all them books? I wouldn't mind taking over for you if you need a change of pace."

"I'm doing just fine. That office and those books are in better order than they've ever been since Sarah left. Besides," Hank added as he poured himself a cup of coffee, "you most certainly would mind sitting behind that desk. Actually, I think this is the way it should be."

"I think you're right. Being out here makes me feel more like a saloon owner and less like a goddamn banker."

Suddenly, Hank snapped his fingers. "That reminds me! You do still own most of this place, so you should go see Charlie Austin."

"Champagne Charlie? What's he want?"

"I got a note from him about some sort of business proposal. Since the Flush is still your baby, I think you should go see what he wants."

"Aw, that sounds like something you could—"

"Just go," Hank said. "I need to run to the butcher and a dozen other places for the missus and kids."

"Fine." Before Caleb said another word, the relief bartender was already stepping up to his spot. It was a little too early for the night rush to start, so Caleb decided to get this meeting over with. Besides, paying a visit to Champagne Charlie was never much of a chore.

Caleb made his way to the St. Charles and looked around. It was just as busy in there as it was in the Flush, which put a proud smile on his face. "Is Charlie around?" Caleb asked the hulking man in the clean white shirt working the front door.

The bouncer stood a whole head taller than Caleb and looked down as if he meant to squash him under his heel. After a moment, the giant shook his head.

"Well, I'm supposed to meet him. You know when I can come back?"

Rather than answer that question directly, the giant lifted his arm and pointed toward the back of the room. When Caleb turned to look in that direction, he spotted a man at one of the card tables waving him over.

Caleb walked across the room and stood behind the single empty seat at the table. The man who'd waved him over wore a black vest over a white shirt, which was practically the uniform of a professional gambler. His bald head appeared to have been recently polished, and the pencil-thin mustache was impeccably groomed. Compared to him, the other men at the table looked like common riffraff.

"Take a seat, Mr. Wayfinder," the man said.

"I'm to meet Champagne Charlie," Caleb replied curtly.

"I'm Charlie's partner. The name's Bret Weeks. Since I'm the one who sent for you, why don't you join me in our game?"

Caleb studied everyone at the table and quickly found that all the other men were wearing guns. "How about you say your piece so I can get back to my own business?"

"Fair enough. Sit down."

When it became clear that Caleb had no intention of sandwiching himself in between the others at the table, Weeks flicked his hand a few times to shoo them away. The gunmen got up and quickly found somewhere else to be. From there, Weeks extended that same hand to the empty seats.

Unable to decide whether or not he felt safer having the other men out of sight, Caleb took a seat opposite Weeks. He would have simply left if not for the questions nagging at the back of his mind.

"So you're the silent partner I've heard about," Caleb said. "Would you also be the one backing that humpback and his idiot cousin before those two killed each other?"

Weeks smirked but made no other move. "I'm a businessman, much like yourself. In fact, it seems that you've been doing pretty well for yourself with that little place of yours."

"It pays the bills."

"You ever think about taking on a partner?"

"Already have one."

"Oh yes," Weeks said. "That would be Hank. I'm referring to the kind of partner who can actually do you some
good."

"Let me guess. Someone like you?"

"Exactly."

"Not interested," Caleb said as he started to get up.

"I'm not your enemy," Weeks said. "In fact, I'm the one
that made your little problem with the Deagles clear up
like the rash it was."

Stopping before walking off, Caleb asked, "How so? I
read in the paper that they got into a fight and tore each
other apart."

"You haven't heard from that old miner for awhile, have
you?"

"No."

Weeks held up both hands like a magician after making
a coin disappear. "And I can assure you, he won't be bothering you, either."

After checking to make sure those other men were still
keeping their distance, Caleb lowered himself back into his
seat. "I'd say it's even money that you had something to do
with stirring up all that shit in the first place."

"If I did, I can assure you it was a mistake. I had no way
of knowing how far those two cousins were willing to go.
Please, accept my apologies."

"Done. Can I go now?"

"You can leave anytime you wish. Just let me know
when you'd like to discuss signing me on as a partner in
the Busted Flush."

Placing both hands upon the table, Caleb leaned forward and said, "Never. Is that a quick enough answer for
you?"

"You get a few good weeks of gamblers' profits, and
you think you're at the top of the heap? Those gamblers
come and go, my friend. A good partner is a smart, lifetime

investment, unlike your friend, Holliday. He doesn't have anything to lose."

"I worked my ass off to get the Flush off the ground, and I'm not about to hand it over because some dandy in a suit asks me to. I appreciate the offer, Mr. Weeks, but I think I'll pass."

As Caleb spoke to him, Weeks didn't move a muscle. It was more than a man sitting still to let another talk. It was akin to the way a snake freezes every muscle in its body just before snapping forward with fangs bared.

"You're making a mistake," Weeks said in a way that hardly even moved his lips.

"A mistake would be handing over a cut of my profits when business is better than it's ever been."

"Then perhaps you're not looking at this the right way." Weeks shifted in his chair until he was perched on the edge of it. "I've extended this same courtesy to every saloon owner in Dallas, and it never fails to amaze me how many times the gesture is slapped down. But, when push comes to shove, those same saloon owners take me up on my deal. Of course, some of them took more convincing than others."

"I was wondering how long it was gonna take for you to threaten me," Caleb said. "So what happens if I say no to your offer? You send these boys after me? Maybe you have them bushwhack me some night when I'm leaving my place?"

"I'm not promising anything. What I can promise is a certain kind of insurance that would prevent any such unfortunate things from happening to you."

"Then it's a protection scheme you're running? I've got to tell you I'm not impressed."

"Then perhaps you will be impressed when you realize that the hell I can inflict upon you is ten times worse than what you're thinking. You see, Mr. Wayfinder, I think on a grander scale than just running saloons and selling liquor.

I think more along the lines of a battlefield general. The smaller skirmishes have already been fought, and this is what you might call our first peace talks. If these fail, than the battles only grow in size, and more people will be caught in the crossfire."

At that moment, Caleb spotted a familiar face lurking in one of the nearby shadows. It was a face that seemed to be melting into the darkness while also oozing out of a wall. He thought his eyes were tricking him at first, but then he realized that the man he saw was the same as the one who'd been in the Flush a while ago. The blue bandanna was gone, but that face was as ugly and twisted as ever.

Weeks glanced over his shoulder to see what had captured Caleb's attention. When he spotted that same face in the shadows, he smiled and settled back into his chair. "Funny you should be drawn to my associate. Mr. Grissom over there has been frequenting your establishment for some time now. My guess is that you've only seen him once. You know why that is? Because Mr. Grissom's orders were to only be seen once."

"What's he got to do with this?" Caleb asked.

"Harking back to my battlefield analogy, Mr. Grissom might be my artillery squadron. If you've been in Dallas for very long, you might already be familiar with his work. You remember the big fire back in October?"

Caleb's eyes narrowed, and he nodded. On the morning of October 8 the previous year, a fire had started in one of the stores at the corner of Main and Market. The cheaply crafted buildings went up like kindling, and the fire quickly engulfed an entire block.

"That fire wasn't an act of God," Weeks said as if he could hear the very thoughts running through Caleb's head. "And it wasn't an accident that it spread all the way to the Alhambra and Thompson's Varieties."

"But those places were on the same block as this one,"

Caleb pointed out. "If you had that fire set, you took an awful risk. Who's to say this whole town didn't go up?"

"It was a risk, but those places burned to the ground, and this place survived. That was no accident, my friend. It just so happens that Charlie over there had already signed on to my insurance plan, which seemed to have worked out for him very nicely. Wouldn't you agree, Mr. Grissom?"

Grissom stepped forward. His eyes flared up within the gnarled layers of skin that permanently drooped over his brow. When he spoke, his voice sounded like a wet croak rising up from the bottom of a rotting stump. "It worked out real nice that this place didn't get doused in kerosene while them other shit holes were soaked in it."

Caleb jumped to his feet. "Folks died in that fire. I don't even think there was a proper count of how many."

"I stayed in the Alhambra for as long as I could to try and count properly," Grissom replied. Leaning forward with a gnarled smile on his face, he added, "Maybe a bit too long."

Caleb had seen the horrors that fire could do to human flesh, but he'd never seen anyone wear those scars with such pride. "You're a sick son of a bitch."

Grissom didn't reply to that. Instead, he just widened his smirk a bit and let his hand drift toward the holster strapped across his belly.

"There's no need for another fire," Weeks said. "You're correct in saying it puts everyone in Dallas in jeopardy. That's why I'm hoping you reconsider my offer, Mr. Wayfinder. After all, that is the quickest way to avoid such unpleasantness."

As much as Caleb wanted to charge across the table and clamp his hands around Weeks's throat, he wasn't stupid enough to play into the killer's hands. It had been a while since he'd worn a gun as a general practice, but he never felt the absence of that iron at his side any more than he did at that moment.

"So, what then?" Caleb asked as he forced himself to calm down a bit. "If I don't pay, you burn my place to the ground?"

Weeks shrugged. "Maybe. Or, to keep the Flush up and running, there might just be a tragedy befall someone of your acquaintance. Someone like that Dr. Holliday who has become such a fixture at your faro table. Perhaps someone else you fancy winds up in the middle of an inferno. Or perhaps even you or your partner wind up choking on all that smoke?"

Smiling even wider, Grissom said, "You won't be so tough once them flames start cooking yer ass. You'll scream just like them others. They all scream, even when their throats crack open."

"Grissom," Weeks said in a sharp, commanding tone, "you made your point." Turning to face Caleb once more, he said, "Sit back down before things get out of hand."

"You've got some burned-up killer working for you, and I'm the one that's out of control?"

"Sit down."

"You don't tell me what to do," Caleb said as the embers inside of him started to burn even brighter. "I didn't get where I am by caving in whenever someone tried to roll over me. If you think you're the first one to try and carve off a piece of what I got, then you're dead wrong!"

"And if you think you can dismiss me so easily, then you'll simply be dead."

Weeks's words hung in the air like gun smoke. Looking around, Caleb was surprised to see that nobody else in the St. Charles seemed to give a damn about what was happening. The more he looked, however, the more Caleb found that the others in the saloon weren't as oblivious as they seemed.

"You got this place filled with hired guns?" Caleb asked.

Weeks shrugged. "Let's just say we won't be bothered. And if something does happen to you, nobody will need to know. You can disappear just as easily as that miner and his idiot nephews. They decided to take matters into their own hands as well and it didn't work out so well."

Caleb nodded grimly and took his seat.

"That's better," Weeks said with a smile. "I'm not unreasonable. I realize there are plenty of shades between black and white. We can negotiate a deal that will be mutually beneficial. Just ask your friend Charlie."

Caleb glanced toward the bar and found Champagne Charlie to be standing with his back to a wall of bottles. Although he was clearly upset with the conversation taking place, he also wasn't moving a muscle to stop it or join in. Then again, there was also plenty of those hired guns sitting within arm's reach of poor Charlie.

"So we work out a deal now or I don't leave this place alive," Caleb said. "Is that what you're getting at?"

"I'll give you time to think it over. But don't take too long, or I'll just have to assume your answer is no."

"Yeah, that would be a crying shame."

"It certainly would," Weeks said gravely. "For you and plenty of others. Let's say . . . two weeks. How would that be?"

Caleb wanted nothing more than to tell Weeks what he could do with his deal as well as his deadline. He wanted to say those words so badly that he could already taste them in the back of his throat. But he knew better than to do that.

It wasn't a matter of courage or even a matter of pride. It was the plain and simple knowledge that Caleb would be killed and buried somewhere if he stepped too far out of line. Something in the pit of Caleb's stomach told him that much was an absolute certainty.

"All right then," Caleb said. "Two weeks it is."

Weeks smiled and extended his hand. "You're a smart man. I had my doubts, which is why I wanted to approach your partner first, but this should work out nicely. Definitely more beneficial than having you both locked up so I could take the Busted Flush for myself."

Those words hit Caleb like a cold fist. They weren't spoken out of anger or even as a boast. They were stated as pure and simple fact.

"Come up with a deal and bring it to me," Weeks continued. "And I'm certain you're smart enough to avoid crying to the law about our little conversation. Not only would that be pointless, but it would make things very painful for you." Shrugging, Weeks added, "I just want to be your partner, like I'm a partner with every other Dallas saloon that's worth mentioning. Take it as a compliment. We can make a hell of a lot more money than if we were all fighting like a bunch of savages." With an unconvincing wince, he added, "No offense."

Choking back the angry bile that rose up into his throat, Caleb shook Weeks's hand. Ignoring every bit of common sense in his skull, he turned his back on Grissom and the rest of those gunmen and headed for the door.

It was the longest walk he'd ever taken, but he managed to step back onto Main Street without getting a bullet in his back.

{21}

Millie's was a little restaurant on the corner of Jefferson and Pacific. It was close enough to the rest of downtown that Caleb could get back to the Flush if he needed to in a hurry, but was far enough away for him to feel like he could actually get some peace and quiet for a change.

He wasn't alone in his exile, however, since there was also a certain faro dealer who'd decided to come along for the ride. Doc's face had gotten back some of its color, and his eyes were as clear as they always were after only draining half the whiskey from his flask. Another little change that Caleb immediately noticed was the bulge of a holster under Doc's jacket.

"You always go to dinner heeled, Doc?" Caleb asked.

"Haven't you heard? It's all the rage in Paris."

"Actually, I was thinking about buying into that fashion myself."

"Does that have anything to do with your conversation at the St. Charles earlier today?"

"Yeah. It does."

"Since I seem to be fresh out of interesting stories, how about you let me know what took place in there?"

Caleb looked at Doc and smirked. "Maybe it'd be better if you stayed out of this, Doc. It's not your business, and getting tangled up in this mess isn't even something I'd wish upon my worst enemy."

"I've known Champagne Charlie for a little while," Doc said as he lifted his tea and took a sip. Wincing as some of the hot liquid slid over the rough patches in his throat, he reached into his pocket and removed his flask so he could pour a bit of whiskey into the cup. "And I've also come to know you. Neither of you two deserves to be as miserable as you've seemed lately."

"It'll pass."

Doc let out a frustrated breath and said, "I pull teeth for a living, Caleb, don't make me do the same just to get something out of you."

"All right, then. You ever hear of a man by the name of Bret Weeks?"

"Sure I have. He's part owner of most every saloon in Dallas. Every saloon but yours, that is."

"I guess I shouldn't be so surprised with how much you know about this. Especially since you've been spending more time in the Flush than I have."

"Beats the hell out of digging around in bloody gums."

"Yeah," Caleb sighed. "It seems Weeks wants to be a partner of mine as well."

"Could be good for you. His other partnerships seemed fairly lucrative."

"A man who negotiates with gunmen and killers backing him up rarely cuts a fair deal."

"Weeks has killers working for him?" Doc asked.

"At least one. He claims to have started the big fire last October."

That stopped Doc cold. "What?"

Caleb nodded. "That's what he claims. Said the fire was started because the Alhambra and Thompson's Varieties didn't fall in line with Weeks's plan."

"You really think Weeks could do something like that?"

"Maybe not him, but one of the men he had working for him sure could have done it. By the looks of that one's face, he's gotten closer to more fires than an old kettle. Besides that, I've had enough men try to threaten me to know when someone's bluffing. This one wasn't bluffing. I can't prove he started that fire, but I wouldn't put it past him."

Doc lifted his teacup to his mouth and took a sip. "My old practice was nearly caught in that blaze." After taking another sip, he asked, "What did Weeks say to you? What were his exact words?"

"Just that I could either join up with him or get burned down. He also mentioned something about locking me up. That struck me as peculiar."

Leaning back, Doc allowed the server to set down plates of the food they'd ordered. Once the server was gone, Doc asked, "What's so peculiar if he was the backer that Jim Deagle was going on about? Then he's already tried to work the law against you."

"Yeah, but those Deagles are dead and buried."

"You certain about that?"

Caleb nodded.

"Interesting," Doc muttered.

"The law's already admitted that the shooting at my place was self-defense," Caleb continued. "There wasn't even much of a trial to speak of. Hell, all I got was a talking to from a judge that didn't even make a ripple around here."

"Folks are too excited about the new courthouse they've been building to worry about any trial that won't make the papers. I just figured it was best not to look the proverbial gift horse in the mouth."

Caleb looked around and leaned forward, even though there wasn't anyone in the restaurant who seemed at all interested in his conversation. "I think Weeks might have an in with the sheriff or the Texas Rangers."

Doc scowled and stirred his tea. "I doubt he'd pull much weight with Sheriff Hopper, and those Texas Rangers tend to think pretty highly of themselves to stoop to being bribed by some saloon owner."

"A very *rich* saloon owner."

"True." Doc said as he picked at the small steak and baked potato he'd ordered. "If Weeks is telling the truth, it makes sense that he'd have some kind of in with the law to keep it all running. Otherwise, Charlie or any of those other saloon owners would have just turned him in."

"That's my point," Caleb said as he used his fork to point over the table. "And no matter which lawman is in on this with Weeks, I'm in one hell of a bad position."

"Bad position?" Doc scoffed. "My friend, I'd say those words don't do justice to where you're positioned."

"Thanks."

"But that doesn't mean we can't stand to gain from any of this."

Chewing on his own steak, Caleb shook his head and scooped some mashed potatoes onto his fork. "Even after all this, you're still trying to think of a way to make a profit?"

After waiting a moment, Doc allowed a smirk to show on his face. "Between you and me, Weeks has tipped his hand. He wants something you've got and is obviously pretty desperate to get it. You tell me how this is any different than a high-stakes card game."

The scowl that had appeared on Caleb's face melted away, and he soon found himself starting to nod. "We can either play it to win or fold our cards."

"Just like our friend Champagne Charlie," Dcc said. "Not that Charlie is weak or cowardly in the least. He just didn't have any cards to play against a dangerous man like Weeks."

"And we do?"

Pointing across the table with his fork, Doc explained, "First of all, we now know that Weeks is the one behind all of this and that he's got no small number of guns behind him."

"Not to mention whatever lawmen are eating out of his hand," Caleb added.

"Which leads me to my second point." The more he talked, he more color appeared in Doc's face. "We need to figure out which lawman that is."

Groaning, Caleb said, "Or if it's both the sheriff and that ranger."

But Doc shook his head with confidence. "Can't be both of them; otherwise, Weeks would have come after you a whole lot harder."

"I guess that makes sense. By the way, Doc, he also mentioned that he could be coming after you as well as me."

Doc shrugged that off without a thought. "That goes without saying. What's important is that we keep our own cards covered without letting him know that he made a mistake in showing his."

"What cards are you talking about? I'm just trying to keep my saloon and skin in one piece."

"You're a bright fellow, Caleb," Doc said patiently. "But every now and then I wonder how much of that is just the whiskey making me see things."

Caleb cut another slice off his steak and dipped it into the gravy pooling on the side of his plate. "I'll take that as a compliment."

"Good. Now how about we take Bret Weeks for damn near everything he's got?"

Nearly spitting out his food in his haste to speak. Caleb

had to drink some water to keep himself from choking. "What?"

"We've got a few weeks," Doc said thoughtfully. "That should be plenty of time."

"And what about those killers on Weeks's payroll? What about that asshole with the melted face?"

"We'll be going against them sooner or later. That is, unless you wanted to save yourself the trouble and just hand over controlling interest of your saloon."

"The Flush is my place. I may have had second thoughts about retiring there, but I'd rather burn it down myself than have Weeks own it."

"That's the spirit! Once we nail down which lawman we need to worry about, we can set a little fire of our own beneath Mr. Weeks."

"No problem there," Caleb said. "Just wait two weeks, and there'll be enough fire around here to turn my saloon into a pile of ash."

Doc waved that off like so much smoke. "Weeks wants to take your saloon, not destroy it. Although the threat of another fire does serve one big purpose: to put a fright into men like you."

"I guess that makes sense," Caleb said.

"Of course it does. If I was in his position, I would do that very same thing."

"You make me nervous sometimes, Doc."

"Really? Then try this," Doc said as he opened his flask and poured a splash of whiskey into the coffee that Caleb had barely sipped. "You'll find this does wonders for making the world easier to bear."

Although Caleb was about to give Doc hell for spoiling a perfectly good cup of coffee, Caleb took a sip and found that it went down just fine.

"With all that said," Doc added excitedly. "I wouldn't bet against Weeks turning his firebug loose on some other target. But that's neither here nor there, since we'll do our best to win this thing before any of that happens."

"It can't be that easy, Doc. Otherwise, someone else would have taken Weeks out of the picture."

"We have the advantage of thinking unlike other men," Doc said without a trace of doubt in his voice. "All we need to do is give Weeks enough to make him relax a bit and think he's got the upper hand while we gather some bits and pieces of vital information. After that, we can make any number of moves to knock him onto his sorry ass."

Even as Caleb chewed on his perfectly cooked steak, he could feel his appetite shrinking in a hurry. "I don't know. That sounds awfully risky."

"You want to live without risk, you've got a safe little saloon to run. It looks like Charlie and the others are making a decent living. Why not remove all the risk and just let Weeks have what he wants? All the saloons in Dallas might just run better with one man holding the reins."

When he thought about that, Caleb felt a cold knot tie in his stomach. Oddly enough, when he thought about keeping the Flush and growing old in Dallas, that knot was cinched up even tighter.

"I've always been a hard worker, Doc. I had my wild times, but a man's got to sink roots somewhere."

Focusing on his own plate, Doc nodded. A lantern flickered on the wall beside him, making his hair look especially light and his skin even more washed out than normal. His blue eyes darted down to the diamond stickpin fastened to his lapel. "Look at us. We're both young men, but you're talking about sinking roots, and I'm trying to make a living sticking my fingers in people's mouths.

"I don't know about you, but winning my daily bread sure beats the hell out of scrounging for it. That's what makes me feel alive, and I think you know exactly what I'm talking about. You've already dragged yourself out of that miserable office you always complain so much about. Why stop there? If anyone needs to be taken down a few notches, it's Weeks. I owe him for nearly burning down Dr. Seegar's practice back in October, and you need to fight for what you built."

Caleb met Doc's eager stare and replied in an unwavering tone, "It would also help you build up the stake you need to take your gambling onto the professionals' circuit."

"Yes," Doc replied immediately. "It most certainly would."

"Well it sure seems like you've been giving this some thought."

"You're damn right I have."

The knot in Caleb's stomach hadn't only loosened. It was completely gone. Cutting off another chunk of steak, he used it to push some mashed potatoes into a pile. "All right then," he said through a full mouth. "How do you propose we find out which branch of the law has got it in for us the most?"

{22}

Steve had a bet placed covering the ten and jack, coppered a bet for the deuce to lose, and of course he didn't forget to place a healthy wager on the eight to win. Although the three came up as the losing card, the jack of diamonds appeared in the top of the box.

"All right," Steve said as his hands flew into motion once more to spread his bets across the felt display. "That's just fine, because there's still three more turns to go."

Jennifer Wright sat behind her husband. Over the last few of Steve's visits to Dallas, she found it helpful for her to keep an eye on him rather than leave the man to his own devices. While her husband's smile never faltered, the circles under Jen's eyes were growing darker every time she showed her face in the Busted Flush. "That's a lot of money, sweetheart."

"I know, but I've got a system," Steve replied.

"You've said that plenty of times already, but we're still behind."

"That's all right, I'm going to win it back. Remember that big chunk of cash I walked out of here with that last time?"

"That was weeks ago," Jen reminded him. "And since then, you've been behind."

No matter how much he wanted to argue with her, Steve couldn't dispute the facts. "Right, but that can all change."

"Maybe you shouldn't place such high bets, Steve. That's all."

"It's all right. I know what I'm doing."

Doc sat in his spot and looked over to the couple after wrapping up a conversation with one of the other players. "All right now, this is going to be the last game for a while, so be sure to make these bets count."

"You hear that?" Steve asked. "This is the last game. Just a few more rounds, and then we can go."

Jen nodded and took in a breath. As much as she fought to pull back on Steve's reins, it was hard not to get caught up in the atmosphere surrounding any of the gambling tables. The money was right out there for all to see. Unlike the rest of the world, fate's face was in plain sight. It was painted onto the cards, roulette wheels, or spotted over the sides of rolling dice.

Steve placed his bets with the skill of a marksman, having learned all the subtleties of betting at faro. Every spot at Doc's table was full, and when Doc called for the end of betting and moved for the dealer's box, all the players felt the same breathless anticipation as if Doc was reaching for the gun under his arm.

After milking the moment for all it was worth, Doc flipped the cards and showed the loser and winner. "Good news, friends," Doc announced. "That is, only if you coppered a nine and bet on lucky number eight."

"Yes!" Steve said as he pumped a fist in the air.

More than half of the other players were just as happy. There were slaps on the back along with a few grumbled curses as a seat was vacated, in no time at all, another hopeful soul sat down to try his luck.

"You see, sweetie?" Steve asked. "This game's got a science to it. All you need to do is figure it out."

Doc smirked at that. "Two more rounds, gents," he said. When his eyes fell onto Jen, he winked and added, "Better make that lady and gents."

Jen returned Doc's cordial smile. Before she could do much else, Steve had laid down his next series of bets, and the cards were being shown.

Although none of Steve's winning numbers came up, he'd coppered a bet on the king, which had turned out to be the losing card.

Nodding and studying the felt tabletop. Steve collected his paltry winnings and quickly counted up his remaining funds. Before he got a total figured out, he felt a tap on his shoulder.

"Mind if I have a word with you?" Caleb asked.

"Can it wait?" Steve asked. "This game is almost over."

"Actually, no. It's about that matter we were talking about before," Caleb said as he shot a quick nod toward Jennifer.

Suddenly, Steve understood and got up. "I'll be right back, sweetie," he said to his wife. "Save my seat, and don't let Doc deal until I get back."

She nodded nervously and started to ask a question, but was sidetracked when Doc asked for her assistance in a card trick.

"How much did you win just now?" Caleb asked as he pulled Steve away from the table.

Steve kept turning to get a look at his chair without seeming to notice that Caleb wasn't about to let him get back to it. By the time he was led to the end of the bar, he let his eyes settle back onto the man who'd led him there.

"How much?" Caleb repeated.

"Um, a few hundred."

"That's not enough to pay me back, but it's a start. Hand it over."

Judging by the look on Steve's face, someone might have thought he'd just been asked to sign his wife into slavery. "But I can't! The next bet is the last one!"

"And when I close up tonight, your first batch of loans are due. Remember our deal?"

Steve cringed and glanced reflexively over to Jennifer. It had been hard work for Caleb to convince him to open his line of credit, but once Steve had more money at his disposal, he'd accepted the next couple of loans without hesitation. Of course, Doc had a knack for feeding him just enough wins to make Steve certain he'd be able to pay back what he owed and still be left with a healthy profit. After a few long nights, Steve had found himself in deeper than he liked to admit.

"Not so loud," Steve whispered. "I don't want Jen to get worried."

"And I don't want to make this ugly," Caleb said with a bit of a snarl. "But you owe me over five thousand dollars, and after tonight, I'll have to start tacking on interest."

Finally, Steve nodded and said, "All right. If I can pay off at least that first loan tonight . . ."

"That would be great," Caleb said before Steve finished. "Since you're such a good fellow, I'll be willing to let the interest slide a bit longer if you could scrape together enough to pay off that first loan. I believe it was two thousand."

"Two thousand?"

"Actually, that's the first two loans, but if I'm going to hold off on the interest, that's what it's going to have to be."

Nodding before it got any worse, Steve drifted toward the table. "All right, all right. I just need to get back there before Doc deals that last round."

"Don't let me stop you," Caleb said. As he watched

Steve run to the table, a grin worked its way across his face.

❦

"Here comes the cat-hop," Doc said, announcing the last round of the game where three cards were dealt instead of two. Apart from the normal betting, there was a special bet in which players could guess the order in which the cards would appear. That one, as Doc was quick to remind everyone at the table, paid double.

"You hear that, sweetie?" Steve said as he sat back down in his chair and his eyes darted to the abacus where the spent cards had been marked off. "Double."

Doc drummed his fingers on the dealer's box as he said, "This is the big one, my friends. Make it good, and don't spend all your winnings in one place."

Nodding to himself, Steve let out the breath he'd been holding before turning to look at his wife. "I've got it figured out," he said. "I know what the order's got to be."

Jen looked at him and leaned in so she could whisper to her husband. "How can you know for certain?"

"I've got a hunch. Look at the cards that have to drop," he said while pointing toward the abacus. "There's a queen, two fives, and a seven left in the deck. Of all the games I've played the last two days, I can't recall the last time a face card has come up dead last."

"So?"

"So, that means it's bound to show up! It's due to come. That's just the odds talking. See what I mean about science?"

She winced and began nervously wringing her hands. "Maybe, but there's still two other cards to bet on."

"Let's get those bets out there," Doc announced.

"There's two fives left," Steve said quickly. "That means the odds should be pretty good that one of them will be first. But, the odds that they'll be in a row can't be nearly as good. It's like in poker! The odds of getting a pair are less than pulling two other cards, right?"

"Yes," Jen said as she began nodding. "So that only leaves one to choose."

"You got it. What do you say, sweetie? Should I go with my gut?"

When she saw the expectant look on Doc's face, Jen started to fidget. Glancing between her husband and the money in front of him, she covered her eyes with both hands and said, "Do what you want. I just can't watch."

"All right, then," Steve announced confidently. "I'm ready to make a bet. Thanks for waiting again, Doc."

"Not at all," Doc said. "Just make it a good one. The natives are getting restless."

Without another moment of hesitation, Steve pushed a few of his chips forward to make his normal spread of bets. The bulk of his chips, along with some money he took from his pockets, went to mark his bet on the cat-hop. The order he'd chosen was five, seven, queen.

Seeing that Steve had all of his money in play, Doc quickly peeled the first card. "Here we go," he said. "I believe this is called the moment of truth."

Even though the final round was designed to be the most dramatic, this one was especially so since both Steve and Jen were holding their breaths and clasping each other's hands.

The first card to fall was the five of spades.

Steve hopped to his feet as his wife began clapping happily. "I told you," Steve said. "Just like I said!"

Doc showed the second card, which turned out to be the seven of clubs.

Jen's hands were in front of her mouth and her eyes opened wide. "Oh my Lord," she said in an excited, muffled voice.

"It's due, honey," Steve said with absolute certainty.

"I'm telling you, that queen is due to fall. It's like I've already seen it happen."

"You have an uncanny eye, sir," Doc said in his easy, southern drawl. As he spoke, his fingers tapped the top of the dealer's box in a manner to which everyone at the table had grown accustomed. This time, his finger also traced along the side of the top card in a motion that wasn't more than a quick brush.

"Good luck to you all," Doc said. With that, he showed the final card.

It was the five of diamonds.

Staring down at every bit of his money lying on the wrong patch of felt, Steve crumpled as if he'd been punched in the stomach. "Aw, hell."

The other players at the table went through their normal mix of whoops, hollers, complaints, and curses as they either collected their money or left it behind. The chairs were emptied as those men quickly found some other way to tempt their fate since Doc was already in the process of packing up his table.

Steve stood in his spot, wearing the faded remains of his ever-present smile. His eyes were glued to the table where the bulk of his money had been. Although he did have a small stack of chips thanks to his bet for the five to win, most of his cash and chips had already been swept up and placed in Doc's lockbox.

"For what it's worth," Doc said, "I thought you had a hell of a system."

Nodding, Steve replied, "Thanks." His voice was strained and cracked, even though he only had to push out that one syllable.

Standing behind him, Jen was only just starting to peek through her fingers. "We lost?" she asked in a trembling voice.

"Yeah, sweetie. We lost."

"But you bet on the five to win, right? Didn't we win that?"

"We did, but . . ." Steve didn't have the heart to finish that sentence. Now that Jen was looking at the table for herself, there was no need for him to say another word.

"Oh my God," Jen whispered. "Was that everything?"

Unable to say the words, Steve just nodded.

Jen was looking around in a daze. She was also starting to wobble a bit on her feet. "Oh my God. Oh my . . ."

Holly was already coming around the table and was in just the right spot to reach out and stop Jen from falling over. The redhead had spotted the glazed look in the other woman's eyes and managed to steady her just long enough for Steve to take notice.

Blinking as if he'd just awaken from a dream, Steve took his wife in his arms and thanked Holly quickly.

Caleb had just emerged from one of his few mandatory stints in his office when he spotted Steve and Jen making their way to the door. "Leaving so soon?" he asked cheerfully.

Although Steve managed to put on a weak smile, he wasn't convincing anyone when he said, "I think we just need to get some rest."

"You look like you could use a drink. How about one on the house?"

"Thanks, but no. I . . . uh . . . we really just need to lie down for a bit."

Steve took his wife outside, and Caleb didn't make a move to stop him. When he turned around, he saw Doc leaning against the bar in his usual spot. Caleb walked around to pour Doc his usual.

"Did he take the fall we were hoping for?" Caleb asked.

Doc reached out for his glass and drained it in one sip. "And then some."

Caleb let out a slow whistle and poured himself a beer. "And did anyone else see you tampering with the cards?"

"I'd be personally ashamed if they had. Especially after all the practicing I've done."

"Great. How long do you think I should wait before having another word with Steve?"

"I don't know. They were both taking it pretty hard."

"I sent Holly over to their hotel to see about taking Mrs. Wright out for tea or something," Caleb explained. "That way, I can talk to Steve without any interruption while the wounds are still fresh."

Doc looked over to Caleb with something of a shocked expression on his face. Once he saw that Caleb wasn't laughing, Doc raised his glass. "I'd have to say that's not only one of the coldest things I've heard you say but a hell of an idea."

A few moments drifted by as Doc poured himself some more whiskey. The silence was broken when Caleb asked, "If I set up a private poker game and extended Steve's line of credit, do you think he'd come by later to try and win some of his money back?"

"I stand corrected. I believe *that* is the coldest thing I've ever heard you say."

Suddenly, Holly burst through the front doors. Her eyes were wide as saucers, and she raced straight over to where Caleb and Doc were standing.

"I thought you were going to comfort Mrs. Wright," Caleb said.

The redhead pulled in a breath and replied, "Too late. She went to the sheriff's office. I couldn't catch up to them."

Caleb pressed his fingertips to his aching head without saying a word.

"This could get interesting," Doc said with a smirk.

[23]

"This is an outrage! What kind of town is this where an honest man can be swindled out of all the cash in his pockets as well as the cash he left at home?"

Ben Mays swung his feet down off his desk and jumped out of his chair. The dark-haired woman had stormed into his office like a runaway bull and had taken most of the deputies by complete surprise. Although he'd heard her furious steps approaching the door, there was no way Mays could have expected the woman to come in swinging.

"Settle down, ma'am," Mays said. "What's the problem?"

"I'll tell you what the problem is! We've been cheated!"

"And who are you?"

"My name's Jennifer Wright, and this is my husband Steve." As she said that, Steve came walking in. He was huffing for breath and reaching to take hold of her arm as if he had any chance of stopping her. She shook him off with ease.

"What happened?" Mays asked. "What are you talking about?"

"My husband was cheated out of his money at one of your saloons."

"Which one?"

"The Busted Flush."

That caused Mays to take notice. Not only that, but the ears of all his men perked up as well. "Go on," the Texas Ranger said.

"It was in a faro game," Jen continued. "He was cheated. I know he was, because that very same dealer took him for enough to force us to sell our business in Dennison to pay him off."

"This sounds more like a local matter," Mays said. "Have you been to see Sheriff Hopper?"

"Yes, I have. He said that gambling is perfectly legal and that my husband was taking his chances when he laid down his money."

Mays shrugged and then immediately flinched. "He does have a point there."

"Maybe for an honest game," Jen explained as tears welled up in her eyes. "But isn't cheating illegal? Isn't there something you can do about this?"

"Do you happen to know who this man is?" Mays asked.

"I certainly do. His name is Holliday."

Mays turned to look at his men and got a few knowing smirks from them. "Actually," he said while facing Steve and Jen, "I may be able to help you, after all. This isn't the first complaint we've had regarding Holliday. Him and several others have been fleecing plenty of good folks out of their hard-earned money, and it's time to put a stop to it."

"Are you going to do something about this?" Steve asked.

"I'll most certainly try, sir. Are you able to prove any of

these claims? Or, do you perhaps know anyone that will back you up?"

Jen looked to Steve and leaned into her husband's arms. "No," she said after choking back a sob. "That's why the sheriff wouldn't do anything."

"Well, you just sit tight and let me handle this," Mays said. "I think we might just be able to help you two, after all."

~~~

The lawmen fell upon the saloons like a plague of locusts. Ben Mays and his men tore through the large and small establishments alike in a sweep that took less than two hours to finish.

It was a well-planned affair and went off without a shot being fired. On the contrary, the gamblers went along quite willingly, since they were used to being hauled in every so often and shaken down for a percentage of their winnings. When they saw how quickly the jail cells were being filled, however, they realized this wasn't just another collection run to fill the city's coffers.

Doc was eating breakfast when the lawmen came storming into the Busted Flush. He barely took notice of them at first, but it was hard to miss them when they made a line straight through the saloon and directly to him. Seeing those men charge toward him with pistols and shotguns held at the ready, Doc found his hand moving reflexively for the gun holstered under his arm.

"Go on and draw it, Doc," Mays said. "That would save me a whole lot of trouble."

That's when Doc spotted the badges on the men's chests. He also saw a look in their eyes that told him they would burn him down happily if he gave them the first excuse to do so. Extending his arms, Doc stood up and allowed his gun to be taken from him as the lawmen hauled him outside.

"What the hell is this?" Caleb asked as he stormed out of the office.

Mays shoved Doc ahead of him as he moved toward the front door. "Town's getting sick of these gamblers cheating its citizens. You want to come along with us?"

"No, but—"

"Then shut yer mouth. Say your piece to the judge. I don't want to hear any of it."

And just like that, the lawmen stomped out of the Flush. And Doc wasn't the only one missing. In their wake, there were a whole lot of confused players sitting at half-empty tables.

"Looks like they made off with Clem and Jerry," Hank said from behind the bar.

"Great," Caleb fumed. "That means we don't have anyone to deal blackjack or spin the roulette wheel! I just got that damn wheel, and now this happens!"

"Hell of a shame," came a voice from one of the tables at the back of the saloon.

When Caleb glanced back to see who'd spoken, he spotted a familiar if unwelcome face. He marched straight for that table with his eyes practically boring a hole through the man sitting there.

"What the hell are you doing here, Weeks?" Caleb snarled.

Weeks sat at the small, round table by himself. Playing cards were spread out in front of him, showing that whoever had been there before had been midway through a game of solitaire. "I wanted to be here to see the look on your face when this happened."

"What? You mean you had something to do with Doc getting hauled off?"

"Not just Doc, but several others who won't come around to my way of thinking. By the way, have you given my offer any more thought?"

"Two weeks aren't up yet."

"Yeah, well, an opportunity presented itself. You wouldn't believe how much better I'm going to look in the eyes of the politicians who run this town thanks to this little move. I may just move into government myself if it starts paying out more than I can make in the saloon business."

After pulling a few breaths into his lungs, Caleb felt his blood start to cool off a bit. "This isn't the first time there's been a sweep like this. Last I checked, it only resulted in a bunch of ten-dollar fines."

"That may be," Weeks admitted, "but there's more to this game than just rousting the likes of you and your pasty-skinned friend. I was interviewed by the *Herald* today. Joining up with me might just be the best thing you could do for yourself as well as this here place."

Grinning, Caleb said, "You can spout off all you want to the newspaper, Weeks. It won't change a damn thing. Folks read that and then line birdcages with it two minutes later. I'm not about to change my mind, since I'll have my dealers back before nightfall. As for Doc, I don't think ten dollars is gonna cause him too much grief."

"Then maybe you should worry more about yourself. Or, more importantly, this place. Grissom's already been here and scouted it out. He's got his heart set on putting this saloon to the torch, and he's even picked out the best spots for the first spark to go."

Caleb thought back to when he'd first laid eyes on Grissom's gnarled face. The burned man had been sitting in a dark corner of the Flush like a ghoul. At the time, Caleb had wondered what the man in the blue bandanna had been studying so closely. Now, he knew the answer to that question.

"I won't give you an answer now," Caleb said. "I'll take my two weeks, just like we agreed. If you can't even hold up that much of the bargain, then I've got no reason to go into business with you."

Weeks stood up. "Fair enough. I know you'll make the right decision. Joining up with me could very well be the break you've been looking for."

"I've been doing just fine on my own. Now get the hell off my property."

Before he took one step toward the door, Weeks took a hard look at the man in front of him. He dismissed the angry glare in Caleb's eyes and focused more on the gun handle peeking out from his waistband. "You going heeled now?" Weeks asked.

"Damn right, I am. I don't intend on being pushed around by you or anyone else."

Weeks nodded and gave Caleb a wide berth as he walked by. He took his time leaving the Flush and was immediately joined by four of his men the moment he stepped outside.

"I don't know what that was about," Hank said, "but it didn't look good. Care to enlighten me?"

As much as Caleb wanted to spell it all out for the other man, he simply couldn't. There was too much going on and too much at stake for it all to be explained in any short amount of time. Besides, there wasn't any use in poking a hornet's nest when the damn things were already so worked up.

"Nah," Caleb said. "Just some prick trying to talk tough. That's all."

Hank's eyes fixed on Caleb. He bit his tongue, though, until his eyes landed upon the gun in Caleb's waistband. "Since when do you start carrying that around?"

Reflexively, Caleb reached for the gun and tried to put it out of sight. "With everything that's been going on around here lately, it seemed like a good idea to have something more than a club on me."

"Yeah," Hank replied unconvincingly. "I guess you're full of good ideas."

{24}

"Should I pay my fine now, or wait until later?" Doc asked as he was herded in the middle of three lawmen.

None of the men answered, although one of them gave Doc a shove in the middle of his back that was almost enough to force the dentist to the ground.

Doc stumbled for a step or two but kept his balance. "I wouldn't mind you telling me what brought all this on."

"You being a filthy cheater is what brought it on," came a voice to Doc's right.

The man who'd just spoken was in his late thirties and had the leathery skin of a man who'd made his living under the sun rather than a roof. He had the walk of a cowboy and the snarl of someone who no longer needed a reason to be pissed at the rest of the world.

"I assure you, I am no cheat," Doc said. With a shrug and a grin, he added, "No more than anyone else, I imagine."

That got a snicker from one of the other deputies, which

was quickly silenced by a backhand from the grim-faced spokesman of the group.

"Don't laugh at this, asshole," the first deputy said.

"You're a gambler," Doc said to the deputy who'd been the one to laugh. "I think I sat in on a few games with you over at Thompson's."

The man didn't respond, but the twitch in his eye was just as good as a nod.

Moving on, Doc looked at the others surrounding him. "I don't know your name," he said to the first deputy, "but I know I've seen you before."

"Shut yer fucking mouth and keep moving," the first deputy snarled as he gave Doc a powerful shove.

Although Doc stumbled again, he kept his balance just fine. "If I recall, you missed the turn for the ranger's office."

"I said shut up."

"Yeah, Doc," Ben Mays said from behind the group. "Keep your mouth shut for a change. It'll make this go a lot easier."

"Go where?" Doc asked. "We're not even headed toward Sheriff Hopper's. What the hell is this all about, anyway?"

Mays stepped past his men and into Doc's line of sight. "You want to know what this is about? This is about troublesome sons of bitches like you who keep things from running smoothly. It's about stubborn assholes like your Injun friend who's too damn stupid to know what's good for him. Now all our hands are forced, and it's come down to something like this."

"No need to get yourself worked up, Ben."

"Don't give me the innocent act, Doc. It's way past that now. Mr. Weeks knows that you and that Injun are in this together. What happened? Did you get all soft on him when he shot down Mike Abel for you?"

"For your information," Doc said in a voice that got

rougher with each syllable, "I think Mr. Weeks is a very generous man."

"Too late," Mays grunted as he shoved Doc forward and got the rest of the men moving as well.

"In fact, I'd be more than willing to have a word with Caleb about working with your employer. In fact, he's not all that opposed to a partnership anyway. Especially since things seemed to have worked out so well with Charlie and the other saloon owners."

Having walked down Main Street, the lawmen turned north onto Houston and were steering Doc to one of the buildings at the end of the block.

"Apart from being a good example to that Injun, you don't have a bit of pull in this," Mays said. "You're just another piece of shit card player who should have stuck to a more respectable job. What's the matter, Doc? Being a dentist just ain't good enough for you?"

Allowing his posture to slip just a bit, Doc let out a cough that soon turned into a hacking fit, which rattled him down to the core. When he was able to catch his breath, he said, "You try sticking your hands into people's mouths for a living. It's not as delightful as it seems."

The group stood in front of an empty storefront that faced onto Houston Street. With all the commotion in town as the other gamblers were swept up, there weren't many people out and about in this area. Some were in sight, but they were either down the street with their backs turned or rushing on their way to see some of the more dramatic arrests.

Ben Mays looked at Doc with a mixture of disgust and pity as Doc strained for his next breath. Nodding toward the empty storefront, be said, "Take him inside, Theison. Make it quick, and try to keep it quiet."

The first deputy nodded.

With everything happening so quickly, Doc had barely even felt his gun get taken from him. At that moment, how-

ever, he was plenty aware of the empty holster hanging
uselessly under his arm. His mind raced with a thousand
possibilities as he quickly figured odds and angles as if he
was calculating the next hand of a poker game rather than
summing up his own chances for survival.

"You're a Texas Ranger," Doc said. "Whatever happened to those men being fine examples of enforcing the
law?"

"I do enforce the law," Mays said without a scrap of
emotion in his voice. "Cheating is illegal."

"What about murder?" Doc asked. "Were the laws
changed on that?"

Mays raised his eyebrows and looked around as if he'd
just woken up and found himself standing on that boardwalk. "I don't know what this is, and I've never seen these
men before in my life." Shifting his eyes to the men surrounding Doc, he said, "Quick and quiet. Especially you,
Cambridge," he added while stabbing a finger to one of the
deputies. "Remember to leave through the back."

With that, Mays turned on his heel and walked down the
street.

"You hear that?" Theison asked. "You belong to us
now."

Doc knew that trying to talk to these men was useless.
He could tell the difference between the dog and the one
holding its leash. Unfortunately, the latter of those two had
already disappeared around the corner.

One of the men reached out to shove the door. It swung
open on rusted hinges and all but smashed a hole into the
wall beside it. The loud bang rattled through the dirty room
inside, which was roughly the size of the drugstore beneath
Dr. Seegar's office. Dust swirled through the room, making the few bits and pieces of abandoned furniture look
more like relics in a tomb.

Each of the deputies reached to pull bandannas over
their faces. Some of them were coughing a bit underneath

the cotton mask, but none of them could be heard over the noise coming from Doc's shredded throat. Whenever Doc tried to pull in a breath, he only sucked in more dust to further aggravate his condition. It finally got to the point that one of the other men took hold of his arm to keep Doc from keeling over.

"Jesus Christ," the third deputy said. "What's his problem?"

"He's sick, Danny," Theison replied. "Ain't you got eyes in your head?"

"I know, but it sounds like he's gonna die."

"Let him. It'll save us the trouble."

Doc staggered forward another few steps until Theison was forced to pull him back. There were two other deputies in the room as well, and they'd both taken up positions in front of Doc.

"You all right?" Theison asked.

Through the hacking coughs which shook his shoulders, Doc laughed and asked, "Does it matter?"

The deputy pulled his arm back, but was unable to take his eyes off of Doc's trembling frame. "I . . . uh . . . I guess not."

"Are we gonna do this or what?" Danny asked. "The more he chokes, the more noise he makes."

Theison's scowl showed through the bandanna, which clung to his jaw and nose. It was also reflected in his eyes.

Sucking in one more wheezing breath, Doc stood up as straight as he could manage and started moving his hand inside his jacket. When he saw the others snap their guns toward him, he stopped and asked, "Do I get one last drink before we go through with this?"

The other two men looked toward Theison, who nodded and said, "Keep yer hands out where we can see 'em."

"My flask is in my pocket."

"Yeah, I figured that much. I'll get it."

"You're too kind," Doc said in his normal, easygoing manner.

Keeping his arms extended, Doc lowered his eyes so he didn't have to meet the pitying gazes of the other two men who were keeping their distance. He pulled another labored breath into his lungs, which filled the dusty air with a dry, scratchy sound.

Theison let out an impatient grumble as he reached for the flap of Doc's jacket. "Let's just get this over and done with. I don't want to catch whatever the hell this poor bastard's got."

Doc struggled to take his next breath as his upper body drooped forward like a wilting stem. The moment the deputy's hand reached into his jacket, however, Doc flew into motion like a trap that had been sprung.

Doc's left hand snapped up to close tightly around Theison's wrist. He then reached out with his right hand to snatch the gun from the deputy's grasp. The bigger man was so surprised that Doc hadn't fallen over that he barely noticed when he was relieved of his gun.

The other two deputies jumped back with a start when they saw Doc make his move. It took them a moment to comprehend what was happening, but the gun that was now in Doc's possession was more than enough to get their minds on the business at hand.

Fuming as he backed away from Doc, Theison shouted, "Shoot this son of a bi—" His words were cut short when the butt of his own pistol was delivered straight into his mouth.

Doc's arm snapped out like a spring to crack the gun's handle flat against the deputy's jaw. A dull crunch drifted through the air, followed by a muffled groan coming from beneath Theison's bandanna.

Just as one of the other deputies took aim, Doc squeezed his trigger. Fire and thunder erupted from his barrel as lead flew through the air. Cambridge snarled in pain as he was twisted around like a top with blood spraying from his elbow.

Danny jumped away from his partner and fired back, only to take a chunk of meat from Theison's rib cage. With his bandanna already soaked through with blood from the knock Doc had give him, Theison crumpled over to let out a violent string of profanities.

Even as more shots were fired at him, Doc stood rooted in his spot. He squinted through the dust and smoke churning through the air to try to pick out his next target. When he found what he was after, he snapped his arm out in a fluid, practiced motion and pulled his trigger. The gun bucked in his hand as it spat hot lead toward Cambridge. His bullet cut a messy path through the deputy's hip and dropped him straight to the floor.

"Toss your guns," Doc said to any of the men who would listen.

Theison was finally mad enough to push through his pain. Now that he could see straight again, he reached across his belly to draw a second gun that had been holstered under his jacket. "You're dead, you skinny bastard!"

Doc took a quick look around at all of the deputies. Each of them was still trying to shoot him, so Doc pointed his gun at each in turn and pulled his trigger in a fluid rhythm. Like the bottles on Dr. Seegar's fence, the deputies fell backward and dropped over as they rushed to find some cover. Thunder filled Doc's ears and he was vaguely aware that the other men were firing back at him.

Even as the incoming bullets hissed past his ears, Doc never felt compelled to run or even duck. He simply looked for his next target, took his shot, and moved on. After spotting his own gun in Theison's belt, Doc walked over to retrieve it.

Theison snarled through his bloody mask when he saw Doc lean toward him. He was set to fire point-blank at the dentist, but before his finger tightened around his trigger, the roar of Doc's Colt filled the air. Hot lead punched the deputy square in the chest, and another round blazed a tunnel through his skull. He was dead before the back of his head hit the floor.

Now that he was using his own gun, Doc was firing his shots even quicker than before. His eyes were narrowed and seeking his next target as he straightened up to stand amid the swirling cloud of black smoke.

Cambridge fired a quick shot but caught a round in the chest, which put him down for good.

That only left one other man. Danny was bleeding from a wound in his arm, but that didn't stop him from squeezing his trigger again and again. His ammunition had been spent in his initial, panicked frenzy, which left him with nothing but a series of metallic clicks as his hammer dropped upon one spent shell after another.

Doc walked slowly up to the last deputy. "Now I remember where I've seen you," he said.

The other man was too busy looking at the bodies on the floor and the gun in Doc's hand to do much of anything but mutter, "Jesus . . . Jesus Christ!"

"You boys are the ones who toss drunks out of the Alhambra," Doc said. "That would mean you're not really the law after all."

"P-put the gun down," Danny stammered.

"Or what? You'll arrest me?" Doc shook his head and stepped back so he had the man in his sights. "Tell me what you were meant to do here, and I might consider allowing you to walk out of here."

Although Danny wanted to hold his tongue, he was too rattled to even look Doc in the eyes. "We was supposed to . . . kill you."

"I figured that much. Now tell me why."

"Mr. Weeks . . . he said to make sure that Injun found you. Weeks arranged for all of this."

"What else is on his mind?"

Danny's eyes wobbled in their sockets as he fought to come up with something to say that would save his life. When he came up empty, tears started to well up and slide down his cheek.

"Toss that gun," Doc said.

Danny let the empty weapon slip from his fingers.

"And any backup you might have."

"I don't have any others. I swear."

Doc's eyes narrowed as he cocked his head a bit to one side and sighted along the barrel of his gun.

Reflexively, Danny cowered and threw up his hands. "I swear to God, I don't have any more guns. Please don't kill me!"

Doc holstered his pistol and held out his hand. "Come on, now. Get up."

At first, Danny seemed surprised that he was still drawing breath. Then, he took Doc's hand and allowed himself to be hoisted onto his feet. "Y-you ain't gonna kill me?"

"Not unless you'd prefer it that way."

Danny shook his head so hard it almost twisted from the top of his neck.

"I want you to take me back to Weeks."

The gratitude in Danny's eyes started to fade and was soon replaced with confusion. "Huh? Why?"

"Just for a little chat. But first, you're going to help me move these bodies somewhere a little less conspicuous."

[25]

Weeks shot up from his chair in the back room of the St. Charles as if he'd been kicked toward the ceiling. "What the hell is this?" he snarled. "What's he doing here?"

Doc walked into the room, accompanied by the man who'd been posing as a deputy.

"Answer me, Danny," Weeks demanded.

The deputy patted the air and stopped where he was, allowing Doc to step forward. "He wanted to have a word with you, Mr. Weeks, that's all."

"Bullshit. Where's Theison?"

"Theison's gone. So's Cambridge."

Weeks looked nervously from Doc to Danny and back again. "What about Mays?"

"He can come visit me," Doc said in a friendly tone. "When I turn myself in to Sheriff Hopper."

"Then what the hell are you doing here?" Weeks asked.

"Simple. I think you've made a mistake."

"A mistake?"

Doc nodded.

"What's he talking about, Danny?" Weeks asked. "And where the fuck are those other two?"

"They made a mistake, too," Doc said plainly. "And I defended myself."

That brought Weeks's eyes to Doc and kept them there. "You killed them?"

"Let's not dwell on that. Instead, I'd like to talk about the future."

"You ain't got no future, Doc."

"That's where you're wrong," Doc said with a grin. "In fact, I see us both having one hell of a future . . . as co-owners of all the major saloons in town."

Weeks was speechless. At least, he was for a few moments. He walked around his small desk and sat upon its edge. After studying Doc carefully, he smiled. "You want the same deal I offered Wayfinder? Unless you're the owner of the Busted Flush, I don't see how that would apply."

"I may not be the owner, but I know Caleb well enough to steer him in a mutually beneficial direction."

"And why should I listen to a damn word you're saying? Especially since I've got men in this very room who'll be glad to burn you down."

Doc looked around and saw the other two gunmen sitting nearby. "If you think these men will fare any better than those supposed deputies, then by all means, give the order. But I don't think that's what you're after. You want the Flush, and I can give it to you."

Motioning for the gunmen to stay put, Weeks asked, "How, exactly?"

"We can arrange for you to win it, fair and square. Well," Doc added, "at least as fair and square as we can afford to be."

Weeks rubbed his chin thoughtfully and kept his eyes fixed on Doc. After a few quiet moments, he asked, "You talking about the game being held at the Alhambra next week?"

"That one's as good as any. I'll need some elbow room and a bit of time to talk him into it, but I should be able to swing it. Once Caleb thinks he's weathered the storm you've sent his way, it shouldn't be difficult to get him into that game. But for this to work, I'll need someone else working with me in the game itself. It should be someone that Caleb already recognizes."

"You have anyone in mind?"

Doc nodded. "Actually, I do."

∽∾∽

The front door to the Busted Flush came open, and a familiar, slender figure walked into the saloon.

"There you are, Doc!" Caleb said as he rushed forward to greet the dentist. "I went down to where they took the rest of the gamblers that were swept up, and you never showed. What the hell happened to you?"

"There was a bit of trouble," Doc said. "And I'll be more than happy to tell you about it over a drink."

"How about you tell me before you start downing the whiskey?"

"Well, I was dragged into an empty building and lined up for execution by three of Weeks's gun hands. I managed to get a gun from one of them and then kill a few to secure my escape. Now, how about that drink?"

Caleb's mouth hung open, and it took a while for him to close it again. "Sure, Doc," he said after a few seconds. "I think I'll join you."

As Caleb poured, Doc gave him a rundown of what happened after he was escorted out of the Flush. When he was done, he drained the glass in front of him and let out a slow, measured breath.

"Jesus," Caleb said. "I didn't have any idea those two would move so fast after leaving here."

Doc let out a choppy laugh and said, "Believe me, I didn't either. Did you manage to catch up to them since I've been gone?"

"Haven't had the time, seeing as how I was busy trying to track you down for the last hour or so. But I'll bet there's going to be plenty of spare time in my future, since folks run out of here screaming about being cheated before the law comes stomping in! I knew I shouldn't get too attached to all those profits this place has been pulling in."

"I find it amusing how you can be so upset when I'm the one who was shot at this afternoon."

"Yeah, well I've been shot at myself through all this. I've even had to sidestep a few knives along the way."

"One knife, Caleb. No need for dramatics. Besides, we both knew something like this would be coming. Weeks did say that he would be coming after me as well as you. We just made the mistake of thinking he would stick to his own timetable."

"Well, he can stuff that timetable up his ass. After all the shit that he's pulled, Weeks can come and try to take my place from me if he wants it so bad." Caleb looked at Doc with amazement. "How can you be so damn calm?"

"How can you not see how exciting this is?"

For a moment, Caleb didn't know how to respond. Then, he gave the only response that seemed to fit. He started laughing. "So what took you so long in getting back, anyway?" he asked once he could catch his breath. "It's been a few hours since those deputies came in here."

"I paid a visit to Sheriff Hopper," Doc replied. "It seems he didn't have the first clue as to why men were getting tossed into his jailhouse. After taking down their names and giving them times to appear in that new courthouse everyone's so excited about, he let them go."

"But it wasn't Hopper or any of his men that came to get you."

"I went to him after I left Weeks. After all, it wouldn't be too smart for me to walk back into Mays's open arms, now would it?"

"I suppose not," Caleb replied, still adjusting to the easy manner in which Doc talked about all of this. "So that means Ben Mays is the lawman in Weeks's pocket."

"Since Mays is the one who handed me over to my would-be executioners, I'd say that is a very sound conclusion. You see what I mean about things working out for the best?" Doc asked as he raised his glass.

"When did you mention that?"

"Somewhere along the line. The point is that we wanted to get that Wright fellow to help us figure out which lawman to trust, and that's precisely what happened."

Shrugging, Caleb said, "I guess you could say that."

"We just need to hope that the lovely couple hasn't left town just yet. There's still some things Steve needs to do for us."

Caleb shook his head. "It's not *we* anymore, Doc. Just me."

"I beg your pardon?"

"You nearly got killed today," Caleb said as he poured himself another measure of whiskey. "Maybe this is all too much trouble to go through just to keep this place. I mean, Charlie and the other saloon owners seem to be doing well enough."

"Charlie would smile through the Apocalypse," Doc said. "That doesn't mean he's enjoying the show."

"Then maybe I don't like having others get hurt when I'm the one that should be in the thick of this mess."

"If you're still referring to me, then you can stop right there. I haven't felt this good in a long time."

"Are you serious?" Even as he asked that question, however, Caleb could see his answer written across Doc's face. Although the slender man never looked like the picture of health, he did have a bit more color in his cheeks than normal, and his breaths were coming and going without a scratch.

Doc lifted his glass and took another drink. The whiskey seemed to be spreading the smile even farther across his face. "This thing is so close to being over that you can't even see it. Weeks has taken a beating from us both, and he's ripe to be plucked from his spot. He's practically begging for it."

Caleb grinned at the excitement in Doc's voice. "What haven't you told me?"

"Just that you and our mutual friend Steve Wright are about to get yourselves into an exclusive, high-stakes game of poker with Mr. Bret Weeks."

"What?"

Doc nodded. "I went to pay Weeks a visit after my little scuffle with those deputies."

"And you got him to arrange a game of poker instead of taking another shot at you?"

"I can be very convincing."

Rather than press for more details, Caleb asked, "How high of stakes are we talking?"

"As high as we want to drive them. Since I'm going to be in that same game, we could steer it any way we want."

Caleb thought that over but wound up shaking his head. "I doubt Weeks will let us take more than a few breaths before turning his hired guns loose on us."

"He'll be more than happy to play if he already thinks I plan on stabbing you in the back to get this saloon out from under you."

"You're talking about betting the Flush in a game of poker?"

Shrugging, Doc said, "If you do that, he'd have to match your bet. That's the beauty of the game."

"I don't know about that, Doc."

"We've got an ace in the hole," Doc said with a grin. "If we play our cards right, there's no way for us to lose."

"There's always a way to lose," Caleb said. "That's the other side of the game you love so very much."

"True. But you've got to admit, there's plenty for us to gain in this." Leaning forward, Doc added, "This game is just the thing we needed. We know Weeks has at least one Texas Ranger in his pocket, so it's only a matter of time before he uses him again."

"And what about Grissom? That burned-up killer surely hasn't packed up and left town just yet."

"He's been around for a while and he'll still be around whether this poker game happens or doesn't. At least we know he'll be kept on his leash if this game does happen. If we keep ourselves covered, we stand a better than average chance of getting away fairly unscathed. The only other way to avoid locking horns with Weeks sooner or later is by packing up and leaving Dallas for good. While I don't intend on staying here forever, I surely don't intend on leaving like that."

As much as he wanted to, Caleb couldn't fight that logic. "So you'd rather run headlong into the jaws of death instead of wait for it to sneak up on you?"

Doc's face took on an expression of grim resolve. "Either way, it'll sink its teeth into you. Might as well put up a fight."

"For a man in your shape, you're a hell of an optimist, Doc."

The darkness in Doc's eyes lifted, and he smiled at Caleb. "Considering the source of those words, I'll take that as a compliment. Are we going to sit in on Weeks's game?"

"I don't like gambling with my saloon, but my luck's held up this far. Why not push it a little more? I'll go pay a visit to Steve's hotel."

"Once this plays itself out," Doc said, "you'll see that luck didn't have a damn thing to do with it."

〜〜〜

The knock on the door marked 204 was so subtle that it was almost missed by the couple inside. It came a little louder the second time, which was enough to induce one of its occupants to answer the call. Steve Wright pulled the door open and almost slammed it right in Caleb's face.

"Who is it?" Jennifer asked from inside the room.

Without turning to look over his shoulder, Steve replied, "It's the desk clerk. I'll go settle the bill."

"Good. Then we can leave this town first thing in the morning."

Steve rushed out into the hall and shut the door quickly behind him.

Caleb was leaning patiently against the wall.

"What do you want?" Steve asked in a harsh whisper.

"I wanted to check in and see if you were doing well. You looked a little pale when you left my place."

Actually, that condition had only worsened. To add to it, Steve was now sweating as well. "I lost everything I had and then I find out I was cheated!"

"There's no proof of that."

"It was in the newspaper!"

"Well, you shouldn't believe everything you read. Anyway, I didn't come to give you any trouble."

"If you're after your money, you'll have to wait." Forcing himself to bow out his chest a bit, Steve added, "I . . . uh . . . should get a refund, seeing as how it was one of your dealers who cheated me."

"If the law was going to do anything about that, they would have done it already. Besides, Doc was already hauled off to jail and will be appearing in court with all the others that were dragged in earlier today. Did you read about that in the newspaper?"

"Actually, yes," Steve replied as he gave up on his posturing and shook his head. "I'm really sorry about that. I didn't want to go to the law, but my wife swore she saw Doc messing with the cards. She's just upset."

"That's understandable. Just to show you there's no hard feelings, I've settled your hotel bill all the way through the next few days."

"But . . . we were going back to Dennison tomorrow."

Caleb draped one arm over Steve's shoulders and lowered his voice. "Would you stay if it meant working off that money you borrowed from me?"

"You'd mark off my loans?"

Caleb nodded.

"How many are we talking about?" Steve asked.

"How about all of them?"

[26]

When Doc walked into Thompson's Varieties, everyone knew he was there for the big game being held by Bret Weeks. Doc was dressed in one of his finely tailored black suits with a gold watch chain crossing his midsection. His wide-brimmed hat fit perfectly on his head and was tipped in a friendly manner to everyone he passed. The holster under his arm was just as much a part of his attire as the string tie around Doc's neck. While a few of the locals turned their noses up at seeing their town's dentist walking the streets heeled, they'd started to shrug it off more and more lately.

"Evening, Doc," said the burly man working the door. "Mr. Weeks is saving a spot for ya."

"Good to know," Doc said cheerily. "Have a bottle sent over for me."

"Will do."

As Doc made his way to the table at the back of the room, he picked out several familiar faces. One of those belonged to Weeks, himself, who was flanked by a few of his hired guns. Another was Steve Wright, who seemed to have regained his sunny disposition and even tossed Doc a wave the moment he caught sight of him.

"Howdy, Doc," Steve said.

Doc nodded and took his seat. "Glad to see you haven't lost your enterprising spirit, Steve."

"Hopefully I'll win back the rest of my money tonight."

Winking, Doc said, "Not if I have anything to say about it."

Weeks chuckled confidently and motioned to the other man at the table. "Have you met Jack Vermillion?"

Doc looked across at the man sitting beside Weeks. Jack Vermillion was well dressed but still looked more like a cowboy wearing his Sunday best than a professional gambler who was born to wear a dark, expensive suit. Jack's upper lip was covered with a bushy mustache, and his dark, close-set eyes were intently focused upon Doc's face.

"I don't believe so," Doc said as he nodded in Jack's direction. "Pleased to make your acquaintance."

"Same here," Jack replied. "You'd be the dentist I heard about? Holliday, is it?"

"Right on both accounts."

"Well, I've got an ache in my jaw that's been killing me for a few months now. Maybe you could take a look at it. That is, if you don't harbor no bad feelings after I win all yer money."

Doc nodded, but in a disinterested way that was half-formality and half-excuse to look in another direction.

"Are we ready to play?" Jack asked. "Or are we waiting for someone else to fill this seat?"

"I believe that someone has just arrived," Weeks said.

Just then, Caleb approached the table and pulled out the last remaining chair between Steve and Weeks. He sat down and introduced himself to Jack Vermillion while nodding politely to everyone else. Everyone, that is, except for Weeks.

"I didn't think you'd actually show," Weeks said.

Caleb looked over and replied, "Why wouldn't I? Should I expect you to cheat in your own place?"

Weeks let out a short, grunting laugh. "I'm just here for a friendly game. Surely no one is anxious to cheat at anything after all the attention that type of thing has gotten lately."

"There is a bright side to that nonsense," Doc said. "Everyone's been going on about how grand the new courthouse is, and I'll be getting a guided tour of that very place in a few days."

"A guided tour?" Jack asked.

After taking a sip of his drink, Doc nodded. "My hearing is scheduled for the twenty-second of this month."

It took a moment for Jack to realize that Doc wasn't kidding. Once that sank in, he slapped the table and let out a loud laugh. "Well, with this sort of company to keep, this should be one hell of a night!"

Weeks grinned and shuffled the cards. "Mister, you don't know the half of it."

Weeks dealt the cards, and the game got rolling. After just a few hands, the five men around the table adopted a kind of friendly rivalry.

Jack Vermillion was quick to joke whether he won or lost.

Doc's disposition rarely faltered from his normal, easygoing manner. The more he drank, the thicker his accent became. Even so, his hands remained unwavering as they tossed out and raked in money as though it wasn't anything but so much meaningless paper.

Steve played frugally at first but soon loosened up after winning a few hands. Even as he joked and laughed right along with Doc and Jack, he couldn't hide the beads of sweat that worked their way down his face as the stakes began to slowly creep their way out of his range.

It was a process that resembled the growth of a tree. While it couldn't be seen by someone staring at every flip of the card or counting the money in front of each player, the game grew all the same. After enough time had passed, the sapling had developed thick branches and sprouted a thick mess of leaves.

"I'll raise four hundred," Doc said in the same tone of voice that he'd called a ten-dollar raise less than three hours ago.

"Four hundred?" Jack asked. "Make it five."

Once Jack had pushed in the necessary amount, Weeks took a gander at his cards and then laid them down in front of him. "Five sounds like a good number." He looked at Doc and spotted a subtle nod that be'd been waiting for the entire night. Glancing over to Caleb, he said, "But I was thinking more along the lines of five thousand." With that, Weeks pushed in a quarter of the considerable stack that looked more like a wall in front of him.

Caleb and Weeks hadn't said much to each other the whole night, but there wasn't much tension between them. That is, there wasn't until that very moment. Peeling up his cards so he could take another look at them, Caleb kept his face completely blank. The first two cards, nine of diamonds and four of clubs, weren't pretty. The ace of hearts didn't do much to bolster his spirits, but those last two cards looked awfully good since they were both nines as well.

"I'll see your five thousand," Caleb said as he pushed in just under half of his own stack, "plus another two thousand."

By now, there was no way short of a mop for Steve to hide the sweat pouring off his face. Still, he managed to look down at his cards without letting them slip through his trembling fingers and push in the appropriate amount of money. In front of him, there was now just about enough to pay for a steak dinner. "I'd like to call, but my wife would have my scalp if I lost again."

"This is a friendly game," Weeks said. "Put in what you've got, and the rest of us can fight for the rest. You'll still stand to double your money."

Although Steve seemed tempted, he set his cards down and pushed them away. "Maybe next time."

Staring down at his cards, Doc had as much emotion on his face as he might show while picking out his socks. With a shrug, he tossed his cards down.

"Too rich for your blood?" Jack teased.

"Make the call yourself," Doc said. "Then you can flap your lips at me."

Jack's eyes darted back and forth between his cards. He then turned his attention to Weeks and the hungry look in that man's eyes. From there, Jack glanced down at the pile of money in front of Weeks, which made his own stack look pathetic in comparison. "To hell with it," Jack grunted. "A man can't be shoved around in this game." With those words still hanging in the air, he shoved in all of his money. "That covers the bet plus another . . . fifty-eight hundred I reckon."

"Count it," Caleb said.

Jack was only off by twenty-nine dollars and nodded proudly at his maneuver.

"Why, Jack," Doc said with a grin. "You made a fool out of me. Steve and I here bet that you couldn't count higher than twenty, and that was only if you took off your boots."

"Twenty-one if I dropped my trousers," Jack retorted. "But I can count as high as you please when there's money involved."

Everyone at the table got a laugh out of that, and Steve seemed even more relieved to be out of the game.

Without batting an eye, Weeks nodded down to his wall of chips. "I'll bet everything I've got left."

Jack started to choke on the whiskey he'd just sipped.

"You're trying to shove us out," Caleb said. "You don't have the cards to pull this off."

"One way to see for yourself," Weeks replied.

"You know I don't have enough to cover that bet."

"Then maybe we can make this game really interesting. You put up your shares in that saloon of yours, and we can see what cards we've been dealt."

"You want my part of the Flush? That's worth more to me than whatever you've got in that pot."

Weeks nodded slowly and said, "Then I guess you're out."

Caleb took another look at his cards. They were still the same as the last time he'd paid them a visit. Shifting his eyes up until he was staring straight at Weeks, be said, "Put up something of equal value to my saloon, and we've got a bet."

"Fine," Weeks said a little too quickly. "What about this place here? I may not own as much of Thompson's Varieties as you do the Busted Flush, but I'd say there's enough to cover the discrepancy between the initial bet."

"My part of the Flush against your part of this place?" Caleb asked.

"That's what I said."

Sucking in a deep breath, Caleb forced himself to nod. "Let's do it."

It seemed as if every other noise in the saloon had been snuffed out. A few of Weeks's gun hands stepped forward as if they'd emerged from the walls, adding another layer to the tension that was unfolding.

Jack's nervous laughter cut through it all like a brick coming through a plate glass window. "Jesus H. Christ, I should've kept my beak out of this one!" he said while tossing his cards away as if they'd sprouted thorns.

"You heard the man, Doc," Weeks said with a satisfied grin. "Pick up that deck and deal us our cards."

Doc set his glass down and picked up the deck. After all the words that had been flying back and forth, it seemed as though he'd nearly forgotten that he was dealing. With the deck in his left hand and his fingers running along the edges, he looked up at Weeks and asked, "How many?"

"Just one."

Caleb felt the knot cinch in tighter around his guts. Although there was nothing on the table apart from the cards, shot glasses, and a mess of money, he knew his very livelihood was sitting in that pot.

Doc's fingers plucked a card from the deck with subtle ease. His movement was so quick that the card seemed to spring into his hand to be launched across the table. It landed neatly on top of Weeks's other four and remained there.

Weeks tapped a finger on the card and grinned like a snake with a belly full of squirming mice.

"I'll take two," Caleb said.

With similar ease, Doc tossed two cards across the table to land in front of Caleb. His job done, Doc set the deck down and took another pull from his whiskey.

"Care to add anything else to the mix?" Weeks asked. "Or should we just show what we've got?"

"I don't have anything else," Caleb replied through gritted teeth. With that, he showed his hand. The only thing that had changed for him was the fact that he now had a deuce and a seven to keep his three nines company.

"Not bad, Mr. Wayfinder. Let's see if I can do any better." Like a true showman, Weeks flipped over his cards one at a time. The king and queen of spades were the first to show, followed by the four and six of the same suit. His smile had already reached its triumphant peak when he flipped over the card Doc had so recently given him.

"Stings, doesn't it?" Weeks said, still keeping his eyes focused on Caleb.

Once more, silence had engulfed the table. Caleb, Jack,

and Steve were all staring intently at Weeks's cards. Nobody seemed able or willing to make a noise. Doc, on the other hand, started laughing.

"Looking for this?" Doc asked as he peeled off the top card from the deck. It was the ace of spades, and when Weeks saw it, he quickly looked down at his cards.

Sitting there next to all those spades was the ten of hearts.

The smile melted off Weeks's face, leaving behind a visage of bitter rage. "What the fuck is this?" He snapped his head up and found Doc already getting to his feet. "What the hell is going on here, Holliday?"

But Doc was shrugging and walking for the door. When some of Weeks's gunmen stepped in his way, Doc merely turned sideways and stepped between them.

Glancing uncomfortably at Weeks and the gunmen that were appearing like flies at a picnic, Steve edged back from the table and looked for somewhere he could disappear.

Jack Vermillion let out a low whistle and shook his head. "I guess the game's over."

"Almost," Caleb said. "But not quite."

{27}

The front door to Thompson's Varieties was flung open to smack against the wall. Exploding from there like an arrow from a bow, Doc stumbled into the street where he quickly regained his footing and straightened his coat. The men who'd shoved him through the door came out next and were, in turn, shoved aside by Bret Weeks.

"You're a dead man, Holliday!" Weeks snarled. "That wasn't supposed to happen!"

Doc shrugged and said, "The cards can't favor you all the time, Bret."

Standing toe-to-toe with Doc, Weeks was breathing as if he'd run a few miles to get there. Sweat dripped along his bald scalp and curved around his narrowed eyes. Shaking his head, he growled, "That's not what I mean, you skinny little prick, and you goddamn well know it!"

Doc looked back at him as if they were discussing which wine would most compliment their next meal. "I didn't make the bets in there. I wasn't even in the hand. You're the one who got in over his head."

As Weeks moved his hand closer to his gun, the men who had clustered around him did the same. "You gave me the signal. You knew it was time to make the move, and you fucked me! You even had the . . ." Weeks had to take a moment to force himself to breathe before he could continue. ". . . had the gall to show me the card you knew I was supposed to get."

Doc's eyes shifted around to all the gunmen who were staring at him with murderous intent in their eyes. Dismissing those men, their guns, and the lethal fire in their eyes, Doc shrugged and said, "I'm sure I don't know what you could be referring to."

Weeks had had enough. He was so enraged that he didn't even think to go for his pistol. Instead, he reached out to take hold of the very source of his anger by clenching both fists around the front of Doc's jacket. Nearly pulling Doc off his feet, Weeks glared straight into Doc's face and hollered, "You were supposed to deal me the winning hand, goddammit! That was the deal! You fucked this up on purpose, and don't try to tell me otherwise!"

The circle of gunmen was closing in around Doc and Weeks, although even they knew better than to intrude upon their boss's tirade.

"We set up the signals," Weeks fumed. "You gave the nod. I raised the bet. I'm supposed to be the owner of that Injun's shit hole saloon right now! Instead, you decided to piss all over the plan, and for what?"

Doc's face was unreadable. The flash of anger that had shown when Weeks grabbed him had passed. Instead, there was just enough of a smile on his face to keep Weeks's own rage burning brightly.

After letting out another breath, Weeks pulled back just a little bit before letting go of Doc's coat. He looked around at his men and nodded at the way they stood there, waiting for the order to pounce. "You want to die. Is that it, Holliday? You're sick of hacking up your lungs every day, and you want me to put you out of your misery?"

"That's not a nice thing to say," Doc replied in a tone of voice that fell just short of singsong.

"I just can't figure any other reason why you'd pitch our deal. You're not the sharpest dealer just yet, but a child could have pulled off picking out that spade and tossing it my way. Now, you don't have your stake money, and you're a few minutes away from the most painful death my boys here can come up with." Leaning in, Weeks added, "To be honest, some of these boys are downright depraved. Whatever pain your coughing fits give you won't be nothing compared to what they're thinking about right now."

Behind Weeks, Caleb tried to walk out of the saloon but was stopped by the gunman standing there. Plenty of other folks were starting to work their way in closer to get a look at what was going on.

"I changed my mind," Doc said. "That's all."

"Stupid move. I'll still get my hands on that saloon. Either that, or I'll just make it disappear."

Doc smirked and stood up straight enough to look down his nose at Weeks. "Since you lost one saloon tonight, I'd suggest you make the best of the ones you've got left."

"That's right," Caleb shouted from the doorway. "This here is my place now, and I want you and all of your hired guns to get away from it!"

Whatever calm Weeks had regained went right out the window when he heard that. "You are dead! I still own enough of this town to see to that!"

"I don't think so, Bret."

Those last words came from outside of the circle formed by Weeks's gunmen. When they heard it, those men turned and slapped their hands onto their holsters in preparation for the worst. Sheriff Hopper walked right up to them without the slightest hint of worry on his face. He might have had fewer deputies with him than Weeks had gunmen, but those deputies already had their weapons drawn.

"What's going on here?" Weeks asked.

"Looks to me like you just confessed to cheating in front of the one lawman who's not on your side," Doc said. "Stupid move."

"You got no cause to harass me or my men, Sheriff," Weeks said.

Sheriff Hopper planted his feet and allowed a friendly smile to drift onto his face. "Well, now there's where you're wrong. I may not approve of the way Dr. Holliday's been handling himself lately, but he seemed awfully convinced that he could get you to trip up."

"This was all just talk. It doesn't mean shit."

Turning to Doc, Sheriff Hopper asked, "Will you testify to Mr. Weeks here approaching you to help him in a scheme to cheat Mr. Wayfinder out of his saloon?"

"Seeing as how I'll be visiting the courthouse anyway, I think that can be arranged. I can even tell all about how Mr. Weeks tried to get every other player at the game in his pocket as well."

"I'll need another witness to testify to that," the sheriff announced "Someone not on the payroll of Mr. Weeks or Mr. Wayfinder."

"That would be me," Steve Wright said as he stepped out onto the boardwalk.

Caleb glanced over at Steve and saw that the gambler was holding up even better than he could have hoped.

"But they were all cheating!" Weeks fumed.

"Can you prove it?"

"Sure I can."

"Then you'll have your chance," Sheriff Hopper replied. "You'll have your day in court. Until then, you'll have to come along with us."

With that, the deputies fanned out to hold Weeks's men

at gunpoint. The gunmen parted like the Red Sea, allowing the sheriff a clear view of their boss.

"What?" Weeks grunted.

"Don't you read the papers, Bret?" Doc asked. "This town doesn't cater to card cheats anymore. Don't feel too badly, though. The cot in my cell wasn't too bad."

Holding his hands up so a deputy could relieve him of his pistol, Weeks locked his eyes on Doc and snarled, "You just signed your own death warrant, Holliday. I'll be out of that cell before breakfast, and then you'll wish you just stuck to the deal."

"Hold that thought," Hopper said as he took Weeks by the collar and dragged him away from the gunmen. "I'm sure the judge will want to hear all about that deal of yours."

"This doesn't change anything," Weeks said. "Thompson's Varieties still belongs to me. It can't change hands if that game was crooked. Isn't that right, Sheriff?"

"If Dr. Holliday dealt those cards fairly, then those bets stand," the lawman replied. "Will anyone here testify that they had another deal with Holliday to see that the saloon changed hands?"

Apart from a few nervous coughs or clearing of their throats, nobody standing around made a sound.

"Check the cards!" Weeks suddenly said with a wide grin. "The cards are trimmed so Doc could find the spade I needed! Would that be proof enough to show that Injun don't have an honest claim to my saloon?"

"Sure it would." The sheriff nodded to one of his men and said, "Go have a look at them cards. Why don't you turn out your pockets as well, Holiday?"

Doc emptied his pockets as the deputy disappeared into Thompson's. By the time Doc was finished, the younger lawman was already stepping back out onto the street.

"I don't see anything here to be worried about," Hopper said after patting Doc down. "What about those cards?"

"These were the ones on the table," the deputy said as he handed over a deck. "I couldn't find any marks on them."

The sheriff ran his fingers along all sides of the deck. "Feels nice and even to me," Hopper said with a grin.

"That's impossible!" Weeks growled. Obviously not too concerned with paying the minor fine that accompanied playing with a crooked deck, he examined the cards himself. The more he traced along the edges of the deck, the more flustered he became. "These aren't the cards! These aren't the ones we played with, goddammit!"

"I trust my deputies just fine," Sheriff Hopper said. "Looks like you'll just have to reap what you've sown."

Weeks gritted his teeth and nodded to himself. He made eye contact with each of his gunmen in turn, lingering only on one of them for more than a second. That single gunman nodded and immediately turned to head down the street.

The sheriff hauled Weeks toward the jail. His deputies followed behind him, carrying the pistols and shotguns that had been dropped by Weeks's men. As soon as the lawmen rounded the first corner, all the owners of those weapons turned and scattered.

In no time at all, folks started walking in and out of the saloon as if it was just another night in Dallas.

"That was beautiful," Caleb said as he walked out to stand beside Doc. "There were a few moments where I thought it was going to head south, but it turned out just great."

Stepping up to them with his hat in hand, Steve let out a shaky breath. "Please tell me there's nothing else you need me to do."

"Take a drink," Doc said as he offered his flask. "Looks like you need it."

Steve did so gladly. As the whiskey burned its way down his throat, he wiped away the sweat that drenched him from the top of his head all the way down the front of his shirt. With a trembling hand, he took a deck of cards out of his jacket's inner pocket. "I don't think anyone saw me take these. As far as I could tell, nobody was paying much attention to me at all. Just like you said."

"Trust me," Caleb said as he took the cards and tucked them away in his own pocket, "if anyone saw you, we would've heard about it. You did a real good job, Steve."

"You should thank Jen as much as me," Steve said. "She was the one who got Sheriff Hopper to be here and wait for Weeks to come out."

"Well, as far as I'm concerned, you worked off your debt and then some. You agree, Doc?"

"I was happy when you brought in so many players to my faro table," Doc replied. "Everything after that was frosting on the cake."

Although Steve seemed happy at first, he became visibly more nervous the more he thought things over. Finally, he let out the breath he'd been holding and said, "I guess I'll just be happy I wasn't killed tonight and leave it at that."

Caleb let out a laugh. "I'll even make sure you leave here with the same amount of money you brought in. How's that?"

"Wonderful!" Steve said as a smile exploded onto his face. "That's just wonderful! It's been a real pleasure meeting you fellas."

"You did us a real service," Caleb said as he shook Steve's hand. "But you might still want to head home before Weeks gets cut loose."

When it was his turn to shake Steve's hand, Doc added, "That is, unless you'd rather try a few more hands to see about doubling your money?"

"No thanks, Doc. Jen will be anxious to get moving."

Caleb and Doc watched as Steve all but bounded down the street. Once the man was out of earshot, Doc said,

"How about we take a look at your new saloon? There's a bottle of imported scotch that I've had my eye on every time I've played here."

"Let's go and open her up," Caleb said. "I think I could use some of that myself."

[28]

Caleb felt pretty good about the way things had turned out. He'd managed to keep the Busted Flush, deal a satisfying blow to Bret Weeks, and even acquire a significant piece of another one of Dallas's more profitable saloons. That night, Caleb got one of the best night's sleep he'd had in some time.

Doc's hearing came and went without a lot of fuss. Although most everyone else who'd been dragged in on that gambling sweep was set loose on a ten-dollar fine, Doc was charged one hundred dollars for the same privilege of sleeping in his own bed that night rather than in a jail cell. He paid it, tipped his hat, and left the newly opened courthouse.

The next few weeks were filled with talk and gossip regarding the arrest and pending hearing of Bret Weeks. Although most folks didn't even know Weeks personally, the charges that were being filed were enough to shock anyone who hadn't dealt with Weeks for themselves.

The most recent tidbit to reach the masses was splashed across the front of the *Dallas Weekly Herald*. It read: "Possible Bribery Charges Link Saloon Owner to Texas Rangers." Caleb was reading those very words when he heard a familiar cough echoing through the main room of the Busted Flush.

"Where have you been, Doc?" Caleb asked after poking his head out of his office. "The courthouse has been closed for hours."

"I had business to attend to," Doc replied. "I am, after all, a prominent, educated professional that still has plenty to offer the citizens of Dallas." When he saw the look on Caleb's face, he added, "At least, that's what Myers said."

T. M. Myers had acted as surety to post Doc's bail. Myers had even gotten Caleb out of more than a few scrapes throughout his time in Dallas.

Doc made his way to his normal spot at the bar, reached behind it, and found a bottle. Reflexively tensing to break the wrist of anyone making such a move, Hank stopped just short of swinging his arm. He grudgingly allowed Doc to take his drink as he slumped back down to read the section of newspaper Caleb had already finished.

"It won't even be much of a trial," Doc said. "More of a judicial formality."

"Weeks will probably have even less to endure," Caleb muttered.

"If anyone on his payroll had a hand in this, Weeks would be free as a bird by now," Doc pointed out. "Also, if that is the case, then there really wasn't much for us to do about it in the first place. I'm fairly satisfied with the irony of being the one to get him arrested for cheating."

"But he'll still have his day, and since nobody was actually killed, he'll walk free sooner rather than later."

After a few seconds, Doc nodded. "You're probably right." As he said that, he set down the bottle and pushed it close enough to Hank for the barkeep to reach out and reclaim it. "And he'll be wanting to take back his saloon."

"If you're talking about Thompson's, I intend on handing over what I won to the man who it rightfully belongs to."

Doc's eyes were focused on the wall behind the bar, although it was plain to see that he wasn't really looking at anything in particular. "That's probably for the best."

Furrowing his brow, Caleb leaned against the bar so he could face Doc. The slender dentist had a bit of color in his cheeks and smelled like shaving cream. Even his clothes were none the worse for wear. "I was just wondering if . . . well . . . if going through all that trouble was really worth it. I mean, as far as Weeks was concerned."

"We did what we could. No matter how crooked that Texas Ranger is, it'll be hard for Weeks to make a move around here without being under someone's watchful eye. Besides, I'm the one he'll be after, and if he wants to find me, he'll have to look a whole lot farther than Main Street."

"Where did you have in mind, Doc?"

"I'm not certain just yet. I was considering Dennison. This place is getting to be more trouble than it's worth."

Caleb nodded and stepped up so he was standing right next to Doc. That way, he could speak without being overheard by Hank or anyone else. "That might not be a bad idea. Considering how things turned out, handing Weeks over to the law rather than killing him might not have been the best idea."

Doc shrugged. "Learn as you go. Next time I'm dealing with a murderous, card-playing saloon owner, I'll know better."

Both men laughed at that one.

Tucking his flask into his pocket, Doc straightened up and extended his hand. "I need to make arrangements for wrapping up my practice before leaving town. If I don't see you before I leave, I'll try to look in on you the next time I visit."

"Sure thing, Doc. I'll make sure to keep the whiskey out of reach."

After one last grin, Holliday turned and strode out of the Busted Flush. His steps were just as sure as a man who'd never had a drop of liquor pass his lips. Caleb still had no clue how Doc managed to stay upright after drinking the same amount it would take to drop a buffalo.

Caleb leaned back against his bar and rested both elbows on its edge. He could see the front door as well as the narrow front window, which had been so recently cleaned. He didn't recognize the men outside right away. After studying their faces for more than a second, Caleb remembered them just fine.

"Hank, where's the shotgun?"

The barkeep snapped to attention while still holding the newspaper in his hands. "Huh?"

"The shotgun. I need it."

As he spoke, Caleb was stepping up to the window so be could get a better look outside. He could still only spot three of Weeks's hired guns but didn't have much faith in that being the final number.

When Hank brought the shotgun out from its spot behind the bar, the few regulars in there weren't rattled by the sight of the weapon. The remaining customers were too wrapped up in their games to worry about much else.

"What's the matter, Caleb?" Hank asked as he stepped up beside him.

Without taking his eyes off of the street, Caleb stepped even closer to the window. The moment he did, he regretted it. As soon as he was within a few inches of the glass, the men across the street started walking forward. Each of them had their eyes fixed upon the Flush as they reached into their long coats.

Too anxious to answer Hank's question, Caleb snatched

the shotgun from Hank's hands. He expected to see the gunmen take similar weapons from beneath their coats, but was even more shaken when he saw what they were packing.

Instead of pistols or shotguns, two of the men carried bottles with rags stuffed into them. The third man stepped ahead of the others, gripping a brick in each hand. Before Caleb could do much of anything, those bricks were already being flung toward the window.

Caleb dropped to the floor. The only part of Hank that he could grab was the barkeep's belt, but that was enough for him to be able to drag Hank down along with him. Both men hit the floor as the first brick smashed through plate glass.

The sound of breaking glass filled the saloon and was quickly followed by the thump of a brick pounding against the bar. A second brick crashed through the remains of the window, sailed over the bar, and made short work of the rectangular mirror that hung lengthwise behind a shelf of liquor bottles.

Caleb winced at the sound of more breaking glass. With his body pressed against the floor, he could feel the patter of broken shards raining down onto him. Just outside the window, heavy steps thumped against the boardwalk.

{29}

Throughout the saloon, folks were shouting or stumbling over each other to get away from the window.

The gunman who'd tossed the bricks stepped aside while fishing a smaller bottle from his pocket. The other two jumped in front of the window, carrying full-sized bottles in their hands. The man at the front of that group extended his free arm and scraped a match along a nearby post and touched the little flame to the end of the rag sticking out of his bottle. After lighting the rag in the other man's bottle, he flicked away the match and cocked his arm back.

The Flush's window was nothing more than an open space with a few rows of stubborn glass that looked more like jagged teeth. Aiming for a spot in between those teeth, the first man prepared to toss his bottle into the saloon. Before he could complete the throw, he saw Caleb stand up, bring a shotgun to his shoulder, and pull his trigger.

The weapon exploded in a thunderous, smoky roar. Hot

lead spewed from the barrel, shattering the bottle in midair while also tearing off a good portion of the hand that held it.

Before the man realized he'd been hit, alcohol from his own bottle sprayed across him, and sparks from his fiery rag set the alcohol on his clothes to burning. With blood still spraying through the air behind his mutilated hand, he was soon engulfed in crackling flames.

Still holding his own bottle at the ready, the second gunman watched in wide-eyed horror as his partner began a stumbling, frantic dance to try and put out the fire that consumed him. When he turned and saw Caleb standing there with shotgun in hand, he tossed his own bottle straight at him.

Caleb gritted his teeth and emptied the shotgun's second barrel while ducking out of the bottle's path. Although he heard a bit of glass chipping, he knew he'd missed his target.

"Son of a bitch!" Caleb shouted as the bottle slammed against the wall no more than a few feet away.

He could hear the roar of a fire and could feel its heat on his face. The next thing Caleb felt was himself being roughly hauled from his feet.

"Get the hell away from there!" Hank shouted as he grabbed Caleb's arm and pulled him back.

Caleb stumbled backward and soon found himself landing hard on his rump. Even as a good amount of air was knocked from his lungs, he was still opening the shotgun and pulling out the spent shells. "Everybody clear out!" he shouted.

Saying those words at that time was less necessary than telling a bird to flap its wings when it flew. Once the front window had shattered, practically everyone had jumped to their feet. By this time, there was already a stampede for the side door with Thirsty leading the charge.

Scrambling to his feet, Caleb dashed behind the bar to

where he kept the box of spare shotgun shells. As he reloaded, he saw the flames licking around the edge of the broken window frame. Fortunately, the fire wasn't spreading much past the window.

"Looks like that last bottle didn't make it through," Hank said.

"That just means the outside of my saloon is on fire rather than the inside."

"Considering what side of the wall we're on, I'm willing to accept that."

Closing the newly loaded shotgun, Caleb gave Hank a quick nod. "Good point. Catch." With that, he tossed the shotgun toward the barkeep.

Hank caught it and swung its barrel toward the burning window. "What about you?"

"I'll do just fine," Caleb replied as he reached for the holster hanging behind the bar. "Serves me right for not wearing this damn thing." The moment he got the holster buckled around his waist, Caleb felt that knot in his stomach finally loosen up. He drew the old Smith & Wesson, took position next to Hank, and watched the window for the first sign of movement.

"We can't wait here for long," Hank said anxiously. "This place is still burning."

"You're right. Stay here, and I'll head out first." Without waiting for a reply, Caleb ran for the window so he could take a quick look at the damage that had been done.

There was a fair amount of smoke billowing into the saloon, but the window was wide enough for Caleb to see the street beyond the flames. By the look of it, the fire was still confined to the part of the wall that had been wetted by liquor. The early evening breeze was still relatively calm, so there wasn't much else to fan the flames.

The next sound to fill the Busted Flush wasn't from gunfire or another burst of flame. It was the slam of the front door being kicked in.

With the door still rattling on its hinges, the gunman who'd tossed the bricks reached inside to lob something else into the saloon. This bottle wasn't as big as the others, but it shattered just as well against the bar, and its contents ignited, thanks to the flaming rag stuffed down its neck.

Reflexively, Caleb turned and fired at the door as flames worked their way up the side of his bar. The pistol bucked against his palm again and again as he sent round after round toward the bastard who'd tossed in that most recent bottle.

Since the gunman had delivered his package, the bullets were whipping past his head and the fires were growing hotter by the second. Rather than trade shots with the saloon's owner, he jumped back out the same way he'd come in.

Caleb didn't think about the fires burning around him or the guns filling the air with blazing lead. Instead, he stomped toward the door with a fire of his own burning deep inside his chest.

The moment Caleb stepped outside, he heard a shot blast through the air. A bullet whipped past him, punching out a chunk of the doorframe along the way. While Caleb twitched away from the shot, it was only so he could snap his own hand up and pull his trigger. He didn't come close to hitting either of the two gunmen outside but managed to force them back a few steps.

"You're through in this town!" one of the gunmen said as the other ducked behind some cover. "If you survive this night, we'll just have to come back some other—"

The threat was cut short by a single shot from Caleb's revolver. It cracked through the air, drilled a hole through the gunman's face, and exploded out the back of his head. For a moment, the gunman just stood where he was, still holding his weapon as if he meant to take another shot. Then, like a puppet whose strings had been cut, he dropped to the ground and crumpled into a lifeless heap.

"Where's your friend?" Caleb asked as he walked over to the twitching body.

The sounds of the approaching fire brigade were growing louder by the second, but Caleb didn't even notice them. He was walking farther into the street and searching for any trace of the third gunman. What caught his eye was a flicker of light from across the way and a few doors down.

That third gunman was kneeling behind a trough with another bottle in one hand and a sputtering match in the other. His face was twisted in an anxious grimace as his eyes darted back and forth between Caleb and the bodies of his partners.

The moment Caleb saw him, he raised his pistol and sighted along the barrel.

"No!" the other man shouted. "Here, see?" With a trembling smile, he stood up and dropped the bottle into the trough. "It's all over."

"Not yet, it isn't," Caleb snarled as he pulled his trigger.

The Smith & Wesson bucked and trimmed a piece of meat from the remaining gunman's neck.

It wasn't a mortal wound by any stretch, but it was more than enough to catch the gunman's attention. He nearly jumped out of his boots as he felt the lead tear away a piece of skin before chipping the post behind him.

Dropping behind the trough, the gunman was just quick enough to get his own weapon in hand.

Caleb aimed at a spot where he would only have to shoot through one side of the trough to get to his man. He squeezed his trigger the instant he had his sights lined up.

Click.

The Smith & Wesson was empty. Judging by the smile on the gunman's face as he rolled away from that trough, he knew that much even before Caleb did.

The gunman hopped to his feet with confidence. Taking his time to walk a few steps forward while taking careful aim, he sighted along his barrel and tightened his finger around his trigger.

A gunshot blasted through the air, only it came from behind Caleb rather than in front of him. Instead of feeling hot lead rip through his body, Caleb got a whiff of burnt powder and the sight of the gunman being knocked clean off of his feet.

Still holding the Smith & Wesson as if it could actually do him any good, Caleb wheeled around to get a look behind him. "Jesus Christ," he said as he lowered his weapon. "You damn near scared the life out of me."

Hank didn't even respond to Caleb. His eyes were fixed upon the dying gunman, and his hands were wrapped around the smoking shotgun.

After letting out a few more pained gasps, the third gunman gave up the ghost and went limp.

"Easy, Hank," Caleb said as he moved to the older man's side. "It's all over. The fire brigade is here."

Hank's face was haunted by what he'd done. His eyes were locked on the gunman's body, and his breathing was so shallow that it was hard to tell if any air was even making it into his lungs.

"You hear me?" Caleb asked. "It's over. They're gone. You saved my life."

"But . . . the Flush. It's . . ."

"The fire brigade is here," Caleb repeated. "Look for yourself."

Hank glanced over to see the fire brigade arriving amid a flurry of shouting voices and clanging bells.

"There's not many of them," Hank said.

Caleb pushed the shotgun down so none of the approaching men would get the wrong idea. "Luckily for us, it's not much of a fire."

"Usually, they come running like a stampede at the first trace of smoke," Hank said. "Where's the rest of them?"

Caleb saw the barkeep's point. The fire inside the saloon was limited to a section along the top of the bar while the flames outside were still mostly around the alcohol-soaked window. The brigade got right to work, and Caleb stayed out of their way as he stepped up to the man who appeared to be in charge.

The man leading the brigade was in his late thirties and had close-cropped dark hair. His skin seemed to have been permanently tinted a darker color thanks to all the smoke that had been smudged on it over the years. "Looks like you've had the same trouble as them others," the brigade leader said.

"What others?" Caleb asked.

The man's only response was to wave down Main Street before rushing in to give his men a hand with their buckets. Hank and a few of the regular customers had started adding their muscle to the mix as well.

Although Caleb wanted to pitch in to save his saloon, he couldn't help but be distracted by the sight a few blocks down Main Street. In that direction, black smoke filled the sky like a fierce storm that had been brewed directly over the corner of Main and Market.

The streets in that area were filled with what had to be the rest of the fire brigade as well as a few reserve wagons. The sky was almost completely blotted out by the smoke and roaring flames that reached upward as if threatening to burn down the gates of heaven. It wasn't even one single building on fire, but several of them. As Caleb watched, he could see new gouts of flame bursting to life amid the sound of shattering glass.

[30]

Doc had been on his way to his office when he'd heard the loud explosion behind him. He was just about to cross Austin Street when the blast rocked through the city like God stomping his foot in a fit of rage. For a moment, Doc couldn't hear a thing. Then his ears were filled with the sounds of screams, cracking wood, and breaking glass. He could also hear the crackle of gunshots coming from farther down the street, but those were the least of his worries at that moment.

Going against the tide of people trying to run from the fire, Doc headed straight for it. Sure enough, his first instinct was proven correct, and Thompson's Varieties was at the center of the blaze. Doc could feel the heat on his face as he ran toward the saloon. The flames were brighter than the sun as they reached up through broken windows to lick the surrounding buildings.

Reaching out to grab hold of one of the men fleeing

from Thompson's, Doc had to shout to be heard. "What happened?"

Turning to get a look at the fire, the man shook his head as if he thought he might be in a dream. "I don't know what happened. I was having a drink, and suddenly all hell broke loose."

"Is there anyone else inside?"

"We all started running after the blast. The ones that didn't were either killed flat out or are dead now."

Doc looked around to find people gathered on the street, gazing in shock at the burning building. Suddenly, his own eyes grew wide, and his breath sped from his lungs. From where he was standing, he could see the fire had already spread to other buildings. One of those buildings on the other end of that same block was the one Dr. Seegar was still using as his office.

"Oh my God," Doc said as he shoved through the stragglers working their way from Thompson's.

"Are you crazy?" the man shouted to Doc's back. "You'll be killed if you go that way!"

Taking a quick look over his shoulder, Doc spotted a group of wagons barreling straight toward the inferno. "The fire brigade is almost here. Tell them to send help after me. It looks like the fire's already spreading."

"Tell them yourself! Get back here!"

But Doc had already turned his back on the man and was running down Market Street.

Instead of following the street, Doc followed a trail made of crackling flame. That trail separated itself from the rest of the blaze to run along the lower sections of each and every building on the same block as Thompson's Varieties. At times, the fiery trail dipped down to the boardwalk before jumping back onto the next building. It made Doc think of the Devil walking down the street, running the tip of his finger along the shops, restaurants, and storefronts, leaving fire and brimstone in his wake.

Looking farther down the street, he could see buildings that hadn't yet been touched by the Devil. Then, in front of his eyes, those buildings went up in flame just like all the others.

People dashed out of their doors as the fire jumped from one structure to another. Most of the buildings were of the older variety and went up like kindling. Even the newer ones lit up as if they'd been constructed of dry leaves.

As Doc sped up in a futile attempt to try to get ahead of the fire, he caught his first whiff of kerosene. Seconds later, he spotted the one man who stood and watched the spreading fire the way a child watched fireworks on the Fourth of July.

Gritting his teeth, Doc ran faster until he felt his lungs burning in his chest. His fists were clenched, and his eyes were fixed upon Grissom's gnarled, grinning face.

As Doc got closer to him, Grissom turned and opened his arms as if to embrace Doc like a brother.

"You son of a bitch," Doc snarled as he threw himself at Grissom. "You did this!"

Grissom reeked of kerosene. He caught Doc and pivoted on his heels to toss the narrow-framed dentist to one side. "You're damn right I did this! I'd say this is the best piece of work I've ever done! Even tops the October fire. Your friend Seegar won't escape this one."

Doc tried to keep himself from falling, but he'd put too much steam behind his first charge to remain upright. Even as his hands scraped against the rocky soil and his knees pounded against the ground, he didn't feel a bit of pain. All he could think about was getting up again.

Grissom watched with amusement. The scarred skin of his face twisted like an ugly mask that had been partially melted in the sun. "I set more fires than I can count. They's all a thing of beauty. You'd see that if you just settled down and took a look for yourself."

Rather than admire Grissom's handiwork, Doc strained

to see farther down the street. The moment he saw smoke billowing up from the end of the block where Dr. Seegar worked, Doc scrambled to get moving again.

"Oh, no you don't," Grissom said as he reached out to grab hold of Doc's jacket. "I said for you to watch this with me, an' that's just what you're gonna do."

Like most everyone else who didn't know better, Grissom assumed that Doc's slender build and pale complexion meant he was weak. He was shown the error of his ways soon enough when Doc wheeled around to send a vicious right hook into Grissom's chin.

The punch snapped Grissom's head back and loosened his grip on Doc. His eyes were wide with surprise, but the smile soon came back onto his face when he spotted Doc running for the drugstore down the street.

~~~~

"Where's John?" Doc wheezed to the first person he could find outside of A. M. Cochrane's Drug Store.

The man had his sleeves rolled up and a dazed expression on his face. After a few seconds, Doc recognized him as one of the store's clerks.

"John Seegar?" the clerk asked.

"Yes. Where is he?"

"I don't know. I heard the explosion and was about to take a look for myself when I smelled the smoke."

Doc was already shoving past him to get to the stairs that would take him to the dental practice upstairs.

"Wait! There's a fire up there!" the clerk shouted. But it was too late. Doc had already charged for the steps, and the clerk wasn't foolish enough to go after him.

The moment Doc climbed the last of the stairs, he reached for the door and had to pull his arm back almost immediately as it was kicked open by someone on the other side. The girl who took appointments had her arm around an older woman who covered her mouth with a handkerchief. Neither of them seemed to see Doc until they walked straight into him.

"Oh!" the younger woman said with a start. "Is that you, Dr. Holliday?"

Doc stepped aside and started helping them down the steps. "Who else is up there?"

"Dr. Seegar was right behind me. He's helping one of the other patients."

"Can you make it the rest of the way?"

"Yes, Dr. Holliday. Thank you so much."

It took a moment for Doc to realize that they were already down the stairs and within sight of the street. He made sure they were safely on their way before turning and racing back up the stairs.

Every breath he took was a painful ordeal, and Doc could already feel the blood at the back of his throat. Thanks to years of practice, he was able to hold back the coughing fit that he knew to be coming, but he knew that wouldn't last long.

Suddenly, there was a loud thump inside the office. The moment Doc heard it, he pictured Seegar lying on the ground or burning alive. Just as he was about to storm through the door, he heard a familiar voice behind him amid the pounding of boots against wooden slats.

"You want to watch this up close and personal?" Grissom snarled as he stomped up the stairs. "That's fine with me!"

Doc's instincts screamed for him to draw the gun holstered under his arm. Even as his muscles started to follow through on that command, his lungs pinched in as if they were being squeezed within a ruthless grasp. It was all he could do to keep from doubling over.

Grissom took hold of Doc's shoulder and pulled him into a gut-level uppercut. He could feel Doc's chest folding against his fist. Lifting Doc's head up using a handful of hair, Grissom sucked in a deep, smoke-filled breath.

"Just so you know, this is all on account of that shit you pulled on Mr. Weeks. You and your Injun friend are both going to be real familiar with these here flames. In fact, he's probably cooking inside that saloon of his right now."

Doc could feel himself being hoisted up. As much as he wanted to do something about it, his strength was being sapped by the sheer effort of trying to hold back the coughing fit. When he gave in to it, the hacking coughs battered him from the inside like a series of punches.

"That's it," Grissom said. "Take it in nice and deep. You'll be able to see your dentist friend sooner that way."

Doc's eyes snapped open, and he clenched his jaw shut. Although the coughs were still kicking blood into the back of his throat, he kept them to himself by forcing his lips to remain closed. Once he was able to breathe, he asked, "What . . . did you say?"

They were well inside the office now, and the air inside was greasy with smoke. Flames crept in on all sides. Grissom held his head high as if he was taking in a cool, sunny day. "Mr. Weeks don't make idle threats. Anyone with half a brain would have known better than to embarrass him the way you did."

Pulling in one more painful breath, Doc straightened his back and tore himself out of Grissom's grasp. He lashed out with a fist aimed for Grissom's chin, but caught only air as Grissom deftly moved away.

"Normally, folks tend to run for the door right about now," Grissom said. "This ought to be fun."

Doc didn't hear a word Grissom said. He was too busy lunging forward to take another swing.

Grissom sidestepped that punch as well and bumped into a wall that was already covered with a growing sheet of flame. His shoulder and left arm dipped into the fire, but he only winced slightly in reaction to it. Letting out a low whistle, he pulled his arm back and looked at the blackened skin.

Compared to his face and a good deal more of his body, the fresh burns didn't even stand out. He flexed his fingers and breathed excitedly at the pain that caused. "You got sand, Holliday," Grissom said as he reached down to draw a hunting knife, using his burned hand. "But you still ain't gonna make it out of here."

The moment Doc saw the knife in Grissom's hand, his mind cleared of everything else. His lungs were filled with pain, but he was used to that. His mouth was full of blood, and every move he made hurt like hell. He was very likely stumbling right into the jaws of death.

He was used to that, too.

Ignoring the wild look in Grissom's eyes and the long blade in his hand, Doc reached down and plucked his father's Colt from its holster. The draw was smooth and just quick enough to get the job done. Keeping his eye on his target, Doc shifted his hips and bent his arm just as he'd practiced.

The Colt barked once and tore a hole clean through Grissom's side.

Fire raged around them like a storm. Smoke filled the air; creeping into nostrils and crawling into lungs as if it had a mind of its own. Now, with the gunshot still rattling through the burning office, fresh blood was dripping onto the floor.

Grissom had yet to move from his spot.

"I been burned too many times to feel much pain anymore," Grissom said as he tossed his knife with a quick snap of his wrist. "Let's see how well you do once the heat fries the flesh off yer bones."

Doc turned sharply to one side so the blade could whirl past him. When he turned around, he saw Grissom draw his own pistol and calmly thumb back the hammer. Suddenly, footsteps dropped like hammers against the floor behind Doc. He'd sucked down too much smoke to tell how many were coming up behind him, and even the sight of the man in front of him was starting to get blurred and smeared by water streaming from his eyes.

Doc gritted his teeth and decided to fill his final moments with as much sound and fury as possible. Aiming at the only target he could see, Doc fired again and again. His hands went through their practiced motions even as his legs started to weaken.

As each of Doc's bullets punched through him, Grissom jerked and danced like a fish on a hook. His own gun went off once or twice, but those rounds merely hissed into the crumbling walls. When he fell back to land in a pool of flame, Grissom still wore his twisted smile.

But Doc couldn't see any of that. Dizziness was overtaking him, and the smoke covered his eyes with a dark fog.

Heat from the fire bit into his arms and legs.

When his back slammed against the floor, he didn't even feel it.

There wasn't even enough air in his lungs for any to be driven out on impact.

Silence wrapped its arms around Doc's shoulders and lifted him upward.

He'd always wondered what it would feel like when the Reaper finally arrived to cart him off.

Actually . . .

. . . all things considered . . .

. . . it wasn't so bad.

{31}

The fire brigade didn't have much trouble snuffing the flames in and on the Busted Flush. Considering the blaze that now consumed the entire block shared by Thompson's Varieties and Dr. Seegar's office, the fire at Caleb's saloon wasn't much more than a sputtering nuisance. Once it was out, Caleb hightailed it down Main Street to see if there was anything he could do to help.

"Gunshots!" someone shouted from the line of bucket carriers. "I heard gunshots!"

Caleb had heard them as well. The shots weren't much more than a few pops within the fire's consuming roar, but they jumped into Caleb's ears as if they were meant for him alone.

Running down Market Street, Caleb felt his senses melt away like most of the nearby buildings. Between the acrid smoke and flurry of hot cinders biting into his face, and arms, it was all he could do to focus on the gunshots that still rattled through the air.

"Aw Jesus," Caleb growled, knowing in his gut that Doc was on one end of those bullets.

Even though there were flames licking out from every window and smoke hanging over the entire block like a shroud, Caleb charged straight toward the drugstore. In his mind, he was already climbing up the stairs to get to the dentist's office on the second floor.

He didn't have time to think about the heat or the dangers that could drop on him from any angle. After coming this far, Caleb wasn't about to stop now. Just as he was about to slam his shoulder into the front door, Caleb saw that same door swing open.

Through the smoke, a large man could be seen hunching over as he ran outside. Once he was outside, it became clear that the man wasn't actually that large. Instead, he was carrying someone else over one shoulder.

"Move aside!" Dr. Seegar shouted as he rushed down the stairs. "This man needs some fresh air."

Seeing that Doc was the man over Seegar's shoulder, Caleb helped the older dentist lower Doc to the ground. The moment he'd set Doc down, Seegar wobbled and started to fall. Caleb took one of the man's arms and eased him the rest of the way down.

Seegar's eyes were full of panic as he looked around. Once he saw he was in the street and away from the burning building, he let out a haggard breath.

"Is he dead?" Caleb asked.

Seegar looked down at Doc and shook his head,. "I don't think so, but how that's possible I have no idea."

"What happened in there? I heard shots."

"I was treating a patient," Seegar said amid a few rough coughs to clear his throat. "I heard someone come into the office. I smelled kerosene, and the next thing I knew, I could smell smoke. My patient went out to see, but . . . he . . ." Seegar's voice trailed off as if the weight of what had happened was just now descending on him. "He burned up. I lost my bearings and didn't know what to do, so . . . I hid.

"I must have passed out, but I woke to the sound of loud voices and gunfire. I don't know who the other one was, but I recognized Henry's voice. All I could think of was to get out and carry him with me." Just then, Seegar looked at the rest of the block, which was almost completely ablaze. "Good Lord."

"What about Doc?" Caleb asked. "What happened to him?"

Seegar snapped himself away from the fire and looked down at Doc. The pale, slender man was just starting to stir upon the ground. "I don't know. I think he came in to check on me, but there was another man in the office with him. He and Henry had guns in their hands."

"Was Doc hit?"

"No," Seegar replied with no small amount of disbelief. "At least I know that much." Seegar's face was haunted as he replayed the scene in his mind. After a few quick blinks, he looked down at Doc and then up to Caleb. "I carried him out of there as best I could. It was the longest walk of my life."

Doc pulled in a weak breath, which immediately caught in his throat. When he hacked out an exhale, he spat up a mess of blood and tried to sit up. No matter how much Caleb or Seegar tried to help him, Doc insisted on clambering up on his own. He never once loosened his grip on the empty pistol in his hand.

"What's . . . where am I?" Doc stammered.

Caleb pushed Doc toward the other side of the street to make way for some members of the fire brigade. "You're safe. So is Dr. Seegar."

Doc looked over at Seegar and then glared up at the dentist's office. There wasn't much to see apart from a blocky shape within a curtain of flame. "It was Weeks's man," Doc snarled. "The one with the burnt face. He did this."

"Thompson's is already gone," Caleb added. "So's most of this block by the look of it."

"What about Weeks?" Doc asked. "Where is that son of a bitch?"

Caleb stepped in front of Doc to keep him from running toward the drugstore. After that, the street was filled with the fire brigade as well as those folks trying to help them. "We'll catch up with him soon enough. Right now this fire is what we need to worry about. You need to stay here and catch your breath."

"To hell with that," Doc rasped. Already, he was reloading his gun and tucking it back into its holster. "I'll stay here and do my part."

"You almost died in there," Seegar said. "I had to carry you out myself."

Doc looked at the older dentist as if seeing him for the first time. "Then I won't stand by and keep letting you do all the work. I can pass a bucket along just like anyone else."

Rather than try to talk Doc into resting for a moment, Caleb and Seegar led the way back to the line of people passing buckets back and forth to either be filled or emptied onto the flames. The fire brigade was hard at work, but it was plain to see that there was no saving the drugstore or the dental offices above it.

Even so, everyone still tried to put a dent in the blossoming flames.

～⌒～

Nearly a whole day passed before the fires were reduced to a thick, greasy haze in the air and a stain on the ground. Locals picked through the remains, trying to find personal items or whatever was left of their businesses.

Caleb sat on the boardwalk facing Main Street, and Doc stood beside him with his back to a post.

"I'm surprised Weeks didn't come along to gloat," Doc said.

"He was probably around," Caleb replied. "But he's gone by now."

"How can you be certain?"

"Because he's not a fool. I saw three more of his men die at the Flush, and you killed the worst of the lot. That doesn't leave much in the way of hired guns."

Doc nodded. "Guess you're right. There's still the matter of his trial."

"All the more reason for him to run. Whatever pull Weeks had with the law must have been used up just to let him get out of here without being caught."

"Caught or worse," Doc said. "I plan on looking in on this place from time to time just to make certain he doesn't get any more bright ideas."

"You becoming a guardian angel to saloon owners now, Doc?"

"No," Doc replied gravely. "I've just got a whole lot of unfinished business with Weeks, and I aim to see it through. If you want the job of watching over the saloons, you can come along with me when I visit Dallas."

"What makes you think I won't be staying?"

"Because that wouldn't make sense. You seemed more relaxed in an actual jail cell than you did when you were running that place. I know, because I've seen you in both places."

Caleb wanted to refute what Doc was saying, but was too tired to come up with a convincing lie.

"There's plenty of action in Dennison," Doc continued. "You could come along with me and scout out some good games. You have an eye for separating the good and bad saloons, and that will come in awfully handy."

"You mean you want someone who can spot a place

running crooked tables before you find out for yourself the hard way," Caleb said.

"Something like that. We worked pretty well together. There's no reason to turn away from a partnership like that."

Caleb took a look around at the streets that he'd known for more than his share of years. Suddenly, every corner seemed as dreary and blackened as the ones that had been scorched in the fire. It was then he realized that making the decision wasn't all that difficult. The challenge was in recognizing that his mind had been made up on the matter long ago.

"Are you asking for a partner or an accomplice?" Caleb asked.

"Does it matter?"

"No. I guess it doesn't."

[32]

Six Months
∽ Later ∽

Champagne Charlie Austin was most definitely living up to his nickname. The St. Charles Saloon had been packed to the gills all night long, and it wasn't until early the next morning that it finally cleared out. Even so, Charlie was all smiles and still busying himself with making certain that none of his few remaining guests could find the bottom on their drinks.

"Happy New Year, Caleb!" Charlie said for what had to have been the hundredth time.

As he'd done every other time, Caleb lifted his glass and replied, "Happy New Year to you."

"Since he didn't show up here, you'd best say hello to Hank. He's been running the Busted Flush into some mighty fine profits. I hear he'll be adding some ladies to work there in the next few months."

"I've already been," Caleb said. "Hank had his hands full, so I had a quick drink and paid my respects. He doesn't need me around to flap my gums. Besides, there was someone else I wanted to see while I was here."

"How is Sarah, by the way?"

"Fine as ever."

"Tell her I said Happy New Year."

"Actually," Caleb said as he drained the rest of his drink, "I'll go and tell her now." With that, Caleb tipped his hat and left.

Apart from a few men passed out at their tables, Charlie was alone when Caleb stepped out of the St. Charles. The moment he knew there was nobody in sight, Charlie's smile flickered out of existence. Sure enough, the heavy footsteps came right on cue from the office behind him.

"Where's he staying?" came a gruff voice from behind Charlie.

"I don't know, Mr. Weeks," Charlie replied.

"Find out, and do it quick. Otherwise, I'll see to it this place goes up in smoke like Thompson's. Grissom may be dead, but I can raise plenty of hell on my own, by God."

"I know, Mr. Weeks. I'll try to find out."

Just then, one of the drunks in the back of the saloon sat up straight and got up. "Maybe I can help you, Bret."

Weeks turned toward the familiar sound of the smooth, southern drawl. "I'll be damned, Doc," he said as his hand drifted toward the gun at his hip. "You are one sneaky little bastard."

"You could only afford one man to look out for you?" Doc asked in a mocking tone. "Times are hard indeed."

"I got more," Weeks said.

Doc stepped around the table and squared his shoulders to Weeks. "I don't think so. And I wouldn't even hold my breath for that one man if I were you. Caleb's already seen to him by now. Your friend Grissom was right. It does pay to study a place for a bit before you make a move."

"What the hell do you want here?" Weeks asked. "I had my trial and paid my fine. You would've known that if you and that Injun hadn't run out of Dallas like a couple dogs with your tails tucked between your legs."

"I came to visit you, Bret," Doc said calmly. "And to toast your new start in another town."

"Other town? What other town?"

"Any one but this one."

Weeks gritted his teeth and started breathing in loud, powerful gusts.

"Or do you need me to drag you through the mud one more time?" Doc asked in a biting tone.

That was all Weeks could take. Just by looking at him, Doc could tell that Weeks wasn't anything close to the man he'd been when he still had all his saloons and men to back him up. The desperation showed in the dark circles under his eyes as well as the strain in his voice. His anger showed in the flexing of his jaw muscles and the way he swore under his breath as he went to pull his gun from its holster.

Doc's hand swept toward the holster under his left arm. He cleared leather in a motion that was every bit as smooth and sure as his Georgia accent. The Colt spat out a brief shower of sparks to illuminate the front of Doc's dark gray suit as a bullet hissed through the air to slap wetly into Weeks's forehead.

For a moment, Weeks merely stood there with a stunned expression on his face. His hand wavered slightly and then became too weak to hold his gun. Weeks's knees pounded against the floor at the same time as his weapon, and then he slumped over to spill the contents of his skull onto the floor.

"The place is yours again, Charlie," Doc said. "Just as it should be."

Slack-jawed, Charlie glanced between Doc and Weeks. "But . . . there's folks still out on the street," he said. "Someone's bound to have heard the shot."

Caleb was already inside and lifting Weeks's body over

his shoulder. "You two were drunk and had some words," he said. "Anyone who knows Doc will believe that one."

Holstering his Colt, Doc added, "What if the shots were just to celebrate the New Year?"

"Just pick one and stick to it," Caleb said as he dragged Weeks into the alley. "I'll meet up with you back in Dennison."

"I don't have the words, Doc," Charlie said. "You just took one hell of a thorn out of my side."

Already, there were men gathering at the front door of the St. Charles. One of them was a deputy and stepped in to get a look.

"Whatever you tell folks that happened here, just keep Caleb's name out of it," Doc said as he set his gun on the bar and turned to face the deputy. "He's got enough on his plate without being an accomplice."

"Accomplice to what?" Charlie asked.

Doc grinned as he removed his flask from his pocket and took a drink. "I've got a few ideas."